Walking the Edge

A Southern Gothic Anthology

Edited by Joan Leggitt

Walking the Edge

A Southern Gothic Anthology

Twisted Road Publications

Twisted Road Publications
Tallahassee, Florida

ISBN # 978-1-940189-16-1

"A Place Called Sickness" was previously published in *Fourteen Hills*. It also appears in the forthcoming short story collection *The Metaphysical Ukulele*.

"Qualities of the Modern Farmer" was first published by *Alligator Juniper* in June 2016

"The Caterer," was first published in *New Delta Review*, Spring 2010

"Dream Location" originally appeared in the short story collection *Winter Investments*, published by The Trilobite Press.

"Pink Moon" was previously published in *Saint + Sinners: New Stories from the Festival 2012*

Earlier versions of "Winnie Nunez on T Cannon" were published in *Apalachee Review*, 2006. No. 56. and *Lochloosa Review*, May 2012. Vol. 1, No. 1.

CONTENTS

INTRODUCTION

Walking the Edge accomplishes what I believe to be the absolute necessary thing. This collection of stories is simply stunning, and in the largest sense counters the silence and refusal that renders so many of our lives unspeakable. These are laugh out loud stories, mouth fall open stories and most of all, damn but I believe that stories.

Read these stories and you will know that our lives are not unspeakable—not us stubborn products of the dusty south or us tentative queer adolescents, us soft-mouthed lesbians looking for a family that will not backhand us into despair or us craggy boys trying to sort out who can be trusted and who cannot. "Tender-hearted," my mama labeled me. And once I heard her tell one of my aunts that she worried I was "too soft at the core". A dreamer, I lived in story, retelling myself what had happened, what had not, what should have happened. I absorbed story and books and movie plots like cool sweet water. This is how it is, I thought, or more often—that's not at all how it is. That's good, I would think but if only they would write about my aunt Dot or my uncle Jack. My people, the ones I understood even as I did not quite understand—my people were so rarely in the stories I read that it makes perfect sense to me that I began to write my own fiction, my counter-myths, and collect stories that met my definition of the true. Yes, we might in many ways be unknown, mysterious or even occasionally contemptible. But we were always good story, and I knew intrinsically that nothing can be changed that cannot first be understood, if only in the smallest way. True stories run counter to all the lies that are told about us, and yes I am speaking about fiction, because it is in fiction that I find the greatest power to evoke our lives.

We put ourselves into the narrative. We claim what we know even if we do not fully understand all we know. We resist violence and denial and that easy contempt we encounter every day. We walk the edge refusing the temptation to sway into the abyss. This is the way it is, we say. Us dreamers, us tender-hearted journal keepers, us soft-at-the-core watchers and recorders. We document. We claim our own. Sometimes what we tell is the smallest piece of a story, but that bit edges right up to the wonderful—the world fully seen and understood.

This is what I love and live for—these truth tellers, these world makers, giving me a vision of the landscape I want to see more clearly. These stories will take you places you may never have imagined before, but in every case the wonder of the narratives will allow you to see over the walls of ignorance and indifference to the heart's core.

And gothic? Gothic to me echoes romanticism; the macabre or the darker elements of our natures and may provoke oddly enjoyable sensation of terror, while the Southern Gothic is said to reflect what is generally labeled the grotesque. I first read references to this when I was quite young and took offense that so much of what I considered everyday life appeared grotesque to outsiders. All right so Carson McCullers did have that woman who clipped her nipples with garden shears, and Flannery O'Connor a traveling salesman who stole a prosthetic leg. I could see the grotesque in those but not so much in the books I loved, the stories that echoed my own family. We were not grotesque, exceptional maybe but not grotesque—except when we were.

"A Place Called Sickness" by Sean Carswell, "Feeding the Dog" by Vickie Weaver, and "Sunflowers" by Sally Bellerose each laid me out—in that way that great stories can do. Having read them I wanted to go out in the backyard and just think for a while, to stay in each of the worlds these writers had given me. They can't all be this good, I thought, but I was wrong.

Here you will find the exceptional, a bit of the absurd, and a lot of the unique, but all in all people who are bluntly making their way in a difficult world as stubbornly as anyone you might meet in a truck stop on the highway headed south. You might hesitate to sidle up to such a person. God knows what they are thinking or plotting or imagining as you approach. The glory of story is that you get to not only approach but step into the fully realized experience of people who might scare the bejesus out of you with a quick wry glance or a gesture of fine-boned muscley forearms. How lucky you are to get them this way, in the safe but scary resonance of story on the page. Lucky you.

Dorothy Allison

A Place Called Sickness

Sean Carswell

The old woman and her daughter were sitting on their porch when Mr. Langkjaer drove up their road for the last time. The old woman, Regina Cline O'Connor, leaned heavy on the right arm of her white rocking chair and craned her neck for a better look at Mr. Langkjaer's shiny Ford ambling down the leaf-strewn driveway. A peacock blocked his path. The Ford slowed to a pace that questioned the very notion of the word motion. It seemed as if forward could shift into reverse without any demonstrative change in progress. The peacock would not hurry. The Ford could not inspire a greater pace in the fowl. The peacock knew his privilege on the farm. Other drivers had confronted the birds, coming close enough to run their tires over the long tail feathers. This was a crime that Mr. Langkjaer knew he could not commit. The old woman's daughter, Flannery, prized her peafowl more than the chicken she had trained to walk backwards two decades earlier. Flannery claimed the eye at the peak of the peacock's tail feathers was the eye of the Almighty come forth to deliver divine grace. Regina doubted it. Regina felt that her daughter simply liked the odd birds, Flannery being an odd bird herself.

Flannery the odd bird did not look up to watch the approaching Ford. She continued to plunk away on her ukulele. Regina found the music to be grotesque. It had its roots in old-time gospel and the Appalachian picking of Regina's childhood, but something else had crept in, something Regina had heard vibrating around the Negro cabins on the back forty acres. The kids of Flannery's generation called this music bluegrass. Regina knew better. She knew jazz when she heard it. Flannery's tiny fingers bounced about the strings and fret board. Regina shook her head. Where was the absolution? Where was the word of the Lord in this racket?

Mr. Langkjaer parked the Ford adjacent to the front porch. He stepped out of the car and brushed the wrinkles off his gray flannel suit. The old woman watched every move. He raised his fedora and nodded. Regina nodded back. He started up the brick path to the porch. The profile of his face was a crescent moon on the wane. What her daughter saw in this Danish textbook salesman was beyond anything Regina could quite possibly comprehend. The man called his sample book with the tables of contents for the textbooks he sold his "bible." Mr. Langkjaer never called the real Bible at all. He strolled with no greater pace than the peacock had shown earlier. Neither man nor bird, thought Regina, knows a mortal sin from a can of Shinola. Both of them wear their pride like a birthright. "I best see about dinner," Regina said. She stood from the rocker and walked inside.

Flannery played her bluegrass ukulele to the beat of Mr. Langkjaer's footsteps, slowing the rhythm as he walked the brick steps leading up to the porch. He opened the screen door without a word. Flannery set the ukulele down and said, simply, "Erik." She gathered her courage. Her day's first challenge would be her rise from this chair. The lupus in her blood threatened to kill her, and the adrenocorticotropic hormone she'd been taking for the past three years leached the marrow from her hip bones. When she stood or when she lay flat, she felt that her life could contain perhaps as much future as it had past, that tomorrows could outnumber yesterdays. When she bent to sit, or rose to stand, she felt that she'd aged three years for every one she lived. The process of standing took her from a twenty-nine-year old girl to an eighty-seven-year-old woman. She bent to stand for Erik. The pain coursed through her. She wobbled for a second on her feet. Erik engulfed her in a hug that was perhaps more supportive than romantic.

Elements of the Old South continued to live at the O'Connor dairy farm. Regina's brother had dubbed the land "Andalusia."

White tenant farmers continued to work the front twenty acres. African Americans—"Negroes," as Regina called them in her more diplomatic moments—worked the back forty. The house itself, while far from the plantation mansions of old, retained the thick white columns and broad front porch of a bygone era. An ancient magnolia from a time when Milledgeville was capitol of antebellum Georgia shaded the house. Every noon, Mrs. Freeman, the white wife of the tenant farmer on the front twenty acres, cooked a formal dinner. If only Regina and her daughter were present, then the two ate with four empty dining room chairs. If company were present, leaves could be inserted into the table and up to six guests could join. Mrs. Freeman dined by herself in the kitchen, and only after the O'Connors and their guests were finished.

The ghost of a ham haunted today's dinner. The black-eyed peas had been slow cooked with the ham bone. Ham fat flavored the collard greens. Even the lard in the cornbread contained hints of salted pork. The main dish, of course, was the best and heaviest part of the ham: its butt end. Mrs. Freeman doled carefully measured spoonfuls of the beans and greens onto the plates of both Regina and Erik. The portions, like the plates that contained them, were small. Flannery's doctor had placed her on a no-salt diet, so she could not join Erik and Regina in the ham-haunted dinner. Mrs. Freeman served her a bland vegetable soup. Flannery scooped the wilted collards out of the thin broth with a wry smile.

Regina said, "Mr. Langkjaer, I expect you plan to take my daughter for another of your famous rides?"

Erik chewed the dry cornbread until it formed a paste in his mouth, then washed it down with sweetened iced tea so full of sugar that it was more syrup than beverage. He cleared his throat. "Well, then, there, Mrs. O'Connor." Erik kept his white cloth napkin close to his mouth to keep the corn bread crumbs from spreading. "I don't know how famous these rides are or what they're famous for, but your daughter has shown me a great deal of the world around Milledgeville, and I look forward to her further tutelage."

"And I expect you don't have a chaperone to take with you," Regina said.

"No," Erik said. "No chaperone."

Regina corrected Erik in her mind: *No, ma'am. I have no chaperone.* Erik scooped a forkful of black-eyed peas into his mouth in what he thought was a friendly manner. He had no way of knowing the offense he caused with his lack of a "ma'am." Erik Langkjaer had learned to speak English in a Danish elementary school. The English was an English dialect. Colloquialisms of the American South were unheard. Never had the word ma'am been uttered that far north of Copenhagen.

Flannery, for her part, had fought this battle with her mother many times. Neither side ever declared victory. There was no point in fighting one more time, and in front of Erik. She ate her salt-free soup and said all she could through her silence.

Regina knew about this Mr. Langkjaer, though. Flannery did not know men. Regina did. She'd married Flannery's father. And it taught Regina an important lesson. Men leave. All men leave. It's in the nature of a man to leave. Her husband Edward had left without having to go anywhere to do it. He didn't even bother to get out of bed to die. He just lay right there in their marriage bed, soul gone to heaven and corpse chilling Regina when she awoke. He could blame the lupus, sure. Flannery would blame that same silent killer. But he left, sure as the day is long. And so would this Mr. Langkjaer. As sure as the pointy nose on his crescent moon of a face, he'd leave. She didn't know for certain that this was the last time he'd visit. She sensed it would be, though.

After dinner, the old woman chaperoned Erik and Flannery as far as the front porch. Flannery carried her ukulele in her right hand and held Erik's elbow with her left hand. The longer she continued the adrenocorticotropic hormone treatments, the more her joints seemed to creak, the more her bones seemed to disintegrate. If Erik had much walking in mind, Flannery would have to subtly suggest a walking stick. Twenty-nine years old may be far too young for a girl to need a cane, but Flannery knew that the hip needs what the hip needs. She leaned on Erik's elbow as lightly as she could while walking down the steps. If Erik noticed, he said nothing about Flannery's heavy hand. He pointed to a strand of flowers surrounding a nearby red oak. "Your geraniums are lovely."

Flannery smiled. Bless Erik's heart. He couldn't tell the difference between a bush and a tree, much less between geraniums and chrysanthemums. He did know Flannery's stories, which was more than Regina could say. For Regina, the fact that Flannery wrote short stories was something short of a scandal, but more than an embarrassment. She would never understand what kind of lady would think so much of herself to think that her daydreams needed to be written down and typed up and sent out into the world. It was nothing short of indecent.

Erik trafficked in fiction. He travelled from university to university, selling these daydreams in textbooks and anthologies. He knew the daydreams Flannery would share, and he knew the first one. It had been a little story named "The Geraniums." And so, on Flannery's front yard, any flower must be a geranium. Even if it was this deep into fall and geraniums never survived that first October cold snap. Even if autumn blooms with that deep yellow had to be a chrysanthemum. Flannery said, "It's not so literal."

Erik helped her down the final step and onto the brick walkway. A peacock bellowed. Erik winced. No matter how many times he'd heard these fowl cry, they always sounded like a wounded child to him. "What's not so literal?" he asked.

"The geraniums," Flannery said. "You can know me a little from my fiction, but I don't tell the whole story."

Erik nodded. They moseyed down the brick path to Erik's Ford. Erik opened the passenger door for Flannery. She and her ukulele settled into the front seat. Erik shut the door behind them and sauntered over to his own door. Time seemed to run at a slower pace on these Milledgeville autumn afternoons.

Flannery guided Erik down the various dirt roads, through farms and fields, pecan plantations and second-growth southern pines that locals looked at as lumber more than trees. For someone who never drove and seemed to lose more mobility every time Erik came to visit, Flannery knew every back road of this county. She could navigate him directly into the gothic past and the hidden beauty. Forget country. This place was a whole different planet from the Denmark Erik knew as a boy. He gawked and asked questions, amazed to find that Flannery could name every tree and distinguish the tupelos from the poplars, the loblolly pines from slash pines, the sweetgums from the black walnuts. Flannery could tell the story of the old white man trudging along the road, lugging a wood box of carpentry tools and Erik could even believe that Flannery knew the old man and that the story was real.

For her part, Flannery kept thumbing through the book of samples that Erik called his bible. She noticed Emily Dickinson's poetry was finding a home in more and more anthologies these days. Just ten years ago, when Flannery attended the Georgia State College for Women, Dickinson was little more than a footnote in literature classes. Flannery had learned about Dickinson from a history professor, of all people. Helen Greene. The very same woman who had introduced Erik and Flannery. "You selling more Emily Dickinson these days?" Flannery asked.

"You know we don't sell individual authors," Erik said. He stole a glance at Flannery. Her gaze was still locked on the bible. In moments like these, when her smile didn't push up the cheeks that were swollen by hormone treatments, with her glasses off and no sense of eyes upon her, Flannery was something like a beautiful young woman. Erik may not have been in love, but he was aware that Flannery was a woman and he wanted to kiss her. Instead, he turned his eyes back to the dirt road in time to swerve around a startled squirrel. He added, "You're a little bit like that Emily Dickinson."

Flannery clenched her jaw. "How so?"

"Living out your days in your family home, watching over your mother in her old age…"

"My mother is not that old."

"…writing these enigmatic little pieces about God and redemption. You could be the twentieth century's own little virgin poet."

Flannery whipped not only her gaze but her whole body so that she sat facing him across the bench seat. Erik had never seen such speed, such agility out of her. He wondered if he'd said the wrong thing, if she might pounce upon him. She glared at Erik, perhaps wondering the same thing. Instead, she produced her ukulele and began to strum a few simple chords. "Greensleeves," she said. She played through the melody. It sounded somewhat soft, but she played with enough force and confidence to be heard over the wind flowing in through the windows. She strummed as she said, "Every Emily Dickinson poem can be sung to the tune of 'Greensleeves.'"

And, to prove her point, Flannery sang first about a narrow fellow in the grass and second about a visit from death, all while playing the same simple melody. When she started into "Wild nights, wild nights!" in that notoriously thick Southern accent of hers, Erik slowed the car to a crawl and parked under a stand of hickories. He listened to Flannery sing about the wild nights that could be their luxury. When she stopped, he said, "With your permission, I would like to kiss you."

Flannery, of course, was no Emily Dickinson. She would not hide behind a curtain and listen to music in another room. She would not lock herself in her room when a suitor came calling. She may not be the most experienced romantic in Baldwin County, and she may be a devout Catholic, but she would not be defined as the twentieth century's own little virgin poet. She spoke softly. "You have my permission."

Erik closed his eyes and leaned in. Later, he would read Flannery's fictionalized version of this kiss. She described the adrenaline that surged through her, the same type that enables a girl to carry a packed trunk out of a burning house. But for Erik, all he felt was awkward. Flannery didn't know how to position her lips, so he ended up kissing her teeth. He grazed his hand softly across her ribs. He could feel the crumbling bones underneath her wool coat, each rib jutting like the ridges in the dirt roads they'd ridden along. The teeth. The ribs. Flannery's sickness flooded through Erik. Where he wanted to feel love, he felt death.

He was at a loss. Should he keep kissing her teeth? Could he stop? Erik dangled over the precipice of panic for one second, then another until, luckily, the sound of a man clearing his throat drifted through the open window. Erik released Flannery. They both turned to see the man who had wandered up behind the parked car. He was a lean white man in his late fifties. He pushed back a black felt hat ringed with sweat. "Y'all doing okay?" he asked. "Ain't got a flat tire or nothing, do you?"

"No," Erik said. "Everything is just fine."

"Well, okay, then." The old man nodded and started again on his way down the road.

Flannery, for her part, could not stop giggling. Clearly, she was just plain tickled by the whole affair.

Unfortunately, Flannery was so flustered when Erik dropped her back off at Andalusia that she forgot her ukulele in his car. The next she heard from him, he'd taken a six-month leave of absence from work and returned to Denmark. Whether or not he took her ukulele with him is not clear. Either way, both were gone.

The autumn turned to winter and the subsequent spring limped in without the usual sense of rebirth. Flannery's doctor took her off the adrenocorticotropic hormone and put her on an experimental drug called Meticorton. Flannery's thirtieth birthday came with a cane that she would need to get around that summer. One year after the kiss, Flannery purchased the pair of aluminum crutches that she'd ride for the rest of her life. These crutches helped her out to the mailbox, where she found her final letter from Erik: the one in which he announced his engagement.

Flannery stuffed the letter in the pocket of her wool coat and hobbled through the magnolias and red oaks, the chrysanthemums back in bloom and the sweetgums carpeting pathways with their fallen leaves until she made it well into the back forty of Andalusia, to a shack that an old black man had built, that Regina knew nothing about and everyone else ignored. The man's name was Coleman. Flannery liked him because he had skin that wrapped around a bag of bones in the same ill-fated manner as Flannery's. She caught sight of then turned a blind eye to the moonshine still he used to make his money. She tapped on his door with the rubber end of her crutch. Coleman groaned and cursed his popping knee joints and kicked over a tin plate that never should have been left on the floor to begin with and eventually opened the door. Of course, he would've known from the knock that it was Flannery and of course he would've known what she was there for. He invited her in. He lit the fire in his little chimney and set a kettle on to boil. He asked, "Would you like some coffee, Miss Flannery?"

"Yes, please, Coleman." She lowered herself into an old cane chair next to Coleman's one table. She hesitated to ask. Surely, Coleman would get to the matter in his own time. She leaned the crutches against the back of her chair and folded her hands in her lap. She could still feel the crumpled letter in her coat.

Coleman watched the kettle come to a boil, then set two mugs of coffee on a slow drip. He smiled wide enough for Flannery to catch a glimpse of his foremost tooth: the lower right canine. He reached from behind a chest of drawers and pulled out his latest work of art: a cigar box ukulele made for his favorite dying girl. He handed it over.

Flannery grazed her fingers across the frets, tapped the soundboard of old, dry redwood, and tuned the strings. It wasn't quite the masterpiece of dark mahogany and tortoiseshell binding that she'd left in Erik's car, but it was beautiful in all the ways it seemed so fallen and lacking. Flannery worried that, if she looked up to smile at Coleman, she'd cry. Coleman said, "Play us a song for our suffering, Flannery."

Flannery plucked through the scale of C, eight simple notes, then let her fingers leap and dance across the fret board. It was a song from a place of sickness. A place where there is no company. Where nobody can follow.

Sean Carswell is the author of three novels and three short story collections. "A Place Called Sickness" is one of several short stories he wrote based upon true incidents in authors' lives and fictional ukuleles. The stories are collected in *The Metaphysical Ukulele* (Ig Publishing, 2016). His work has appeared in *The Southeastern Review, The Rattling Wall, Los Angeles Review of Books, The Millions, Flipside, Razorcake,* and *Thrasher.* He is an assistant professor of writing and literature at California State University Channel Islands.

Feeding the Dog

Vickie Weaver

Mama woke us up not talking. She roused me and Roy by shoving at our sleeping shoulders and walked out of our room in hard steps. While we was getting our clothes on, the sun was moving through the window, but it could not warm away the mopes that mama had left behind. Me and Roy ate milk and crackers for breakfast and made ourselfs small. When I saw that mama had run a comb through her hair and changed her dress to go to the grocery, I did not ask if we could go too.

It didnt surprise me when mama come home from the A&P dragging that black dog by her ankle. Me and Roy was doing like we'd been told, staying close to the house. I could watch him because I was nine, the big brother. We was by the kitchen window, driving our cars in the dirt. The window was tall as a door, and when it was raised, me and Roy could walk in and out. But only when mama wadnt looking. The dirt was worn soft and fine as the ribbon edge of Roy's blankie. I saw mama first, and something fell down inside me, because that dog only showed itself when mama was mad. I shushed Roy with a finger to my lips. Mama had a brown bag of groceries on each hip, and her dress was hiked up on one side. Her steps was long and fast, even with that dog on her. Me and Roy put our heads low and shifted down to first gear.

That dog wadnt no licking dog.

We kept a sideways eye on mama as she stomped up to the porch, step-drag, step-drag, on into the house. When that black dog come to our house he stayed for a while. I wisht I didnt feel sorry for him because I knew if he ever did let go of mama he would eat me and Roy alive.

From our roadways, we peeked on mama unloading the groceries. On our hands and knees, we drove our cars, careful of curves and dips. We slowed our cars when we passed by grandma's house, where we wadnt allowed to go. If daddy wadnt welcome there, we wadnt none of us going.

I thought of what all we saw on TV. Did mama buy Van Camp's pork and beans? Libby's fruit cocktail? My ears watered for the rustle of a bag of Fritos. When she opened the refrigerator door to set a carton of milk on the shelf, she slammed the door shut. I shivered like I could feel the swoosh of cold air that pushed into the kitchen.

Mama stopped with her back to the window. The dog's mouth was wrapped around her ankle, and his squinty eye staring at me made sure I stayed right where I was. I did, I stayed there, between him and Roy. I jumped when mama yanked the dog away. The back screen door squawked when she walked out on the covered porch. I recalled this morning, while me and Roy was still abed, that door slamming when daddy left the house.

I brushed me and Roy off. We traveled around and went in the front door. In the bathroom, we watered our hands clean. From the kitchen, we could see through the screen door to the back porch. Mama was there, fists on her hips, every so often jerking that dog when she kicked the leg of the wringer warshing machine. "Piece of shit," she said. "This thing isn't any better than a rusty bucket!" The dog did not come aloose from her and I give him some credit for that. I worked powerful not to pet him. I learned that lesson before.

"Ungrateful sonsa bitches every one," mama said in the way she had of talking to the dog. Them sonsa bitches, that was me and Roy, and daddy. "If they only knew what I gave up for them," she shook her head. I wisht she would tell us what that was.

Mama plunged her arms into the warsher tub, and pulled out a pair of my jeans. She twisted them tight, wetting her good blue dress, water running down her legs, dripping on the dog. It made me think of rain, and all of a sudden I longed for the smell of it, when the first round drops mark the dirt outside the kitchen window, but are slow to muddy it.

"What do you want?" mama asked. Dirty clothes was scattered all around her and the dog. "Your grandmother was right," she said, "it's nothing but heartache to marry a footloose man."

"We're hungry," Roy said. I was glad for Roy to be there. He detoured my mind from knowing that I had a footloose daddy who gave my mama heartache.

Her sigh was so soft I hoped maybe the dog had let go. Huh uh.

"There's bologna in the refrigerator. Make yourselves a sandwich."

"Did you get any strawberry Jell-O?" Roy asked before I could clamp my hand over his mouth.

"Do you children think we are made of money? Why don't you tell your daddy to bring home an honest-to-God paycheck!"

I helped Roy put baloney between white bread, and ran him a glass of faucet water, all the while watching mama. I went out on the porch, the screen door creaking like somebody on tiptoe.

I kept clear of the dog, and reached into the thick gray water. Catching one of my daddy's shirts, I drawed it out, and squeezed it, gritting my teeth, forgetting to be careful of my loose tooth. For days I had been thinking of the dime that would be under my pillow for that tooth. I stood there, sawing on it with my tongue, and nearly fell over when mama snatched the shirt out of my hands.

"Now look at what you've done," she put a blame on me. "Got your clothes all wet." She showed me how she could bring more water out of the shirt. "How on earth do you think you are helping? Get back in there and eat." The dog's lips jittered when he growled a warning around her ankle.

While Mama wrung out that tubful of clothes, I made me two samwiches. The white bread balled up in my mouth real nice. After we ate, I set Roy on the couch for reading time. Mama walked us the three blocks to the libary every Saturday to borrow books, even in the rain and snow. She said this was so we would not grow up footloose. This week we had a book about Henry and Henry's dog, Ribsy. Every afternoon I read out loud till Roy fell asleep. Then I would read some ahead, to myself, but I always backed up for Roy the next day. I liked Ribsy but he shore got Henry into trouble. Henry got allowance, for taking out garbage. If I got allowance, I would buy ice cream, and hamburgers, and Hershey bars that we could break off and eat, square by square. I would buy mama's black dog a bone so he would quit looking at me and Roy like he wanted to chew on us.

The rest of the day mama muttered to the dog, and made a pot of Folgers coffee, but didnt eat a bite. She holed up in her bedroom, and opened her Singer sewing machine. She run Roy's cowboy pajamas under the needle, with that dog lockjawed on her ankle. When I stepped too close, to go to the bathroom, he showed the whites of his eyes.

Daddy was hunting work, so it wadnt nothing for him to get home near dark. That sure made those dog days long days. Afternoons, me and Roy played with our cars, but it wadnt fun like in the mornings, when we had made up new roads with no pot holes or dead ends. With that old dog here again we couldnt get easy.

After supper, fried taters and white bread, there was daylight yet. Me and Roy was setting on the porch steps, thinking of something sweet. Mama was on the metal glider, not gliding. A strange car stopped in front of the house, and we saw our daddy was driving it. When he got out, the car door swung backwards. He slammed it and come whistling to us.

Our daddy was a tall man, and his sharp knees and elbows stuck out everywhere. He gave me and Roy a Dutch rub, which is what daddy told they did over in Holland. Holland was pink on our geography map at school. "How's my cowboys?" he asked us, looking over at mama, frowning at the dog.

"What's eating you?" he said, and my taters went hard in me, like the peel had come back on them, because daddy was feeding the dog.

"Where's our car?" mama asked, like a bark.

"This is our car now. You said we couldn't afford the Chevy, so I traded it off this noontime to a guy I met at work." That got all's our attention, and even the dog's ears showed curious.

"You got a job?" Mama's eyes changed, and I could tell she caught herself before she petted the dog.

"Roofing crew. Cash money every day for a month. Things go good, I get on the regular payroll." He took some paper money out of his pocket. "I got off early today, but there's times it'll be daylight to dark."

Mama took the money from daddy's hand, even though he didnt say she could. We all stared at the car. I bet daddy thought it was as ugly as I did.

"The washing machine quit."

"I'll fix it."

"What if you can't fix it this time?"

"I said I would fix it."

"Our clothes need washed."

"So warsh 'em."

"Don't be an ass." Mama said this slow and even. Don't. Be. An. Ass. Me and Roy knew not to say *ass*, because daddy would get out his Jesus belt.

"We'll go to the laundry mat." Daddy put up his hand. "Don't say it. We can afford it tonight." Me and Roy watched them decide, us both itching inside.

The dog choked a little, but he didnt let go.

"I could fry you an egg," mama said, but I could tell she didnt want to. I didnt want her to, either. I was ready to ride in that ugly car.

"Forget it. Ain't hungry right now."

Mama and daddy looked each other over careful, like neither one of them was sure the othern wouldnt bite.

Crowding mama's left side, away from the dog, we filled up wooden bushel baskets with the dirty clothes from the back porch. Daddy toted one basket of wet clothes and another basket. Mama carried one.

Out at the curb, daddy laughed because mama didnt know the trunk of this car was in the front. The motor was in the back. "What kind of car is this?" she demanded.

"Renault, r-e-n-a-u-l-t," daddy spelled it out. "But you say it *ren-oh*, that's the way the French say it." Even though the car was old and wadnt nothing to brag about, at least it had come from a fancy country across the ocean. I had seen that blue ocean on a map at school, and France was green, the color of the car.

Only one of the baskets would fit in the trunk, because there was some tools in there, and a extra tire. When we made to put the other two baskets in the car, mama screeched: "Where the hell and tarnation is the back seat?" I noticed the dog roll his eye to see around mama's ankle.

Daddy swore how the feller who'd sold him the car had the back seat in a barn somewheres, and promised to get it to us. Though he told most of it to mama's back because she was already walking away.

Me and Roy got in the car like daddy told us, me pressed tight on the floor with a basket to each side of me, and Roy standing between my legs, holding on to the front seat. Daddy slammed the door on us, and went after mama. I prayed, being the oldest, and soon the hollering stopped. Daddy come back to the car, alone, carrying a box of Duz, and us sonsa bitches drove away.

The laundry mat was at the edge of town, not built like a house, but all square and flat out of cement block. There was a restaurant in one side of the building. I had seen it before, when we was driving out to the country, not stopping at grandma's. Daddy carried the baskets in. Then he walked through the door cut in the wall to the restaurant to get quarters for the warshers and dimes for the dryers.

The light in the laundry mat shined brighter than the light in a empty refrigerator. The floor squares was yellow and white, every other one, pretty and new. When daddy come back, he let me and Roy take turns sliding quarters in the six machines full of our clothes. The heavy clean smell made me and Roy giggle. It was hard for me to believe that mama didnt want to come here with us, but daddy said so.

While the clothes warshed, we all three of us went and got up on red stools in the restaurant. Daddy had to pick Roy up and set him on one. There was a chocolate cake on the counter that somebody had already been into. It had a clear glass cover over it, and you could see three tall layers with runny brown icing. I reckoned the cover kept slobbers off the cake. Nobody ordered cake while we was sitting at the counter. There was other customers besides us, a family with a mama at a table, and a old man who stood by the cash register and waited to buy a white sack of hamburgers. He was Mexican like the ones we saw every summer picking tomatoes in the fields along the highway. Mexico was orange on the school map.

The cook, who was short and brown, said "Call me Tío," and he fried thick hamburgers that he salted from a box that had a little girl and a umbrella on it, Morton Salt. He could not stop frying because everyone loved his hamburgers. They sizzled loud and made good-smelling smoke. Roy ate half, I ate one, and daddy ate one and Roy's other half. Daddy asked for lettuce, tomato, onion, pickle and mayonnaise on his. That was deluxe, he said, and deluxe was the American way. America was tan on the map. The buns was soft, and warm, and that was the best hamburger I ever ate, partly because I was sitting on a slick stool, and my feet could touch the bottom bar on it.

When we went back through the door to the laundry mat, a gray-haired Mexican grandma was sorting clothes. "Hola, señora," daddy said, and I swelled up for all that my footloose daddy knowed of the world. The woman did not answer. He pulled our clothes out of the warshers, and piled them into the carts on wheels. We put the clothes in white dryers along the wall. For a while, me and Roy sat near the door. It was propped open with a cement block. Bugs came in to drive around the lights in the ceiling. It wadnt long until we was cross-eyed from watching our clothes turn in circles, so daddy said we could go outside.

The rest of the Mexican family was in the parking lot, far out, where it was black night. A daddy and a grandpa was setting on the back of a truck. There wadnt any tailgate. Two boys my size, and a girl Roy's size, played barefoot in the yellow light of the laundry mat. I couldnt see no mama, but a skinny dog was sleeping by a back tire.

"What's your name?" The black-haired girl spoke to Roy. She was round with dark eyes.

"Roy Rogers Smith." Roy didn't talk to strangers, so he surprised me, talking.

"What's your name?" She pointed at me.

"Tom Mix Smith."

Before we could ask her name, the brothers run over and we started a game of hide and seek. Our daddy stood in the doorway of the laundry mat, his hands in his pockets. Me nor Roy was as good at hide and seek as the Mexicans. They said they come to do their laundry twict a week. They knew all the hidey places, and would hide in the night outside the map of light in the parking lot. Me and Roy wouldnt go there because of the dog even though he didnt pay us no mind. Neither did the daddy or the grandpa. I seen the grandpa was the old man who bought the sack of hamburgers while me and Roy and daddy was eating.

Too soon we was called to help fold clothes, and we knew better than to make our daddy holler again. We stacked clothes in the baskets, while the grandma sat in a red plastic chair, watching us with her eyebrows pulled up. She saw mama's old print dresses and daddy's work pants, Roy's shirts, our thin Duz towels, and my underwear. I wadnt too happy for that.

Daddy loaded up the car, and called out, "Adiós, amigos," to the men on the truck as we drove away. They raised a hand and their teeth showed like a smile. We wadnt no sooner out of the parking lot than Roy climbed over to the front seat and said he had to do number one. Daddy pulled over to the side of the road, the car on a tilt, and when Roy opened the door he rolled right out on the ground.

We all peed there between the car and a corn field. Daddy said for us to look at the night sky. Me and Roy greatly admired the stars when we saw that was what our daddy wanted. He was trying to find the serious one, he said, though he finally give up on it.

"It is the brightest star," he told us. There was a grabbing chill around our ankles, coming off the corn. "My daddy showed it to me when I was about your fellers' size, but now I think on it, maybe we saw it of a morning. We got up near daylight to milk the cows. They say that star is what makes it so hot in the summer." I wiggled my loose tooth, thinking about how much money the Tooth Fairy might leave. Acourse I was too big to believe in such a thing, but not too old to want the money. I craved for a whole quarter like the boy in the book.

When we got home, daddy made two trips to haul in the baskets. Then he stripped us down to our underwear, and saw that we crawled into our beds.

"I want mama to kiss me good night," Roy whined, taking his blankie out from under his pillow. I knowed we didnt never get no kiss with that dog in the house.

"She's surely asleep, so we'll leave her be," daddy said, giving us a pat on the shoulder.

Next thing I knowed, daddy was shaking me awake. It wadnt all the way daylight yet but I could see him good enough. The birds that lived on our block was waking up and singing good morning.

"Tom," he whispered, his bad breath going in my ear. "Your mama's gone awhile."

"To the A&P?" I couldnt think where all mama could go.

"No, your Aunt Noleen come and got her."

"You mean over to Crossville?" I sat up in bed. "Are you taking me and Roy there?"

I could tell it saddened my daddy to say mama didnt want none of us, but once she got in her right mind, he said, he was sure Aunt Noleen would bring her on back. I didnt have to ask him if she had drug that dog along with her. I could feel him gone.

Daddy left for work in the French car. I thought about mama, and about the money daddy said he left for a treat at Karo's. I meant to keep my eyes open, but they went shut. Me and Roy stayed in bed late without a mama to holler us awake. When we got up, I did like daddy said, and fixed cold breakfast. Then me and Roy drove our cars on the roads we made, walking in and out of the window whenever we needed to, and even when we didnt. We had baloney samwiches for lunch, which is when Roy saw we was still in our pajamas. They had got too dirty to sleep in, so we throwed them under the bed, and put on blue jeans but no shirts.

After lunch Roy wadnt ready for a nap. Instead, we took the twenty cents daddy left on the table for us, dropping the dimes into two empty Mason jars, and walked down the alley to Karo's. She had a candy store, which wadnt a real store. There was big glass jars filled with different kinds of candy, lined up on shelves in a shadowy room at the back of her house. The room had three tiny windows, high up like basement windows was set.

Karo was a big woman, about as big as my mind could make one. She smelled strong enough to make my nose water. Mama said Karo used camphorated spirits like a lady's perfume, to cover up the liquor on her breath. That was why she didn't have a steady boyfriend. Daddy said Karo used camphor to dry up all the warts on her face, and that he heard she did have a steady boyfriend. When I said Karo didnt have no warts, daddy smiled and said, see, it's working.

"Well, hello there cowboys," Karo said, setting a straw broom aside. "Name your poison," she smiled, trying to talk to us like John Wayne. We shook the dimes into her hand, and gave her our jars, too. She would fix anybody a glass of ice and Pepsi for a nickel, in their own glass. "I heard your daddy got himself a good paying job." Karo bent to pat me on the head, and I was close enough to see her moustache and smell the camphor.

"Yes ma'am," I answered, my attention on all the candy.

"Our mama gone away," Roy offered.

"Is that a fact."

"Yes ma'am," I answered again. "But daddy expects she'll come along home when she gets in her right mind."

Karo scratched in her orange hair. "It's true enough, this time of year, people acting out, dogs going mad. Might be your mama needed to go somewhere to rest her mind." She carried our jars into her kitchen, then come back to us. "Drinks are on me today, how's that?" We spent both dimes on candy: jawbreakers, Bazooka bubble gum, Tootsie Rolls and Kix.

When me and Roy got back home, I set Roy on the couch and I read some more about Henry. Henry had loose teeth like me, and his mama called them canine teeth, which she said means like sharp dog teeth. Roy laughed good at that. We drank our Pepsis so slow the ice cubes in them melted before we was done. We had already broke up our candy in two and ate it. Roy had a little gut upset after that, probably because we was not used to all that good candy at once. We laid on the floor and watched TV till there wadnt nothing else to do but sit on the front porch and wait for our daddy to come home and cook us some supper.

Roy cried for mama, mostly in the bathroom before bed time. I made sure he scrubbed his rusty ankles and neck, with Ivory soap on the rag when I remembered. He was on the scrawny side, hunched there in the tub, and I could see skin crawl over his ribs when he cried. My throat would fill up knowing how much a little boy needed his mama.

I took to reading to him at night, too. One night daddy came in and fell asleep with rough snoring, on the floor, while I was reading about how Henry's mama gave him a bad haircut. Our mama had always cut our hair, and daddy's. We had to sit on the back porch and wear a tablecloth around our necks.

Nowdays it was me and Roy by ourselfs, and I felt bad to say sometimes it was better. Because days when mama was here, dragging that dog around, she wouldnt hardly spare us a word. Since daddy was working, he left us a nickel or a dime apiece every day, and it felt like allowance. Us sonsa bitches cooked supper together. We sat at the table without shirts and ate Spam with ketchup on it three nights in a row.

That third night without mama, we was setting on the porch after supper.

"Let's go for a ride," daddy said, just like that. We left the house wide open, the television set on, and I figured how mama could walk in if she took a notion. I wanted to believe that her mind was rested by now. Karo never let on how long that might take. We got in the car and drove off, me in front, and Roy hopping around in the back, which still didnt have no seat.

We headed out to the highway, like we was going to not go to grandma's, because we knew we wadnt going there till hell froze over. We turned into the laundry mat parking lot. Daddy jerked on the brake and liked to knocked Roy into the front seat when he stopped beside the phone booth. Daddy stepped in the phone booth and dialed O, clinking coins in. When daddy started talking, he pulled the door shut and motioned us away. Me and Roy skipped out close to the highway and kicked rocks. Hurrying cars blew hot dirt on us when they drove by. I tried to hold in my head what it felt like, so I could make my cars do that at home, outside the kitchen window.

"Cowboys, come say hi to your mama." Daddy had folded the door open and stuck his head out. "Hurry!"

I let Roy beat me to the booth, and daddy held him up so the cord would reach the phone to his ear. "Mama come home," he said, before handing the phone back to daddy.

Daddy set Roy down, and I squeezed in with them. When I put my ear to the receiver, I said "Mama?" but the line was dead. Daddy was out of coins, and I had to hang up the phone.

"Is mama coming home?" I was up against daddy, looking high to see his eyes.

A knot in his neck moved up when he talked. "No, son, she ain't quite feeling like it yet." He shuffled us out. "Here, Tom, get some change from Tío, and come back and call your mama." Setting Roy down, he pulled a dollar from his pocket. "Go on, now."

I took the dollar and run to the restaurant. It was coming on night, and the hamburgers smelled their way out the door. Even though I had ate my share of Spam for supper, I was hungry. It felt wrong, but I hiked myself up on a stool and ordered me a hamburger, the American way.

It wadnt long before here come my daddy and Roy. Daddy's arms was stuck low in his pockets, and he stood there at the door, Roy beside him, daddy giving me a look over. Directly he come over and put Roy on a stool between us, and asked Tío for them a hamburger. "Fries, too, Tío," he said.

On the way home we stopped for ice cream cones. All around the building there was yellow lights that was supposed to keep flighty June bugs and little brown moths away while we stood at the ordering window. We bought vanilla cones, and they was only half gone when we got home. I run up in the yard first, through the grass instead of taking the steps, and my foot slipped. I dropped my cone. The smell of dog doo-doo sickened my nose. I motioned Roy and daddy away from the pile I had stepped in. For a minute, I knowed we all thought the same thing. We set our eyes to the front door. The light from the TV set shifted white, then gray, through the open windows, like mama and that dog was pacing the floor for us to come back safe.

But it wadnt so.

"What is it, cowboy?" I must have made a noise, because daddy asked what was wrong. He looked where I was looking.

There was buttery light around us from the street lamp on the corner so's we could make out a dog under the bushes. My mama couldnt be anywhere near, because this dog was white like what a polar bear might be. Polar bears was from the North Pole, white on the map. How would a body see a polar bear in the snow? I had never thought on that.

"Don't you cowboys pet no stray dog," daddy warned. "He could have the hydrophobie. Go on inside." Me and Roy moved slow, and I left my shoes on the porch. "Git!" daddy hollered, clapping his hands at the dog. The dog did not even bark, but hightailed it down the street.

When daddy come in, he put Roy on his shoulders and carried him into our bedroom. I sat down there at the screen door, mournful for my ice cream cone. I got to counting lightning bugs that showed theirself down by the curb. I had got to twenty five when I saw something shine in the dark, and it was the dog. He moved low on his belly up close in the yard. He pawed my melted ice cream, and licked the grass clean like he hadnt had no supper. He swallowed the cone in one bite.

When he looked straight at me, I know my heart showed that I always felt sorry for a dog, even the snarliest one around. But I slammed the door, because any kindness I had ever give to any like him had nearly cost me my hand. I worked on being mad at him, for his doo-doo on my shoe that made me drop my ice cream, and for him making me think my mama had come home. I closed my eyes to hold in my lonesome hurt, and when I opened them, the dog was gone.

I had read to Roy today that Ribsy yanked the string to pull Henry's teeth, and now I was wanting to know what come next, but daddy said lights out. We did not even take time for baths. I left off the sheet, feeling smothered by it. Roy slept with his blankie wrapped around his sweaty neck, and his thumb in his mouth.

I wallered all over my bed, one side and the other, and switched places for my head and my feet and switched back. What was my mama doing, I wondered. Aunt Noleen had a new, two-floored house, and no children. I could not think what might keep them busy all day. I knew the black dog was not there, because Aunt Noleen would not let a dog in her house. In my mind I could see our mama eating Hostess cupcakes and riding around in Aunt Noleen's car that was not missing a back seat, wearing a white dress and a red lipstick smile. She was not worrying on what me and Roy might be doing to get along. I wanted a way to tell her that I was big enough to take care of me and Roy, but that Roy was too little to understand why she would leave us. Maybe if she knew Roy was sucking his thumb again, she might come back for four or five years, until Roy was growed up, like me.

When I slept, my dreams was stirred up. Tío sat at our table. "I like Spam, you sonsa bitches," he said, smiling. When daddy drove him back to his restaurant, Tío tumbled in the back of the renoh with

Roy. We drove by the phone booth, and it was filled with Milky Ways. "The serious star will melt those," daddy sighed, shaking his head. He jumped out of the car and slammed the door.

I waked with a running heartbeat. I wadnt by the phone booth. Thunder cracking had woke me up. My tongue had been sleeping next to my loose tooth, and when I moved it, the tooth sucked into the curl of my tongue.

I heard breathing next to me. I figured Roy must have dreamed, too, and come into my bed. But when lightning filled up our room, I saw it wadnt Roy. It was the white dog.

I couldn't holler for daddy and hold onto my tooth. My heartbeats was as loud as the thunder. I wiggled some away from the dog, slow and easy, but when lightning hit again, I saw his eyes was shut and he was giving out a little snore. Ever time lightning hit, I checked to see what he might be up to. But he wadnt up to nothing far as I could tell. I plucked my tooth out of my mouth and held it close in my hand. I did not move a muscle or blink my eyes.

Rain was filling up the window next to my bed. It smelled good, nothing like warsh water. I pondered about my and Roy's dirt roads, and the cars that was getting stuck in the mud. Me and Roy could make a ocean tomorrow, without mama there to tell us no. But our ocean would be brown, and we didnt have no boats. All that thinking wore me to sleep, but it couldnt have been for long, because when I pulled up my eyelids it was dark yet, and still storming.

Lightning flashed on the dog now standing beside me. He brung his head close to mine and his cold nose plugged my ear, his breath as hot on me as the fast cars driving by on the highway. Would he give me the hydrophobie? I thought of canine teeth, like the one in my hand. If he chewed on me, who would watch out for Roy? My brother, hardly bigger than a bite, called out in his sleep for our mama who wadnt in her right mind.

Some lightning hit that was brighter than the stars in the sky over the cornfield. The dog hunkered down and trembled, pushing in close to me. I trembled, too, but I throwed a arm over him to stop his scare. I hummed a little, not a song, just a peaceful noise. I waited for him to go back to sleep, my tongue searching the hole where my tooth had been.

Vickie Weaver's novel, *Billie Girl*, won the 2009 Leapfrog Literary Press Fiction Award. Her recognition includes: 2014 Lush Triumphant Contest; 2009 fellowship at Spiro Arts, Park City, Utah; 2008 semi-finalist, Mary McCarthy Prize; 2006 Pushcart Prize nominee. Her short stories have appeared in various literary journals, and she's honored to be a part of this anthology.

Sunflowers

Sally Bellerose

"This the most boring hood in America." Sixteen year old Ramon dribbles a basketball on the decaying driveway that belongs to the old ladies who live next door. He slips on a patch of ice on the mostly clear blacktop and rights himself. Ramon grins at his friend TJ as if not falling while he's dribbling is an accomplishment that might get him a spot on the varsity team. When TJ doesn't grin back, Ramon does his chicken dance. The boys' adidas are wet from walking in the snow.

TJ wags his head. "Hood? This ain't no hood. This is a Puerto Rican Dead End, ugly old white ladies in a falling down house on one end of the street, ugly young white ladies with ugly kids on the other end." TJ steals the ball and shoots at the hoop on the side of the driveway. "You spend half your life playing basketball and you still suck, man." TJ dunks the ball a second time. "Hoop ain't even got a net. Fucking embarrassing. This street ..." He snarls at the street. "ReeCans up and down the middle, gringas on both ends. We're the filling in a white lady sandwich."

"ReeCans? Talk normal. Say Puerto Rican. Nobody says ReeCans."

"I just did." TJ makes his ugly face and tosses Ramon the ball.

Ramon dribbles. TJ and Ramon are tight, but TJ's got a lot of problems "at home" as the adjustment councilor with the big titties says to explain why he sometimes acts likes a dumb ass at school. She only sees him at school, when he goes to school. This morning TJ met Ramon at the bus stop, but TJ walked away when the bus arrived and Ramon followed. Mostly TJ is okay when it's just him and Ramon. Usually TJ saves his mean streak for jocks. He likes messing with punk jocks, which means messing with whatever team the punk is on. Weird because TJ would be on the basketball team, he's good enough, if his grades were better. Mostly, TJ goes after assholes who deserve it, but man there are a lot of assholes, you can get real messed up, waste your whole life going after assholes, especially assholes with teams to back them up.

Ramon wonders what he sees in TJ. Like right now, TJ's getting all strung out because Ramon's taking so long to shoot. One good thing about TJ, he likes to screw around, act a fool even, when he's not at home or at school. Today should be an okay day for TJ. He and Ramon are shooting baskets in the neighbor ladies' yard. Ramon's grandmother will make them maizena if they go over to her place. TJ likes to eat it slow and tease Ramon's grandmother about the two of them getting married and moving back to the island. But this morning TJ is acting like a ten inch prick.

Today TJ's not going near Ramon's grandmother or her maizena, if Ramon can help it.

"Well, you're the only one who says ReeCan, Little Man." Ramon is short and skinny. TJ is even shorter, but not as skinny as Ramon. And TJ is a lot stronger. "You getting your rag on, or what, TJ?" TJ's arms are roped with muscle, his chest broad for his size. Even under the two hoodies he's wearing anyone can see that TJ has a kick ass body. Both TJ's hoods are off. The head of the serpent that inks its way from his shoulder to the back of his thick neck and right up into the shaved edge of his hairline is visible.

Ramon shakes his head. With all that going for him TJ is still sensitive about being short.

TJ stares at Ramon who just keeps shaking his head until TJ wails the ball at Ramon's crotch. Finally, TJ smiles. His smile is butt-ugly today. Ramon turns sideways taking the blow on his hip. "Why are you doing me like this?" Ramon means to sound tough, but the hurt in his voice bleeds through. "Serious, what's your problem? Why you fucking with my manhood?"

"What manhood?"

Ramon slams the ball at TJ's chest. TJ catches it easily. Ramon turns, giving TJ the double finger as he walks away. When Ramon is all the way down the driveway TJ yells after him, "She's dead," like a threat or an insult, like it's Ramon's fault he doesn't know what the fuck TJ is talking about. Like Ramon killed whoever it is died.

Ramon freezes and asks without turning around, "Who?" Not TJ's mother. TJ wouldn't be playing basketball if it was his mother or one of his sisters. His grandmother in San Sebastian, maybe?

"The butch one," TJ says.

Ramon spins on his heels. "One of the old white ladies?" He nods at the house in front of them. "Jackie? We saw her yesterday."

"She had a heart attack." TJ squeezes the wet ball between his chapped hands. He looks like he might go for Ramon's crotch again, but puts the ball down on the driveway and sits on it.

Ramon walks back up the drive and crouches next to TJ. "We helped them tie that dead Christmas tree to the roof of their car yesterday." Ramon lives closer to the old ladies than TJ does. He can see them coming and going out their front door from his bedroom window. He points to their car which is parked at the curb.

"She died after we saw her, dumbass."

Ramon frowns. "That old lady is flat on her back, with the TV on, snoring like a beached whale." Ramon points his chin to the side of the house. "Right there in that window."

"Papi says she's dead."

"Your papi never says shit about anything." Ramon pulls the sides of his unzipped parka together and thinks about TJ's father. It's true, TJ's papi has next to nothing to say. When he bothers to talk, he says what needs to be said, bare minimum. The man could not be bothered to open his mouth to tell a lie. Ramon nods and says, "Shit. Only one white lady now."

"What have I been telling you?" TJ's eyes dart around. Ramon knows it's because he wants to run, but TJ is hanging on. Only his eyes are running. For now.

Ramon feels like crying, but TJ might get crazy for real if he does that. TJ loves that old lady. That's the truth. TJ spends a lot of time inside the old ladies' house when his father isn't home and his sisters go at it. He slept on the old ladies' couch just last week. TJ's the baby of the family and the only boy. Maybe that's why TJ gets crazy; all those women making all that noise, his papi gone half the time making money somehow, somewhere, barely saying a word when he's home.

The boys squat. TJ's ears are turning red. Ramon starts to tell him to pull up his hoodies, thinks better of it. Pulls the hood of his own parka up instead. Come to think of it the old lady, the dead one, is quiet like TJ's papi. The live one talks enough for them both. The dead one, Ramon wants to laugh, one of those horror movie laughs, the dead one will talk less than TJ's papi now. Jackie, her name is Jackie. The other one's name is Regina. Seems to Ramon, someone dies, you call them by their name. Someone's wife dies … Ramon can't finish the thought without barking out a laugh. The old ladies got married. What's he supposed to think about that?

TJ doesn't even flinch when Ramon laughs.

Ramon studies TJ while TJ studies a crack in the driveway. Ramon knows exactly how many nights TJ spends on the old ladies' couch. The whole neighborhood knows who sleeps where. They know that TJ's father slept in a third floor apartment with TJ's mother's ex best friend one time. They know Ramon's father kicked Ramon's brother Oscar out of the house for smoking marijuana in front of their little sister Evone and now Oscar lives with their grandmother and gets to eat her maizena every morning. Everybody knows every damn thing. But Ramon keeps his mouth shut about TJ staying with the old white ladies. Sometimes the only privacy you get is not having to talk about your own personal business.

"Only ever was one lady in that house," TJ finally says. He sounds like somebody else. Someone in a trance who might cry without having to punch out the person he cried in front of. His voice is soft, like when they walk in the woods behind the strip mall.

Ramon knows what TJ is saying. Jackie was barely female, buzz cut, men's pants, work boots, on an old lady. A really old lady. "What's going to happen to her, the pretty one?"

"Pretty?" TJ is back to being a dick. "She's poor. She's old. She's white. She's a dyke. Pick any two and it don't add up to pretty."

"You got a white girlfriend," Ramon says. "She ain't old," he concedes. Reconsiders. "But she's poor." He runs a finger along the crack in the blacktop wondering how TJ, with his shit for personality, got a pretty girlfriend. Must be his body. He wonders what the girlfriend lets TJ do. "This is why you've been ugly all morning?"

"How am I supposed to know what's going to happen to the pretty one?" TJ looks like he might spit on Ramon. Not that he would. Probably not. He spit on Ramon's sneaker one time. TJ's shoulder starts twitching like it does when he's trying not to hit someone or trying not to cry. Ramon has seen him cry, but not since TJ's favorite cousin got killed by a hit and run and even then TJ crying meant TJ crazy after he stopped crying. Ramon can see the shoulder moving right through the layers of hoodies. He pretends he doesn't see TJ's arm spazzing.

TJ jumps up. "Let's go see."

"See what?"

"If she's in there, sitting on her chair like a beached whale, like you said. Maybe Papi got it wrong. People on this street." TJ's voice lifts with the thought of how wrong people on this street can be. "You see an ambulance? You hear sirens?" TJ's excited like he hit on the essential point that's going to save the old butch white lady from being dead. Like his papi, maybe this one time, carried a rumor without checking it out, without making sure it was true before it came out his mouth.

"Sirens every night." Ramon thinks a minute. Maybe TJ has a point. "You hear them, same as me, but never on this street, hardly ever." He stops, yeah, maybe TJ is right. "No ambulance next door, not last night."

TJ sprints around to the side of the house, stops dead in his tracks, stands with his back against the faded clapboard a few feet from the window. Ramon stands shoulder to shoulder with TJ. If she's not dead, Jackie should be sleeping on the ratty chair inside the house at this time of the morning, not five feet from the window.

"Look inside," TJ hisses. He crouches and hugs his knees, his butt against the house. Ramon would tell him that the mold on the clapboard is going to rub off on to his jeans, but TJ would be disgusted if he knew Ramon even thinks about this stupid shit.

"You look inside." He slides down next to TJ. "She was your girlfriend." Ramon winces at his own remark. He didn't mean to say *was*, didn't mean to disrespect the dead, not with TJ looking so messed up, his arm twitching, his chest heaving like he ran a mile. Ramon is afraid of looking and finding an empty chair, too. "TV ain't on."

"How do you know?" TJ stands up. "The window is closed. How do you know the TV ain't on?" TJ's voice is a loud squeak.

Ramon shakes his head. "She likes the TV on loud, man." TJ knows this. They've spent enough time slumped against the side of this house by this window to know you can tell if the TV is in on or not even with the window closed. Even on a cold day they can catch the score of a Patriot's game by listening near the window. "Let's get out of here. Your girlfriend is dead." This time Ramon says girlfriend and dead on purpose. He figures if he can piss TJ off by repeating the shit about Jackie being TJ's dead girlfriend TJ will go just a little crazy and they can fight instead of looking in the damn window, not seeing Jackie sitting on the chair, and having TJ go full blown crazy.

"Shut up fool." TJ punches Ramon in the biceps but there's no muscle behind the hit. He stops breathing and listens hard.

There is noise coming through the screen window. Not snoring, not the TV. Whimpering. Ramon leans forward on the tips of his sneakers so his stick-out Obama ears can catch the sound. "Jackie," he whispers.

TJ shakes his head. "Regina." TJ, on his feet, squints through the window. His hand shades his eyes from the glare that bounces from the snow to the glass.

Ramon stands behind TJ, puts a hand on his shoulder. They stare in at Regina.

Regina, who handed them cookies like they were little kids, just yesterday or maybe the day before. She's sitting on Jackie's chair. They see her in side view. Between the screen and the fact that there is no light on in the room, the boys can't see her very well. They can tell it's her though. She's on the edge of the seat, staring straight ahead, an old lady zombie making a sound that's getting louder or maybe just sounds louder because the boys are listening so hard. She's so close that if the window was open and they leaned way in they could touch her.

The pane barely rattles as TJ puts a hand flat against the window, but Regina cocks her head responding to the sound.

They watch Regina's slow-mo move as her head swivels in their direction. They watch her frown as she fights with the sash to unlock and raise the window. They watch her close her eyes and bite her lip as she manages to move the stuck screen. Ramon wants to yell, "Never mind the fucking screen." Something is happening in his chest, like somebody shoved a fist in and is squeezing his lungs, maybe his heart. It hurts bad.

When the screen is finally up the old lady says, "Oh, TJ. Oh, Ramon."

TJ and Regina stare at each other. TJ's mouth is open. It makes him look stupid. Ramon feels like he's doing something bad, watching the old lady's sad face and TJ's open mouth. Regina looks older by the second. TJ's hoodie gets wet in the front. Ramon wonders if TJ knows he's crying. He wants to run, but he can't leave TJ.

"Remember the time Jackie caught you peeing on the rhododendron in the back yard?" Regina says. "And that bouquet of sunflowers you picked for her. She still has those, on a vase on our dresser, all dried up." She smiles, a far-off looking smile that scares Ramon. "Ten years of dust, all the seeds fell out a long time ago." She sighs. "I tossed them in the trash, but she pulled them out."

Ramon takes a step back. Shut up about the fucking dead sunflowers, he wants to yell, TJ doesn't know the difference between a rhododendron and an oak tree.

"You were about six years old," Regina says, almost happy. "So cute."

TJ nods and his fists curl. Ramon wonders if TJ remembers it was him, Ramon, and not TJ who got caught pissing on the rhododendron. Ramon can't remember if it was him or TJ who gave Jackie the sunflowers. TJ's fists clench and uncurl. He is fighting his hands so they won't try to put themselves through something.

Ramon stares at Regina wondering if she'll have to move. Where's TJ going to go when he can't hack it at home if she moves? He can't stay with Ramon. Ramon's father doesn't understand that some people live in places they have to get out of once in a while.

Regina leans closer and puts her fingertips on TJ's cheek. The pain in Ramon's chest pokes at him. He sees Regina's face clearly, her hair uncombed, the wrinkles deep. "She loved you. She would never say it, wouldn't want to embarrass you or herself, but I will." Regina's lips are dry. She usually has pink lips and cheeks. Her face is all the same grey today. Her voice sounds younger than usual, a girl's voice coming out of an old lady.

Ramon tries to breathe the knotted fist out of his chest. The old butch one is dead. He has known people who died, young people. He held a baby once, a little girl who lived right down the street, held her while her mother picked up the shit that fell out of her purse. A few weeks later that baby died. Ramon kind of liked holding her. She smelled good, but he didn't panic when that baby died. His cousin died. Ramon tries to calm himself by thinking of all the people he knows who died and all the times he didn't panic. He sucks in a big breath and holds it, a trick his father taught him. If Ramon doesn't stay cool he can't help TJ stay cool. Old people, Ramon reminds himself, that's what they do, they die. But Jackie, somehow he thought Jackie would wait until TJ got better. Who's going to help Ramon help TJ get better now? He holds his jaw to stop his chin from shaking. Ramon closes his eyes, hoping TJ and Regina keep staring at each other for a minute so he can think of something to do to get them all out this, some way to get the pain out of his chest, but all he can think about is their future. His and TJ's.

Ramon has been holding back visions of their future for a long time. They're only sixteen so, if neither of them dies young, there's a lot of future pressing hard, breaking through his thoughts at the wrong times. He sees them, him and TJ next week or next month, maybe tomorrow or later this afternoon, after TJ stops falling apart and comes back together, and he will, TJ will fall apart and he will come back together, maybe crazier than before, but he will come back, he always does. Ramon tries, but he can't hold back his worst thought - TJ losing the fight to keep his fists down, going after whoever is closest. That's what Ramon is most afraid of - TJ not able to keep his fists at his sides until he finds a punk who deserves them. TJ wailing on whoever is closest.

Ramon wonders when his mom and the rest of the neighbor ladies will come with rice and beans and cake and mass cards. The old dykes have lived here since before the boys were born. The neighbor ladies will turn out for them.

He realizes his mom doesn't know yet, none of the ladies know. TJ's papi wanted TJ to know first. So TJ could pay his respects before everyone else got there. He tugs on TJ's hoodie. TJ shakes him off. "Say sorry, say sorry to Regina." Ramon can't remember using her name before and he says it like a punk now, in a high nervous voice. "Then we gotta go TJ. Sorry for your loss." Ramon wishes he didn't have to look at Regina when he says this. If Jackie was TJ's old lady girlfriend, Regina is Ramon's. "I'm sorry. Real sorry. We gotta go." He grabs a piece of TJ's arm when he yanks at the hoodie this time.

"Get off me," TJ growls.

"She loved you too, Ramon." Regina is wearing some kind of a nightgown that she forgot to tie at the neck. The pepperoni skin on her upper chest shows. Ramon cries, not hard, he thinks he can stop. "But TJ ..." She puts a spotty hand over her heart.

TJ grips the window sill, turns on his heels and runs.

Ramon follows him. He's never been as fast or as strong as TJ, but Ramon catches up and tackles him on the front lawn. They roll over each other, bodies slamming together, hanging on like they'll drown if either one of them lets go. Then there's the moment that both boys long for and dread, when their eyes meet, when the rage and fear hang in the air and everything stops.

"TJ. I don't want to fight you. I don't want you to hurt …." Ramon voice is too tender for either boy to bear, "anybody."

"Get off me," TJ shrieks. The boys are on their knees. Ramon locks his arms around TJ's chest. TJ struggles, but he's fighting against too much, he collapses, an old trick to make Ramon put down his guard for a second while TJ rallies then busts out of the hold Ramon has on him. But Ramon knows this trick and before it happens, Ramon puts his head on TJ's shoulder and kisses TJ neck softly, right there on the frozen lawn next door to Ramon's house, right there in the neighborhood, not out in the fringe of woods a mile from here, where no one has ever found them, or only the one close call when TJ waved around a comb that the other boys thought was a blade, making the punks scatter and TJ laugh like a maniac.

Ramon knows kissing TJ's neck is wrong, the wrong thing to do in the old ladies' yard with the butch one dead and the almost pretty one crying in her too big nightgown. Everything is wrong. Ramon pulls his lips away, holds TJ just tight enough so he won't slip to the ground, taking what he can get, one last time he thinks, but then he thinks one last time every time he kisses TJ. Ramon holds on and waits for TJ to bust out and start swinging. They both wait for TJ to explode. For a long moment TJ stays limp and spent in Ramon's arms.

TJ doesn't burst out. Ramon stops holding him and says, "Sit up, man." Ramon puts his arm over TJ's shoulder, like Ramon's father does to Ramon once in a while. "Fuck all of this, TJ." He means fuck one old white lady being dead and the other one looking tired as death and talking in a little girl voice. He means fuck TJ going to see his pretty white girlfriend after he and TJ have sex behind a tree near the strip mall. He means fuck TJ being crazy. "Jackie's dead. I'm here, man, but I'm done with crazy." He knows it's the wrong thing to say to calm TJ. He knows it is exactly the wrong time to say it. He knows he and TJ will both die some day and if he doesn't say it now he never will. "Done babysitting." Ramon wipes the tears off his face with the sleeve of his parka. "Done fighting you, TJ."

TJ's broad back and shoulders stiffen. "What about fucking me? You done with that, too?"

Ramon takes his arm away. The question hangs there. Ramon pulls his head back. The boys stare each other down. They have never talked about what they do in the woods. Ramon thought TJ put it out of his mind as soon as it was over. He thinks what they do in the trees behind the strip mall is part of why TJ is crazy, but it can't be all of why TJ is crazy, because he was crazy enough before they started going to the mall.

"If I have to be," Ramon says.

TJ wipes the tears and snot on his hoodie. "I got your back too." His voice is close to calm.

Ramon nods, almost smiles because he's not sure if TJ means in the neighborhood and at school or in the woods when he lets Ramon cry on his shoulder without giving him shit about it.

"We should do something," Ramon says. "Flowers or some shit like that for Jackie. She liked those big yellow ones. The ones that grow by their back fence."

"Fucking sunflowers," TJ says. "Why you pretending you don't know they're called sunflowers."

In her writing, **Sally Bellerose** loves to mess with rhythm, rhyme, and awkward emotion. Bellerose writes about class, sex, illness, absurdity, and lately, growing old. Her novel *The Girls Club,* Bywater Books, won many awards including an NEA Fellowship. Her poetry has been widely published and is featured in Lady Business, Sibling Rivalry Press. Bellerose is working on a novel titled *Fishwives,* which features old women behaving badly. http://sallybellerose.wordpress.com/

Open Your Mouth for the Mute

Shane Stricker

I'm back and forth between walking dogs and bathing dogs and tying bows in cats' hair and I don't know if you know this but cats don't much like having their hair tied up in bows so I'm getting myself scratched to pieces and every minute getting hotter and hotter. The bell rings. Over and again. Another owner to retrieve their pet.

I can't be having an exposed tattoo. Dr. Track's told me about that. Over and again. Him explaining the kennel's policy, meeting with me, scrawling his grievance on slice after slice of yellow paper. But it's summer and he don't pay to run the AC. Got twenty semied-dogs and cats at any one time and he's a cheap some bitch. Won't hire no one else. Won't pay no one we've got to help with the pickup on Sundays. Just me. Running the kennel duties and releasing animals to their owners both at the same time.

But it's not another owner coming to get their animal. This time. At the door, it's Dr. Track and he's forgotten his keys. He's got a sick cat and its owner that's brought him up to the office on a Sunday and that's the fourth time. Asks me, what's so damned wrong with me that I need reminding of the office's policies every three months?

"Starting right here and now," he says, "Next thing comes up, it's your job." I didn't think that much fair especially with it being a Sunday and me sweating and blood covered from working so hard and getting eaten and scratched alive but the doctor's shorts were uncomfortably short and I didn't much care for standing there next to him any longer than I had to. I about-faced and went about the rest of my day.

On Monday when I showed up, my mailbox held yellow paper. On it, the watermark of a sad kitten stared back at me. Like the times before. Dr. Track had scratched: *exposed tattoo: cat exposing realistic sphincter*. I'd never had a mailbox before the good doctor started writing me up for my tattoo. And I got nothing else delivered there. My pay stub was e-mailed.

Dr. Track made eye contact with me after I wadded the write-up. When I looked up and saw him looking back at me, I was glad that's all I'd done, that I hadn't wadded and tossed in the same motion. He was pissed but I'm an optimist. It could have been worse. It can always be worse.

That's how I looked at the tattoo when I woke up the morning after getting it. I didn't remember an awful lot but I knew I'd gone and drunk and took some pills and pushed some old friends of mine to go to the shop with me and though I couldn't remember either of them getting tattoos, I knew I'd gotten one and by the way my forearm felt, I knew where it was.

Blood had dried to the clear plastic covering but I could see that asshole anyway. Honest to God, my first reaction was to laugh when I ripped the wrapping away. I laughed as if it had been done to someone else and I laughed for upwards of two minutes. Two minutes doesn't sound like very long but try it. Time yourself. Go.

Like a good buzz coming on when you try to stand, it toppled me. Literally, I had to lie back down with the realization that I'd be walking around with the worst reverse shot anyone'd ever found lifetimed to their skin. But I got over it. That same morning. It could have been worse. It could have been a person's asshole. And I worked at a vet's office. So the tattoo sort of made sense. If you think about it.

But the doctor didn't approve and some of the vet techs liked to rat me out when my sleeve came up or if I left one of my beer bottles in the trashcan. If I forgot to bag and transport a dead dog from exam room two to the deepfreeze in the back. That's just them though. They already had their misconceptions about me, already thought a man in his thirties working minimum wage as a kennel attendant was creepy. They wanted rid of me and I'm not paranoid. Those sentiments came directly from Anna's mouth. "That man gives me the creeps," she said.

Lilly told her I smelled terrible even when I showed up in the morning and Anna said, "You know we can get Dan fired. Dr. Track already hates him. And that tattoo—"

Lilly cut her off by saying, "Can you imagine?" and they went back and forth like that on my various misgivings. To clear up the smell issue, my washer and dryer had been broken and I couldn't hardly afford to fix it. By that point, Dr. Track had already caught me up at the kennel with my clothes in the dryer and he didn't much care for me using their machines so I'd been washing my laundry in the sink at home. I wasn't very good about doing it. Not after working all damned day. Anyway, unless it was Sunday, I wasn't coming into to contact with any people but the staff so what did it matter what I smelled like? I was about to ask them that, ready to tell them all about my real world truths when Anna said, "excuse me." I was standing in front of the fridge and her break was up and she needed some insulin or some other shit from there to give to a cat.

I got out of her way and damned if I forgot what all I had to say to her until much later when I was putting my hand inside a little black baggy and reaching down for the chipmunk-sized load left for me by a big ole Doberman who was walking me around the block. I got pissed. Inordinately so and I threw up my hands. I sat.

Mitch looked at me and I told him he was free to roam the wild, free to jump a fence and find some little bitch to hump until he had his fill. But even when I unhooked his collar, Mitch didn't run away. He turned two full circles and plopped there at my feet. Let out a deep breath. A sigh. I think his jumping and humping days might have been through.

For half an hour, we sat like that. Me on the curb, him in the street. I do not profess to know what dogs chase in their sleep but he was gone after something and by the look on his face when he stopped kicking his legs, I think he caught it. I watched him. He was content. I grew so as well. Until a car pulled up, quick, real quick and slammed on its breaks about three feet from us. Mitch creaked to a stand and got behind me. I sat there trying to figure out exactly how far a foot was and decided three of them wasn't all that far.

The car's driver wore a hat like he was from the 1950s and selling insurance. He didn't get out just immediately, either. He sat there. And then he sat there. And he, you know it, sat some more. In fact, it took me getting pretty damned uncomfortable and getting up, walking Mitch away for that man to exit his vehicle. A few houses down, I looked back and he was quick-stepping toward the door, staring after ole Mitch and me.

That's what it took for me to shave my mustache. I'd been thinking about it for some time. Not as hasty a decision as it sounds. But when I finished, my upper lip bled—it had not seen razor run smooth against it for what, five years?—and even after I'd removed the strip of toilet paper I'd pressed against it, I couldn't recognize me. At least with toilet paper there, I'd had some covering. Free of it, my lip was a blank page and damn was that a big page to fill. I thought of going out and buying a fake mustache but I didn't know how I'd sell that decision to folks who already hated every part of me including the shadow I cast on their walls.

Tuesday morning, I presented lip for inspection. I mean, I didn't actually walk around the kennel and announce I'd shaven it or tell folks to look at me, ask them if they noticed anything different. More like, I walked around with my lip's shoulders back, its chest puffed out. I was almost daring folks to comment. But no one took the bait. I couldn't even catch them glancing when I turned real quick.

The dogs didn't seem to notice either. Depending on whether or not the mustache had helped me become their pack leader, I thought maybe I'd gain or lose authority with them. Not the case. They looked at me as they always had. Looked at me and said, "Get me a cup of Purina, asshole." They didn't actually say that. It was more of the way their heads tilted as I opened their chain-link doors.

The cats, the cats were a different story. Cesar and Juarez—owned by the same elderly white man—pawed at my face when I opened their door. Normally, we don't put two cats to a cage but these cats are good together and anyway, they were both in there taking turns reaching for my face. They weren't trying to get me, no front claws, you know, but just sort of rubbing at my lip.

I didn't have any problem with what they were doing and sat there and let them have at it until Anna opened the door and called me a freak and told me she'd be back when the cat room was a little less crowded. I don't know if she thought I was kissing on those cats—which I mean, people do, normal people—or if she was just keeping up the mantel of hatred she had for me. Either way, I hollered out, "Rude" at the top of my lungs and Cesar and Juarez tucked themselves small against each other and the back wall.

I'd scared them and I felt terrible and no one came back to the cat room just right away so I let them be and went on to the next cage with a fresh towel for Jesus—not owned by the old white man and pronounced like some folks' Lord and Savior. She was the cat that'd drawn Dr. Track up to the kennel that Sunday. Little Baby Jesus, I called her. She wasn't actually a kitten or that small, really, but that's always been my favorite Jesus, the one that's swaddled and whatnot. She wasn't looking too damned good. She'd pissed the towel again and some had puddled beneath the plastic cage mat. It smelled to high heaven in there. Sulfur.

As I took up Little Baby Jesus, I made sure her IV cord didn't pull at her leg. She flopped over my shoulder. Unable or unwilling to keep her head up. I scratched behind her ear and she purred. A soft, sick purr. I let her ride on me as I sprayed everything with disinfectant. As I wiped the cage and mat dry. When I finished, I settled her back inside on a fresh towel and turned to fill her water. I turned back and dropped the bowl.

My tattoo. Little Baby Jesus's tail end and asshole twinned it. I held my forearm next to the cat. I turned my arm this way and that way and every damned way—trying as hard as I could not to bother Little Baby Jesus because I knew she felt something awful—and you guessed it. Anna at the door. Looking in the window when I turned around. Her eyes big. Whatever comes after saucers. She turned quick but I saw those eyes. Fear. Or at least, something approaching fear. Something like fear.

She was already talking to Dr. Track when I got over to them. "He was trying to feel up, to, to, to molest—"

"I wasn't. I was not. That is not what you saw."

To me, she said, "Don't tell me what I saw." To Dr. Track, "World's full of 'em Doc and you've got yourself one here. You've really got yourself one."

Their looks of disgust made me not really want to explain myself. If they thought I was the type of man to sexually assault animals—I didn't even know what kind of man that would make me—in what way were they deserving of an explanation? I tried anyway. I had to. Because I needed the job. But let me tell you, the right way to begin a defense if you're ever thought to have molested a cat is not with, "I really care deeply about cats" because that does not go over well.

That statement ends in Anna talking over you and Dr. Track telling you he doesn't want to hear anymore, that he's heard about all he's ever going to hear from you. And that's it. Sent home. Fired. Not even an actual pink slip to go alongside all the yellows I'd received.

I fetched my stuff from the back—an extra pair of shoes, a few pens with the kennel's logo on them, a mug with the same logo, my clipboard I'd brought from home because Dr. Track had never followed through on the promise he made when I got on two years before—and came back to the front. Lilly had unstacked my mailbox from hers and Anna's and Dr. Track's. When I walked by her, she slapped me in the gut with it. She said "You can have this too," and I don't know why she thought she had the authority to give me it to me but I took the mailbox.

Under my breath, I said, "I guess that means you're not coming with me," and it must not have been that under my breath because she heard it and told me I should be sterilized. "Castrated," she clarified and I didn't stay to discover the finer points separating the two.

"Thanks for the memories," I said to waiting room. It was empty but for a man, middle-aged, long, jet-black hair, and his dog, Chuck, a red mini pin. He was jumping around and his red rocket was out. Chuck. Not the man. And he smiled at me and asked if he knew me. Chuck reached and pulled for me because he wanted to hump my leg I figured from past experience and I told the man he did not know me but I knew Chuck and had taken real good care of him.

I played my best Johnny Carson and put my fingers to my head. "Gets fed half a cup, twice a day. Shivers when he gets through eating. Tries to bury his business when he's done making it." His mouth was open in awe of my display of knowledge. I told him how much I appreciated his business. "But we've had a difference of opinion here," I said. "If you want to continue receiving the same high quality treatment for Chuck, bring him over to the House of Dan."

"Do you have a card?" He said. I did not. The House of Dan was just my house and my name put together. It wasn't a real business. And I guess that didn't matter right then anyway because as soon as I shook the man's hand Lilly, Dr. Track, and Anna stepped into the waiting room. Dr. Track apologizing to Chuck's owner for the disturbance I was causing and telling me to leave, that I had no place there anymore. Lilly yelling at me to go and Chuck clutching after the ladies' legs. Then I was out into the humidity and it was quiet but for the dogs barking back in the kennel. No telling what was said about me in my absence.

I placed my belongings in my bicycle's basket and the urge came on strong as hell to make The House of Dan a real place. The right way to start may not have been with the business cards but Chuck's owner asking for one had gotten me to thinking. My thinking led me over to the library where I signed into a computer and started into searching. Finally, I found a website allowing you to design your own logo and have it printed on a business card and that's just exactly what I did.

I admit it took me entirely too long to come up with an idea and in the end, I might have just been knocking off the kennel's silhouette of a dog and cat nuzzling one another. Before scrolling down the ordering page, I went ahead and gave myself a doctorate. Then, I skipped over the fifty card trial pack, the two, four, and six hundred count boxes, purchasing a thousand with my home phone number and address and the kennel's logo. I was now Dr. Dan Gilbert, DVM, of The House of Dan.

On account of becoming a doctor, I thought I was deserving of a graduation party. For it, I would need cocktails and so I pedaled over to the Rhodes 101 Stop. Under normal conditions, I would not have allowed myself to, but this was a special occasion. I splurged. I went with the King Cobras and I bought two of them.

I waded into one of them immediately. The other one sat in the basket sweating beneath the low evening sun. I got to feeling pretty good on that ride too. I rang the bell on my handlebars. I was worn from being out of shape and I'd just gotten fired but hell, the world wouldn't keep ole Danny Gilbert down for too long. I passed the UPS man, his door open for a breeze and I gave him a little ding ding with the bell and he acted like he didn't hear me, which normally would have brought me way down and kept me from the ringing the bell the rest of the way home but I said, "Shit. He's the one with the burrs in his ass" and I let him slip away. I turned and dinged a white haired woman with a hose in her hand and she smiled at me and waved. I didn't even know her and that gave me hope that maybe shaving the mustache really was working and that maybe there wasn't all that much wrong with me that made folks scared just instantly when they saw me.

I rode that high of feeling good about myself on home and through the second King Cobra—it had grown warm from the ride and I can't hardly handle warm malt liquor but that's how good I was feeling about myself—and I kept on riding that high of feeling good on back to the Rhodes 101 Stop, a dinging all over everyone the whole way, and I got about halfway back home with a couple more King Cobras before my keys fell from my pocket and I was lucky to have heard them over all the dinging. I turned around and pedaled back for them.

I kept trying to bend and I haven't been able to touch my toes ever—not in middle school for the Presidential Fitness Test and sure as hell not as any thirty year old man—and so I tried to pick them up with my foot but all that idea did was push them closer to the curb. Finally, I consented to stepping off the bike. I cursed the keys the whole way down and the whole way up. Literally, I was motherfucking them out loud and I could see the guy backlit by his flood light across the street staring. I got back on my bike before he could ruin my buzz and tried to get my keys back in my pocket. They fell. Again. This time I saw the silver key—the only one of that color I possessed—and realized they'd forgotten to take my key to the kennel.

Hell, this day kept on giving. I had myself an honorary doctorate. My business was making its way in the mail. I was halfway through my third King Cobra. I was feeling downright salty. I spun my bike around real quick and dinged the hell out of the man with the flood light, waving and laughing like I had something wrong with me. Because he was still turned toward me when I stopped watching him, I kept on dinging until I turned at the next block.

My plan wasn't fleshed out before I arrived to the kennel but I knew it had to do with shit and Dr. Track's office. I'll admit that night didn't exactly start out about me being the bigger person or turning the other cheek or any of those other idioms relating to my situation, but you try getting fired and being three King Cobras deep into the night when you find out you still have the key to your former employer's office and better still, you have a readily available, never ending supply of dog and cat feces, and the time to figure out what to do with said surplus. You try that situation on for size and you get back to me before you level that cross of judgment at me.

I started on the fourth and last of the King Cobras when I was hiding my bike on the side of the building. Walking to the door, my neck kept wanting to jerk in all directions on account of being drunk and paranoid over people spotting me. I tried real hard to keep my eyes front and center until I had the door unlocked. I got it turned finally and walked on back to the kennel and more than a few of the dogs had shit their cages because no one had walked them. Figures. Dr. Track, Anna, Lilly—all of them too damned good to tear off a black baggy from the roll and pick up a pile of fresh shit. No sir. Someone might see them. And it might have gone on like that for some time because Dr. Track wasn't about to hire anyone else for as long as he could get by without them.

Mitch was back in the corner cage—his preferred run where he could look out over his kingdom—that's how I always thought he looked at the rest of us, anyway, like we were his servants, peasants— and I figured I'd check in on him while I was there. But I didn't even get to his cage when I saw half the dogs on that side didn't have water. What the hell was wrong with those people up front? I was all charged up to smear a big shit rainbow across Dr. Track's wall but there was just too much damned work to do right then.

I walked the dogs and shuffled them around so I could clean their cages. I fell a time or two on the wet concrete and three different shih tzus tried taking chunks from my hand but I didn't hurt myself when I fell and the dogs didn't get me either. I was thankful for all that. Mitch looked thankful too, that I'd cleaned the piss from his run and given him a fresh blanket. Like a thank you, he licked my hand as I put his food down. I drank all but a quarter inch of that last forty. The rest, I dripped down to ole Mitch because I appreciated him standing by me.

It didn't matter that I threw the bottle in the trash. Not anymore. I no longer worked there. What the hell did I care if some assholes found my bottle? So I dropped it in the trashcan. I'd taken the back trash out too while I was at everything else so the bottle made a loud thump at the bottom of the can. As soon as I heard it, I felt stupid for not keeping any of that shit I'd picked up walking the dogs or cleaned from their cages. That feeling didn't hold on for too long. I remembered the cats and cat shit smells worse than dog anyway so I was still on target of completing my goal for the night.

I took the cat room key from the second drawer to the left of the sink in exam room one and unlocked the door. Juarez and Cesar immediately got up and checked me out. They'd forgotten or forgiven my yelling in their ears earlier and let me swap them from their cage to another for a minute. I gave them a temporary bowl of water while I cleaned their mess. I had already sprayed the blue disinfectant, was about to spray the yellow one when I heard it from two cages away.

Little Baby Jesus was suffering something awful. Crying. A pained cry like stabbing. Other than a soft purring, it was the first noise I'd heard from her in the three days she'd been there. I opened her door and she dragged herself toward me. Like a wounded soldier in a movie. Crawling to be comforted. Held. So that's what I did.

I picked her up and let her drape over my shoulder as I had before. Trying to soothe her and it being the first song to pop into my head, I sang, "Look out Momma there's a white boat comin' up the river" and for a second it seemed like my calm tone and Neil's lyrics could be enough. But they weren't and she kept crying out. Each one digging further and further into me until I could take it no longer. I sat her back in the cage and I left the cat room.

Dr. Track's number was pinned beside the phone but I had it memorized. I dialed him and he answered. He sounded groggy, asleep, and I disguised my voice when I said, "Dr. Track," or I thought I had until he said, "What in the hell do you want, Dan?" I told him Little Baby Jesus needed his help and I didn't know how bad that sounded coming in the middle of the night from the guy he'd just fired until I heard the click.

I didn't even say hello to it. I knew he'd hung up on me but I was committed. I called him back and it rang several times, and I brought my forearm up and studied my tattoo, and then it rang a dozen more times, and I looked back to the cat room, and I let it go a whole bunch more times after that too and was about to hang up when he answered by screaming into the receiver. Not words. Not angry curses directed at me. Just this high pitched squeal. I guess he was trying to hurt my ear but I got the phone away from it fast enough there wasn't any damage done. When he stopped, the phone didn't go dead, so I put my ear back to it. Quiet. I said, "The Cat—" and he started with the high pitched sound business again.

This time I was too pissed off by his childish behavior to not let him have it. "Look, you piece of shit," I said, "I'm standing in your office," and his noises stopped. "Jesus, the cat, who I call 'Little Baby Jesus' needs your help. There's something wrong with her." He started in with his questioning about what I was doing up at the vet office and I told him he was worried about the wrong part of my words. "If you're half a veterinarian," I said, "you'll get your ass up here."

He told me he was on his way and he'd have the cops meet him there. I hung up. I'd heard all I needed. I went back to the cat room and slid on a pair of gloves. Little Baby Jesus was still crying but I'd done all I could for her. I picked through Cesar and Juarez's litter box, grabbing me a couple of prime ones. If I was going to jail anyhow, I might as well finish the goal I'd set for the night. As I rubbed the shit across Dr. Track's wall, I wondered how long it would be until my business cards arrived and The House of Dan could officially open.

Shane Stricker is originally from Sikeston, Missouri but completed his MFA at West Virginia University. He is currently in Morgantown teaching writing. His work appears in Midwestern Gothic, Whitefish Review, Lake Effect, Crossborder, and Moon City Review.

Something Merciful

Dawn S. Davies

I left Waycross, Georgia just before sunset, saying goodbye to no one, save the flame-lit sky that I doubted I would see again in that particular light. The Georgia sky is common and not blessed with beauty, but it was all I had known. I was headed as far south as I could get in Granny's old Fury. I had a mind to see what it felt like to jump off the tip of the earth and Key West sounded like a good place to do it. I could have headed west over 99 to Valdosta to say my goodbyes, then down 75, but the sun was in my eyes so I headed east and picked up I95 instead. Granny always said I was prone to mistakes.

On the gentle curve of the onramp I was distracted by the clump of tall heathery grasses that bent like thin ladies with judgmental elbows and droopy necks, who seemed to say to me, "You shouldn't have done this."

"Mind your business," I wanted to say back, but I didn't because that would have been silly. Just as I passed them, a butterfly dove into my car windshield and impaled itself on the edge of my wiper blade. Its wing spasmed wildly in the breeze before ripping off, and it was a good five minutes before it gave up the ghost, with only me as a witness. I drove on and did not look at the edge of my windshield, but reflected instead on my journey. I was going straight to Key West. I had a bikini on under my dress. I was going to jump off the tip of the Earth into the sea.

Since I was a little girl I've imagined that trees were like people. They grow out of the ground with particular, familiar bodies, and sometimes remind me of people I know, or people I had once known. They have personalities, too, if you take the time to notice. They can be warm and humorous, or stern and foreboding. They stand quietly there, rooted in their private lives, amused that we think we are superior because we can move through space and talk out loud. I've imagined that they've thought about us, too. That would be a funny thing, wouldn't it? If things were like that.

Just south of Woodbine a tractor trailer came up too close behind me and passed with an attitude, so I moved into the right lane. I felt offended, to tell you the truth. People don't give people time to make adjustments anymore. It's a fast-moving world and it was the first time I had ever been on the highway. I rolled over the white bumpy lines between the right lane and the shoulder, which made the car tires go bap bap bap bap as I recovered and tried to pick up speed. It was getting dark so I turned on the headlights. About seventy yards away from a white reflecting pole, I noticed a blown-out tire on the side of the road, and as I drove closer, time seemed to slow and I saw that it was not a shredded piece of rubber, but a crow that had been hit by a car, twisted in a heap with one wing flapping in the breeze like a black flag. By the time I got to it, I was driving so slowly I could have been going backwards, so slowly that the breeze took physical shape and swirled like snow around the bird, so slowly that the blinking of my eye took five deep breaths and the words in my throat were low and growling, and I heard myself say, "Oh, no," like a machine. The bird's feathers glistened purple and blue-black in the dying light. I saw its beak open and close twice, and when I looked in its eye, it looked back helplessly. My heart was pounding in my chest as I pulled over and turned the car off. I knew what must be done. Sometimes you have to do a terrible thing for the sake of something merciful.

I walked a few yards to the edge of the woods and found a thick, heavy rock, then walked back up to the crow, knowing that this was necessary, yet still, not wanting to do it. I squeezed my eyes closed, took a deep breath, raised the rock above my head, and just before I brought it down on the bird's skull, I smelled something rotten and I peeked. I had been mistaken. The bird was long dead. Other animals had already been at its carcass, and the only thing intact was its head and spine and that blowing wing in the air. When I looked into its eyes, they were plucked out. Cars sped by me like bullets, making my dress fly up around me. I don't know what I was thinking. I dropped the rock, got back into my car, and drove. I had to keep driving straight. I was going to Key West to jump off the tip of the Earth in the green bikini that I was wearing instead of underwear. The ties of it were visible behind my neck. Nobody who saw me would think it was a bra. Bras are for full-grown women with heavy breasts who need them, which is dirty to say and dirty to think about.

I crossed the Florida state line by about eight-thirty, and was into that kind of dark where the night is just deciding to be itself. The sky was a dome of deep blue with pink scalloped edges in the Southwest corner, beyond the tree line, and as the light grew silver and black, the trees closer to the road began to change shape and intention, folding into the car as I drove past them, breathing their hot breath on me. I screamed out loud, or maybe it was in my mind. It was hard to tell. The trees should not move toward me, I knew that much. It's called personal space. When they do this, you are allowed to notice them, but you can't talk to them. I was tired and I wanted to say, "Leave me alone. You're not the boss of me," but just thinking that was another mistake. When they hear what you are thinking it is as good as saying it out loud. My breasts felt heavy and were beginning to ache from the bikini that Uncle Oscar had bought me. I plucked the strings and adjusted the cups and kept on the road to Key West. I was going to jump off the tip of the Earth because I wanted to see what it felt like.

When I was younger I was prone to blue spells. They would grab me in the mind, slowing everything down terribly, leading me to worry about being misunderstood and accidentally conscripted to hell instead of heaven for minor, simple offenses, such as talking back to Granny, or making eye contact with strange men in the street, or forgetting to offer tea to Uncle Oscar when he visited. Or the trees would start showing their true faces, the ones most people don't notice but are there if you look. In this state I could hear them speaking, which few people are privy to. Sometimes God puts a blessing with a curse, Granny had said. She knew. She's the one who schooled me.

She's the one who took care of me when I was like that, when trees talked and people turned into machines. She looked after me until my system righted itself and I felt better, and she understood, she said, because Mama had been just like me. *Know ye not that the unrighteous shall not inherit the kingdom of God*, is what she would say to me, and it helped. Eventually, the trees would become mostly trees again, with a nudge and a wink here and there when I looked out of the corner of my eye, just to let me know that they were watching.

I was tired. I hadn't been sleeping well and I had to concentrate to stay on the road. I decided that I wouldn't stop except for gas, that I had to keep going straight because I had promised Granny that I would not swerve to the left, nor to the right and I would always turn my footing from evil like the Bible says. My bikini strings stuck out of the top of my cotton dress, the kind of dress Granny would have called a shift, a dress that works for all figures, she would have said. I could feel the strings on my neck now that my hair was short. A man is not supposed to look upon a young lady's neck, but I had cut my hair early that morning, with the old Gingher sewing scissors that were sharp enough to cut off a finger, or a tree branch, or a cord so rubbery and thick that the butcher's knife wouldn't hack through it. When I first woke up, I wore a braid that I had grown for most of my life, and by two o'clock, I had a straight bob the length of my ear. I was going to Key West in the Fury and I didn't want to get sand in my hair. I was going to jump off the tip of the earth in my immodest bikini, pushing off with my calves and toes, and arcing up and out like a seabird before I hit the water. Then I would let the water hold me like a mother holds a baby.

I had woken up early in the morning to the sound of a rainstorm pounding hard against the west side of the house. It wasn't even light yet. I got up to close the window in the bedroom, which must have let in the puddle of cold, muddy water that was on the floor, and thought I heard a cat mewing. I listened hard, giving it all of my ears, and heard nothing but the rain, and the growl of thunder in the distance, when I noticed that the back door was open, too. No wonder I had been so cold and wet, my braid so full of mud when I woke up. I closed the door. Lightning flashed and I saw the oak that spent its days hunched over us, watching over the cottage, and its eyes flashed and it grimaced, with one gold tooth winking at me. "You did it," it told me, like it had any claim on my life. Like it had any right at all. I closed the window and walked away. You can't talk back to them when they start up, or else they take over immediately. I have learned that the hard way.

Later, when the weather cleared and the sun was drying the crystal balls of water droplets back into the air, I heard the cat again. I went outside and looked under the end of the sleeping porch. All I saw was a pile of rocks and gravel and the deep blue blanket with pink scalloped edges that Granny had made when I was little. When I stood up the frosty evergreen by the washtub looked back at me, moved in the wind and said, "Where's the baby?" "Shut up," I wanted to tell it, and the thought alone was another mistake.

I went inside and got back into bed. My stomach was hurting and there was blood all over that I had not noticed. I put a towel in between my legs, which was a dirty way to ruin it. Then I went to sleep. When I woke up, the rain had started again so I cut my hair and laid the braid under the porch on top of the blanket. It seemed like the right thing to do. Then I put on my bikini and Granny's shift, and started up the Fury I had never been allowed to drive alone. I would go to Key West, I decided then, and jump off the tip of the earth and cleanse myself in the brine of the sea.

I stopped somewhere north of Daytona for gas. My cotton shift was stiff underneath me. I must have spilled coffee on it earlier, I thought, when I was trying to get out of the house, and then I thought no, this must be dried blood from killing that crow on the side of the road. The air was hot and sticky and my skin began to itch. When I went inside to pay, I noticed people staring at me because of my new haircut. I handed over two twenties to the clerk and she said,

"Are you alright, hon?"

"I'm fine," I said. "Do I *look* like I'm not alright?" I was offended.

"You have blood all over you," she said. The place was silent and expectant, as if all these strangers had to do in this world was stick their straw in my Kool-Aid.

"It's not blood. It's mud, see? I stopped by the side of the road. I helped a crow," I said. The pot of Swedish ivy in the window looked at me. It winked and nodded.

As I walked back to my car, my dress stuck to my legs from all of the blood I had wiped on myself after putting the crow out of its misery. Those strangers didn't need to know such private business.

I wasn't back on the road for fifteen minutes when I saw a possum dead on the side. It was belly up, stiff and puffy and perfect, like an upside down footstool made out of a possum. Like with the crow, the car seemed to slow down against my will. I got out and looked at it, leaned over it, blew the flies away, and saw her stiff brush of hair, her white, vase-shaped face with wide whiskers and soft, dark ears and her pointed pink feet and tail. In the black night air, I saw five baby possums clinging to the teats in her belly pouch, writhing pink and shiny, sucking desperately for that last bit of nothing. They would soon be dead, too. A mother's milk dries up like *that*. Even if I helped them, they would probably not make it, and besides, look what had happened with that crow when I tried to help it. What was I going to do? Let them suckle me? I was wearing a bikini, for Pete's sake. You can unclip a nursing bra and show your breast to a baby and she will take it and drink, but you can't do that with a bikini. It's not modest. I drove straight on down the road.

Somewhere around midnight, when the Southern night goes still and closes in on a body's lungs and makes it hard to breathe, I had a pang of regret. I should have stopped in Valdosta, I thought. I should have said goodbye to Mama and Granny. Maybe they would want to know where I was going. It was too late to turn around, because I had promised Granny that I would always drive straight on my path, and not stray to the left or to the right, and I was going to be in Key West by sunrise to jump off the tip of the Earth. A stretch of street light appeared and illuminated a patch of sabal palms that had no reason to bare their teeth at me the way they did, and I saw their chins jutting, chewing rough, biting something tough. All trees are secret meat-eaters. They ignored me, and I refused to acknowledge them. I am not supposed to ever acknowledge them. "You fight it," Granny had told me. "Never give in to it."

Before I got fat like a dirty pig, and before Granny got sick, we would go to Valdosta and visit Mama. She was buried in our family cemetery. Her gravesite had many good, strong protective trees that stood watch over her at night and gave her shade during the day. Granny would read a book and I would talk to Mama. Granny said it was fine to do that. Then Granny got sick.

Right before she had died, she told me, "Lindy, you can't raise this baby by yourself. You are touched in the head like your mama. Call the county and do the right thing. Give it up," and she pressed a navy blue blanket with pink scalloped edges into my hands. "I made this for you when you were born. Send it with the baby. Promise me."

"What baby?" I had asked her. Granny was senile thinking I had a baby. How would I even get a baby in me? Granny had said I was common and not blessed with beauty. Granny had said I would never be the mother of nations. She died the next week because her heart gave out. She had told me she would die on that day and she did. We buried her in Valdosta, too, and when she was laid next to Mama, the oaks sang a dark version of *Abide With Me* that I didn't like at all, and swished their mossy hair around, and none of the people noticed because they had turned into machines. I wanted to scream stop, because the machines kept asking me when the package was due, and the trees were singing that distracting, tyrannical hymn. I just smiled because Granny told me to never be rude. Uncle Oscar drove me home. He drove me home, then gave me his special machine treatment right there in the daytime and he didn't have to come in through the back window because Granny was dead. I didn't say no because Granny told me to never be rude. Uncle Oscar's whiskers brushed my face when he kissed me goodbye on the mouth, which was very, very dirty. When he left, the live oak in the front of Granny's cottage said, "There is in each of us a proneness to wander spiritually," and I understood. I whispered thank you, because I was not allowed to talk out loud to it. Granny had told me that since I was little.

I woke up later that night to a stomach ache and found the cat in my bed, but I fell back to sleep. I never asked for a cat. I didn't say she could come inside Granny's cottage even if it was raining. Granny never could abide a cat in the house. In my dream that night, the cat turned into a crow and flew away to roost in the live oak, and she looked down at me from the arms of the tree, offended at what I had done, as if a common cat could turn into a crow and judge me. In the morning, when I woke up, the cat was gone and I knew what I had done was bad. I should have extended basic hospitality to that cat, for she was one of God's creatures, just like me. When I heard her mewing I went back outside, but I never found her and the mewing eventually stopped. That's when they all bent down over the house, breathed their hot air on me, and told me to go to Key West. "Shut your damn trap!" I shouted into the woods, and those were mistakes. You don't cuss, and you don't talk back to them at all, ever. But I listened, though they made me so mad I cut off my braid.

Somewhere north of Okeechobee, I saw the body of what looked like a small domestic animal on the side of the road, and I knew that I needed to pull over, even though I was going to Key West and my dress was stiff with dried blood and my breasts were full and hot and I needed to cool them in the ocean. Time slept while I pushed my way through the thick air to reach the corpse. It was slow going, and the rocks pushed through my thin flip flops and cut my feet, only the blood ran up my legs because everything was backwards, and blades of grass hissed insults at me in tiny voices as I passed. It was a baby, the poor thing, wearing the pelt of a cat. The baby's face was tiny and grim, half hidden under the cat's broken jaw and skull, and her arms and legs were hard to make out from under the fur.

"You poor baby," I said, as a train of cars blasted by us, nearly knocking me down with the wind. Behind me, a group of scrub pines cackled and pointed at me.

"You shouldn't have done it," they said.

"Shut up!" I said. "I didn't do anything!" But I was lying and that was another mistake. I should never lie.

It was during a storm, and I was lonely in the night because Granny was gone, and Uncle Oscar had gone, and the cottage groaned like a man in the wind. I woke up wet and muddy and there was a cat in the bed and they told me to put it outside under the sleeping porch. I wrapped it in my blue blanket with the scalloped pink trim so it wouldn't get wet in the rain, and did what they said, because that's what I do. I do what they say. I had no business taking care of a cat. I'm touched in the head like Mama and if there ever was a cat, I wouldn't want her to suffer like Mama and I have suffered. I wouldn't want her to have to obey them all the time because they never give you peace. Sometimes they pretend like they are leaving you alone but they never really do. Sometimes they make you crazy. Sometimes you have to do a terrible thing for the sake of something merciful.

As I stood over the small body on the side of the road, they closed in on me with their arms, their whiskers brushing my face, and they said, "Go ahead. You know what you have to do." And I did. I picked up a rock and I put that baby out of its misery, only when I stopped, it wasn't a baby, it was just the carcass of a cat.

I got back into my car and started it. I didn't want to go to Key West wearing a racy bikini under Granny's shift. The cups of the bikini wrapped my aching breasts like cold cabbage leaves. But they had told me to go, and this is what I knew would happen: I would jump off the tip of the Earth. I would float in the brine until the sharks bit my breasts, mixing my hazy milk with salt water. I would feed the creatures of the ocean on my milk and I would become the mother of nations. Then a platoon of seaweed would rise up and swaddle me, declaiming my sins, dragging me down to the bottom where I belonged, because they had told me so and I had to listen.

Dawn S. Davies (www.dawnsdavies.com) has an MFA from Florida International University. She was the 2013 recipient of the Kentucky Women Writers Gabehart Prize for nonfiction and her essay collection, Mothers of Sparta, received the 2015 FIU UGS Provost Award for Best Creative Project. She was recently featured in the Ploughshares column, "The Best Short Story I Read in a Lit Mag This Week." She has been awarded residencies with the Vermont Studio Center and Can Serrat and was finalist in nonfiction for both the 2015 SLS Disquiet Contest and the Fourth Genre Steinberg Essay Contest. Her work can be found in The Missouri Review, Fourth Genre, Ninth Letter and many other places. She currently teaches writing at USC Upstate in Spartanburg, South Carolina.

Rosemary

Dorothy Place

Her eyes were the color of the blue flowers on the rosemary bushes cascading over the edges of the planter outside *La Petite Belle*, the restaurant on the corner of Pine and Williams. When Cricket first saw her, he was distributing leaflets advertising the Capital Grille over on Nassau. She came out of one of those cranky looking buildings near the stock exchange, headed directly for the curb and, with one long step into the street, challenged traffic, stopping every taxi going west. Then she was gone, quick as that, leaving the memory of those blue eyes, her one long leg as she disappeared into the back seat of the cab, and a shadowy image of a woman he named Rosemary.

You might say it was love at first sight. Whimsical thoughts of love, of course. He never really had a girlfriend unless you counted Audrey, the only girl who dropped a valentine in the brown paper bag that Mrs. Russ' third graders decorated as mail boxes. Crippled and homeless, he didn't have much to offer anyone. But he liked to fantasize about having a steady during the long days on the streets, during the wretched nights in the tunnels, during the rainy afternoons sheltered in doorways, during the long painful walks to the next station where the lost stopped for respite.

His fantasies about women were fueled by the nighttime reminiscences of the other homeless men's descriptions of depraved sexual encounters that helped him secretly release his frustrations into a plastic bag, a poor substitute for a warm body. Even though he sated his lusts on their misadventures, he was sure of one thing: he wasn't like any of them. If he had someone he'd never abuse her, never describe her as cunt or bitch, never brag about knocking her up. If someone would have him he'd treat her right, take care of her, maybe bring her presents.

His leaflets had been distributed by five and the financial district crowd was disappearing into the suburbs, leaving the streets to the disinherited. Cricket shouldered his string bag and began the long journey over to West 17th Street to collect his seven dollars. Although he was in a hurry, his twisted foot forced him to walk slowly. Faster, it sometimes followed its own path and, if he wasn't careful, sent him into an unexpected tumble. He had once owned a cane but someone had stolen it. That and his grocery cart with his plastic tarp, bedding, the nearly perfect wool sweater he found in a box left for Goodwill, and the extra pairs of socks he bought from a street vendor for a dollar. It took an entire summer to get enough stuff back to see him through the winter.

Eager to collect his pay, he pressed on against the office workers spilling from buildings through the spinning glass doors and through the hot air pushing the subway noises up through the grates in the sidewalk. The pavement rumbled under his feet and the unfaltering staccato of jackhammers bounced off the buildings. He held his breath against the stink of full garbage cans lining the sidewalks. Garbage workers on strike again. The piles of waste were an invitation for the rats to come out of the buildings at night. Bad time to be sleeping in doorways. He was thankful for the hideaway he found this summer.

One thing New Yorkers could count on, there was always someone on strike. Last week it was the parking garage workers, the week before the public transportation people. It amused the homeless to see the New Yorkers competing for cabs, jaywalking to gain a few minutes, jostling each other for position at the curb. It was like watching spoiled children from whom a favorite toy had been snatched. At least the homeless were sure of where they stood. No matter who was on strike, their lives remained pretty much the same.

Guys like him who distributed leaflets worked under the table, collecting their wages at the end of each day. Gracie, who handled payroll, said cash was better. No taxes. Whatever taxes had to do with the homeless. He quickened his pace. Had to get to the office before she closed. If they let their pay ride, she shaved a few cents here and a few cents there. Handling fees she called it.

"Finished," he called out as he entered the office. As usual, he was one of the last ones in.

Gracie sat behind a counter at an old oak library desk. A ceiling fan whipped the smoke from a cigarette burning in the ash tray around the room, forcing its acrid odor into every corner. She looked up from her newspaper and grumbled, "How many you shoved down the sewer today?" Her voice was as hard as her bleached hair and pancaked face. The guys said she was once a stripper over on Third and that she sometimes did tricks if the price was right. Gossip, but she had that look about her. Wasn't homeless, but you could tell she knew the streets. Cricket fidgeted while she pulled out the metal cash box and inserted the key.

"Good thing you got here. I wasn't gonna wait, you know." She counted out seven ones with fingers yellowed by a life-long acquaintance with cigarettes. "Aren't you tired of earning chicken scratch? Why don't you get a regular life?" She shoved the money across the counter.

"See you in the morning." Cricket smiled and picked up the money.

"Don't be late," she called after him. "I ain't holding nothing for you just because you're a cripple." The cover of the metal box slammed shut as the door closed behind him.

Get a life? He had a life on the streets. Since he was twelve. First in the abandoned high rises in the Bronx with kids his age, then migrating to lower Manhattan when he had heard that things were better for the homeless. But a regular one? How could you get a regular life when you never had one? No matter. Had to stay on her good side. Distributing's better than panhandling. Someone had once told him that vets got more money, especially if they came home without an arm or leg. So he made a sign, "Wounded Vet Needs Help." Didn't pay. Too many vets out there asking for money.

He crossed the sidewalk outside the office and sat down on the curb, rubbing the persistent pain that spread from his foot to his lower leg. It was times like this, after he handed out all the leaflets, after he got his money, after the streets emptied, after his leg gave out and he could hardly walk that he wanted to give up. Wanted to lie down next to some building's heat vent and sleep until they came, picked him up, and hauled him off somewhere.

After a while his stomach complained. He grabbed the light pole, pulled himself up, and headed back toward Little Italy where Anthony's Restaurant was located a couple of blocks south of the posh places that crowded the sidewalks of Mulberry Street, places with tables covered in white cloths and wine glasses so shiny that they reflected the candlelight.

What would Anthony say if he strode by his restaurant one night with Rosemary on his arm and sat at one of those pretty tables, ordering food and maybe a bottle of wine? Not the cheap stuff Anthony served. Stuff from France. He imagined the candlelight casting a shine on her black hair and making her blue eyes glisten. Cricket knew that all the waiters would be wondering how a dropout like him was with such a classy doll, but they wouldn't say anything. Not like Anthony. The first thing he'd ask Cricket the next time he saw him would be, "Where'd you find the Babe?"

Anthony's was the first restaurant he came to after he rounded the corner onto Mulberry. Outside, a chalk board advertised, "All dinners under $15." Today's special was mussels with marinara sauce. Although it was summer, a string of red and green Christmas lights winked through the restaurant's plate glass window that was permanently smeared with city soot. A faded Italian flag hung limply from the casement elaborately carved with vines full of hanging grapes. Yesterday's leaflets advertising the daily special collected in the grate surrounding the curbside tree that struggled to survive against the onslaught of urinating dogs.

Anthony, owner, maître d', and sole waiter was standing inside the open door holding a stack of menus, waiting for customers. He wore a white shirt and black vest and pants, much like the waiters in the tonier restaurants. Unlike them, he also wore a long, white apron that reached his ankles, a tradition he said he brought with him from the old country. The strings on the apron wound twice around his waist and were tied in a neat bow in front. He raised his chin when he saw Cricket and welcomed him with a wink.

"Hey, Anthony, it's my birthday today," Cricket announced as he heaved his way up the steps and into the restaurant. Food was free on his birthday.

"I thought you said it was your birthday last week. Ya pulling my leg?" Anthony yanked his apron aside and scratched his crotch. "How many birthdays you got a year?"

"As many as I can get away with." Cricket grinned and sank into the chair at his regular table in the back near the kitchen and put his twisted foot on the empty seat. He tucked his coat under his sore leg. The smell of cooking tomatoes, garlic, and basil was so comforting that it lured his mind away from his aching leg. It was still early and the place was empty except for the chef sitting with his toque resting on the chair beside him. He fingered his mustache as he worked a crossword puzzle.

Anthony followed Cricket into the restaurant and disappeared into the kitchen, returning with two pieces of pizza left earlier in the day by the lunch customers, a basket with bread and butter, and a large coke. One pizza slice was generously covered with sausage. Cricket sighed when he saw it.

"Twenty-five cents," Anthony said. "And don't forget the tip."

"But my birthday's coming."

"So's Christmas." Anthony turned to the chef, "Ignatius, put that down and turn up the soup. I don't pay you to play games all day."

Anthony stopped by each table and lit the candles set in old Chianti bottles covered with melted wax that had hardened into colorful stalactites, then returned to his customary place by the door. Most of the passing public consulted the day's special on the chalk board, then slowly walked on down the street toward the fancier restaurants. A few, attracted by the bargain price, entered. Anthony herded them to a table and pulled out a chair with a grand gesture, all the while calling out instructions to Ignatius in Italian. He had once told Cricket that yelling out to the cook was another tradition he brought from home. Made the customers think they were in a trattoria in some small Italian village in Sicily. Atmosphere, was what he called it.

Cricket greedily consumed his meal and wrapped the leftover bread and butter in several paper napkins. Anthony might need his table. Besides, a homeless guy like him could give the place a bad name. Before he left, he went into the kitchen to thank Ignatius and snatch a few anchovies to eat with his bread.

"You won't miss these, will you?" Ignatius turned a blank and sweaty face toward him and shrugged. "Grazie," Cricket mumbled. He nodded to Anthony as he left the restaurant.

Traffic had thinned and squares of light appeared in the skyscrapers that were slowly silhouetted against the fading sunset. Except for Sundays in August, the city was about as quiet as it ever got. Cricket turned toward the on-ramp to the Brooklyn Bridge where he had stashed his stuff and holed up for the night. He liked that spot, away from the other homeless, away from the dirty streets, away from the curious eyes of strangers. And when darkness wrapped him in a blanket of safety, he lay back and squinted his eyes, so that the bridge lights came together like the stars in the Milky Way, transporting him away from the noise and filth of the streets and into the unviolated emptiness of space.

Winter was the hard time for the homeless, but Cricket was one of those most distressed when the autumn days shortened. Bad weather forced him into the tunnels where things sometimes got dicey. Last winter, all Dog-ear's stuff had been stolen when he went to the rest room in the subway station. Even swiped his dog Fanny's dish and food.

"Christ," Dog-ear had complained. "If you are in dire straits and got kids, every damn social worker in the city comes out and gives you something. But if you are in dire straits with a dog, you get nothing. The world's full of assholes."

Hal had changed Rupert's name to Dog-ear because his ears were pointed like Fanny's. Hal was a big man around the homeless, quiet and respected. Even when he panhandled, he rarely spoke to anyone. Just sat with his collection can placed at a discreet distance, his knees drawn up to his chest, his round granny glasses low on his nose, sort of scholarly looking. Never put "seed money" in the can. Said the public was onto that trick. Never looked up from the book he was reading, even when a coin clanked. Never said thank you for what he thought he was owed. He had given Cricket a new name, also. "It's the way you hop and leap along," he said. The name, like all the names Hal bestowed on the homeless, stuck. When he slept in the tunnels, Cricket stayed close. No one messed with Hal.

Across the street from the on-ramp, Cricket paused to make sure no one was around, then hobbled toward his digs, ducked behind the shrubbery, fell to his knees, and crawled up to the place where the supporting bridge trusses rested on concrete pads. He took out his leather pouch that he had stashed inside the junction of two I-beams and put in his day's pay. With the $6.75 he had left, he had a total of $31.50. He kept out a dollar for the next day's emergencies, and returned the purse to its hiding place.

Then he pulled several blankets from under the low hanging superstructure, spread some newspapers on the ground, and prepared his bed. He folded his pants and placed his shoes near his head. Next, he took the bread, butter and anchovies out of his string bag, wrapped the food in plastic, and stuffed it inside his shirt next to his chest so that the rats wouldn't get into it. He lay back, grateful that he had made it back to his place. His twisted foot pulsed in concert with the automobile tires as they crossed the separations in the concrete ramp. To keep his mind off the pain, he thought of the woman with rosemary-blue eyes.

She was tall and carried a large black bag over her shoulder, hugging it tightly to her side with one arm. The bag was so large, Cricket could have carried almost all his worldly goods in it. She wore a navy blue suit, a purple scarf, and earrings that waggled and caught the rays of the sun, spreading an occasional blue-green rainbow across her shoulder. Her black hair bounced as she walked purposefully, like a person with somewhere important to go, and slipped into taxis with practiced ease, her right leg, straight and strong was the last in before the door closed. Two good legs. Nice. He imagined her snuggled to his back, those beautiful legs tucked against his, easing his pain with the warmth of her body. "Rosemary," he whispered.

He switched position to ease his hip, and pulled the blanket to his chin. A siren sounded nearby. Police or ambulance? Sometimes it was hard to tell. No matter. Neither boded well for street people. Cops harassed the homeless. And after Connie had gone to the hospital last winter after nearly freezing to death on a park bench in Washington Square, he had never come out. Alive, anyway. Cricket remembered the gray blanket that Connie used to cover his head, even when he was sitting straight up on a bench, even when it was summer and he must have been sweltering inside. But in winter, well … just not warm enough. The traffic coming from Brooklyn slowed, and came to a standstill. Must have been an accident. Cricket crossed himself and thanked whoever it was that watched over him, happy to have gotten through another day without a mishap.

He slept late, waiting for the sun to dry the dew off the nearby hedges and warm his aching bones. His teeth were fuzzy and his breath smelled of garlic and sausage. He pulled yesterday's newspaper from under his blanket and opened it to the city section. He unwrapped the bread, buttered it, and added the fish from Anthony's and ate slowly, looking for news about the homeless.

The word on the street was that the mayor was threatening to clean up the parks and subways again, forcing the homeless into the city-run shelters. That was bad news. Another millionaire making decisions for the homeless, putting them in shelters that were often as dangerous as the tunnels, with staff that had everyone up and out by 5 a.m. What does a homeless person have to get up at 5 a.m. for? The days were long enough as it was. But where else? Charity places with do-gooders hovering over you? Once they gave you a bed and meal, they expected you to pray and collect clothes and furniture from the wealthy who would replace what they donated with things that would soon become cast offs so they could buy more. Not for him. Not unless he was sick and had nowhere else to go. The traffic quickened. Time to start the day.

On the way to pick up the day's leaflets, he detoured to the Presidential Hotel where his friend, Sidney was doorman. Cricket had first met him in the tunnels. Back then, Sidney's name was Half-verse, the name Hal had given him because Sid was always quoting poetry but never remembered the entire poem. When Half-verse got a job as doorman, he took back his former name because it was better suited to his new position and the splendid uniform the job required. The best thing about Sidney was that he never forgot that he was once homeless.

When Cricket arrived at the hotel, Sidney was standing at the curb, the braids on the shoulders of his coat swinging freely as he bent over to open a taxi door. Cricket didn't approach until the guest entered the hotel.

When Sidney saw him, he tipped his hat, like Cricket was an important person. "How's it going?" he asked.

"Can't complain."

"The guys all right?"

"Not any worse."

"Anything new?"

"Heard Jake left last week for some tent city out in Seattle. Says he's gonna hitch all the way."

"Good luck. That foot any better?"

"Some days." Cricket glanced around uneasily.

Sidney handed him a key, turned to the revolving door and raised his hand to salute a departing couple. "Taxi," the man said. Sid walked to the curb, blew his whistle. A waiting cab rolled forward.

Cricket went around back to the delivery entrance and when the door opened to admit a truck, scampered into the building undetected by the security guard. He went directly to the service personnel washroom and let himself in, leaning against the closed door until he caught his breath. When his anxiety subsided, he turned the lock, stripped, and checked himself in the mirror. Beginning to gray around his temples. He tugged out a few hairs, as if it would stave off old age. The older guys were the ones who took a beating. He had some to go yet. Only twenty-nine. But the gray hairs worried him. He brushed his teeth with his finger, washed, and dried off with paper towels. He left the building as he entered.

"Thanks, Sid." He gave the doorman the key and a ten cent tip. "Got to get to seventeenth before all the leaflets are gone. You know Gracie. She's merciless." He couldn't miss a day's pay. Had to save so he could hibernate this winter. His foot couldn't take the cold, and each year it was harder to navigate the icy streets. Some guys went south when the weather turned, but he stuck around. Heard that life on the road was more dangerous than the tunnels. Couldn't take the chance.

He saw it on his way to Gracie's. A shop window full of bathroom stuff with a bar of soap nesting on a white fluffy towel, and surrounded by sprigs of fresh greens. The sign said, "Rosemary Scented Soap. Pure Glycerin. $7.95"

He carried the thought of buying the soap and giving it to Rosemary the entire day. The more he entertained the idea, the more it seemed reasonable. He wouldn't say anything, just hand it to her. She would smile at him before she hurried into her cab, taking the bar of soap with her. Perhaps she'd think of him when she used it, understand how much it meant to him to give to her. By the time the leaflets were gone, it was decided. He'd purchase the soap the next day and give it to her that night.

He rose early the next morning and took ten dollars from his stash. As soon as the shop opened, he entered, reached into the window display, and picked up the soap. He cradled it against his cheek, inhaling its fresh spicy smell, conjuring up her look of surprise when he gave her his gift.

"And what do you think you're doing?" A clerk stood behind him, his arms crossed over his chest, the way snotty kids on the playground do when they dare someone to make the next move. Although his voice was high and tremulous, a tidal wave of fear engulfed Cricket's chest. He cringed and his face flushed. He felt guilty as hell.

"No. Look," he stammered, struggling to take the money out of his pocket with his free hand.

"Take-your-dirty-hands-off-that-soap." The clerk ground out the words. Then, raising his voice, he said, "And get the hell out of here before I call the cops." By the time he got to the word cops, he was shrieking.

"But I ...." Cricket held up the ten dollar bill.

The clerk walked with little mincing steps until he stood between Cricket and the door. He pulled a cell phone from his back pocket and dialed.

Cricket dropped the soap, squeezed past the clerk and, crab-like, scrambled up the street, pushing himself with one hand along the building, dragging his twisted foot, cursing himself for being such a fool, fearing that the cops would arrive before he got away.

"Don't let me see you around here again," the clerk called from the doorway. "I won't forget your face."

That night Cricket pleaded, "Anthony, you got to do me a favor."

"Not another birthday." Anthony was straightening the candles in the Chianti bottles.

"No, this is something you got to do for me. It's important."

"What is it, kid?" He lit the candles as he listened to Cricket's request.

The next morning, Anthony met Cricket on the sidewalk near the bath shop. While he was inside purchasing the soap, Cricket hobbled back and forth outside, hoping that the clerk wouldn't recognize him and call the police. He kept his head down, avoided passing the open doorway, and resisted looking in the window to see how the transaction was going.

When Anthony came out, he handed the package to Cricket. "See," he said, "I even had them gift wrap it for you."

"Gees, Anthony. If there is ever. . . ."

"Hey, forget it. Just cool it on the birthdays." Anthony grinned and walked away.

Cricket carefully wrapped the soap in plastic and placed it in his string bag. When he finished distributing his leaflets that day, he didn't go to Gracie's to collect his pay. He'd let it ride. He had something more important on his mind, so important that it was worth letting Gracie shave a few cents off his pay.

Thirty minutes before the office workers began shoving their way through the revolving doors, Cricket was outside her building. He took the bar of soap out of the plastic, folded the wrapping, and carefully placed it back in his string bag. He clutched the soap tightly, and waited.

About 5:20 she came striding across the sidewalk, focused on reaching the curb, moving so fast Cricket feared that he wouldn't be able to intercept her. Panic caused his heart to race. He called out "Rosemary" but of course, she didn't respond. Pushed by people streaming by, he zig zagged his way toward her, his arms doing a sort of breast stroke as he struggled against the workers heading home. As the woman with the rosemary-blue eyes slowed to step into the street, Cricket scuttled to her side. Breathless, he touched her arm, and held out the package with the bar of soap.

She turned and for a moment their eyes met. Instantly, her head snapped back and her eyes turned toward his outstretched hand. With a decisive swing, she smacked him with her large bag. The package with the soap fell into the water gushing down the gutter, splattering her legs with sodden pieces of blackened waste.

"Jesus Christ," Cricket heard her say. "You'd think the city would do something about these people." She opened the cab door and her long right leg disappeared just as the soap swirled into the sewer.

Dorothy Place lives and writes in Davis California. Since 2002, she has published nine short stories in literary journals. One, *The Full Moon,* won first prize in the Mendocino Coast Writers short story contest (2010) and the Estelle Frank Fellowship. Another, *Rosemary,* was awarded honorable mention in the Southern Gothic Revival short story contest. nopHer debut novel is currently under consideration by an independent publisher.

Qualities of the Modern Farmer

Emily Franklin

Somewhere between two and three in the morning, hours before the police showed up, Miller sat in the field on a metal folding chair. Luna had offered a cushion but he'd turned her down and there he was, cold ass and nearly drained coffee seasoned with Nubit, the liquor Luna made from the pecans nobody wanted to buy.

The sky was a hush of black and stars so tightly plotted together they looked tangled, Miller's shotgun an afterthought on his lap. From the chair he could just about make out the porch and its filmy overhead light, possibly someone moving in the kitchen. Luna was inside making icebox cookies for the swap the next day, all the wives and girlfriends getting together in the afternoon instead of the evening because of the thieves and someone needing to be in the house if trouble started. At dinner, Luna had served some fish she'd done in a green sauce. Miller thought it tasted like bait but ate it because he was hungry and the nights stretched out too long, messing with his senses, his needs; he often pictured Luna inside the house doing something perverted or uncharacteristic – performing a striptease in his fishing gear, waders against her bare skin or inviting the Mormon missionaries who once in a while wandered onto the property to stay overnight, no doubt throwing their beliefs out the small windows and seducing his girl while he was out minding the harvest.

Crime had gone up – at a nickel a nut with 30,000 pounds to harvest in the next few weeks – and Miller knew he should focus, listen for boots on the cold ground or a pick-up with its lights off, perhaps in neutral, men pushing it onto the field to unload a crew with bags or buckets at the ready, sometimes as many as fifty men at once. Just last week Mitch Faber down in Lorraine had gone inside, eaten supper, and come back to find over four hundred pounds stolen.

Luna told Miller he could take comfort knowing that everyone nearby hovered with heavy limbs from one sleepless night to the next, brains coiled like wet laundry. He'd come out in his underwear the night before, rolling a mobile spotlight Luna bought at the bulk club with credit he wouldn't be able to pay off. He'd scanned the dirt drive and gulch where someone might park a truck, but didn't see anything out there in the dark.

Miller shifted in his chair, wriggling his fingers the way he'd done when typing too much on his unfinished dissertation stored – permanently, he figured – on the computer stashed in his father's old roll-top desk.

He found no comfort in knowing every single farmer was doing what he was right now, stretching the minutes with leftover supper biscuits or sandwiches, thermos of coffee or booze nearby. Some men made a party of it, uncles gathering with grown nephews or fathers next to a portable grill, someone with a sweaty tallboy pulled from a cooler, stories or news radio heckling until morning.

But Miller was alone. A peculiar loneliness opened up in the fields at night and instead of communing in the tick-tock of swaying tree limbs, and plotting against potential thieves with friends he didn't have, Miller thought about bears. He'd read about brown bears, each over a thousand pounds, all addicted to gasoline huffing. He could picture them in some Russian nature reserve. They'd stick their snouts into containers left from helicopters and power generators, inhale aviation fuel and paw at the dirt to make a napping place when they'd ingested enough.

In his mind the bears were comical, dipsy with fumes, one with a red tutu extending a paw the size of a shovel to ask him to dance. But just as quickly Miller could see the bears intoxicated and mean, coming at him ill-balanced, ready to smack him, smother his scrubby face into the ground.

His phone dinged; Luna sent a message that she was showering despite the late hour. She liked to give him a play-by-play in real time most days. *Now I'm washing the dishes. Now upstairs. Water pressure still sucks.* He didn't know what to write back so switched the thing off instead.

Every time he typed *pecans* into the phone Luna bought him it autocorrected to *oceans* which seemed cruel and unnecessary.

The field at night smelled part like pie baking in the end of summer, scent elbowing its way through the grass alleys, and part like something dying. The last thing Miller made besides testing pecan recipes was dessert; baked damson plums, brown sugar scorched on top, with a heavy slop of cream. He'd scooped the wilted fruit into a chipped mug for his father, and brought it upstairs to the side bedroom, stood there with his knuckles burning as they pressed into the mug's too-small handle.

There was his father, sheet shitty and damp, food in his beard though he hadn't eaten in days. At the end, Miller had frozen chicken stock in an ice tray and held a cube in his fingertips as his father tried to suckle it. The season was just starting then. Out the window Miller had watched the green nudging him, the nuts whispering to him that this was now his, every last bud on all twenty-nine hundred trees, the largest farm in Walbarger County, everything needing his supervision.

"Who's there?" Miller asked now. He knew it could be someone or nothing. Around harvest, the pecans seemed their own society, able to communicate with odd twisting sounds, the lazy breeze loping between them, creating conversation that Miller struggled to understand.

No answer. Miller swallowed more Nubit, toyed with the idea of bottling it for retail, small armies of snack mixes, liquors, and oils. Hadn't he dreamed of working a cash register as a kid? He could set up a shop in one of the out-buildings, do it up with curtains and a sign out front, take the farm to the next level with tours and products for shipping. Just as fast as he has designed the store in his mind and type-set a brochure, he imagined standing up right now, setting everything down: gun, Nubit, even his coat, and walking away from the place for good, away from the life he's inherited under duress.

The wind swept through the branches, cast a few ready pecans to the ground. The Pawnees were always the first to go, heaviest, best for baking and easy to peel but prone to Pecan Scab. The ugly poetry of diseases; Downy Spot, Fungal Leaf Scorch, Powdery Mildew, each one its own ruin.

Now Miller was sure he heard something. His shoulders twitched. A fox squirrel could be disastrous, with whole families at the ready to raid and chew wires, crops. Miller stood up, pivoted, checked all sides for scurrying, or footsteps. What was it? He headed to the Cheyenne crop, trees heavy on the bottom and huddled close together like church ladies, each overlapping with more to say.

Was it foolish, being out there at night, waiting for something? Miller pawed at his face, wishing to wake up back in his tidy apartment in Somerville, surrounded by books piled into skyscapes or in the lecture hall going on about grammar and syntax in scientific writing. He stopped to pull up a sock sliding past his ankle and when he stood up, he saw something dark in the brush past the folding chair.

Miller grabbed the shotgun, hoofed it back out there, his boots crunching on fallen pecans, his mind calculating loss. He shouted, thinking Luna would hear him and call the cops, then blame him for not having his phone on and doing it himself.

He fired a shot between the trees, then stopped. His wrists shook. Mitch Faber had shot first, questioned later, and wound up hitting his fourteen-year-old neighbor in the thigh. Miller didn't want to be that guy, but he'd shot already.

"Come out here," he said, his voice sounding like his father's in a way that was both comforting and horrifying, deleted years scratching at him. "I called the cops," he lied. There would be a crew of them, thieves all younger and stronger than he, possibly with ropes to tie him to one of the trunks, the bark needling his back while they took everything. "So you better just –"

"I am here." A man, hands up in a stadium wave, hedged out from behind one of the Cheyennes, slim and tidy in dark jeans and a button-down. Had he dressed up for the robbery? In one hand he held a pillowcase. King size, Miller noted, but still – a pillowcase! Like he'd come Halloween trick-or-treating.

Miller stuttered with the gun, his stomach tight, hands ready. "Are you alone?"

The man nodded but too subtly for Miller to see in the dark so he asked again. Miller's eyes metronomic, he checked for a crew. "You're alone?"

"I am alone." He flagged the air with the case. "I bring only this." He took a few steps closer.

"Are you hurt?" Miller scanned the man's legs for seeping blood, his shoulder for wounds. The man shook his head. His father would've scorned him for caring, for asking about the guy's well being, but Miller couldn't help it.

"I am unharmed." His accent was thick, soft on the consonants. Miller wanted him to leave, and also wanted to hear him speak more, read aloud perhaps. Close to the man, the shotgun between them, Miller snagged the pillowcase and threw it to the ground.

"Who takes one bag? What'll that do?" Miller spat the words out, critical more of the man's process than his intent to steal. Only someone truly desperate would take so little. The man had no jacket, nothing but the limp pillowcase now at Miller's feet and a cheap belt that held up pants a size too large but pressed.

What would one bag cost him?

"You want them?" Miller wiped his forehead on his sleeve, the man stayed very still at first and then nodded. How did Miller know the man was unarmed? That he wasn't lying about having an entire crew lurking on the outer grounds? He herded the guy to the folding chair, the shotgun a question mark between them. "Sit here." What should he do with this man? Fragments of ideas, each one Miller chucked to the ground.

Atif approached the chair as though it was a boar or a bear, something not to be trifled with.

"Just sit," Miller said. What is the protocol? Was he meant to demand answers – who this man was and how he got here and why?

Miller inhaled through his nose and then, when the guy settled in, hands clasped on his lap, all he could think to say was, "It's for sale, you know."

Determined not to examine the gun, not to drift back to other guns pointed at him, Atif worked at appearing calm, slowing his breath, keeping still. "Oh?"

"Oh? Yes, oh. Why, you want to buy a farm?" Miller didn't feel great about listing the farm. In fact, he hadn't signed with Shelty Realty just yet. He paced in front of the chair, wondered if Luna heard them or if she was watching reality shows. He hadn't been consulted about owning the farm, there'd been no other plan in place, no buyer at the ready, just pecans that needed harvesting and his father dying in the bed his mother had wanted to die in but hadn't, instead dying early and fast in the local hospital with no one next to her. Miller mumbled, unsure who he addressed – himself, the man, anyone back East. "Here's the shit you don't know about pecan farming, guy."

"My name is Atif."

This caught Miller off guard. "Oh. I'm Miller." Did he feel like an asshole for introducing himself to the thief who was moments before set to haul off part of the season's harvest? He shrugged. "Just sit there and listen." That was something his dad would have said.

Miller described the two separate tracts, six hundred acres and three hundred acres, each flush with pecan trees. "Three different varieties right here – I bet you didn't even know that. Wichita, Pawnee, and –"

"Cheyenne," Atif said. Atif had done his research, finding Miller's place after visiting others, slipping onto the fields at night, once being chased by two men with dogs, a shot fired nearby. Why didn't Miller grow Desirable pecans, large and disease-resistant? "Wichita is excellent variety pecan. Paper-shell pecan. Lots of oil to make great taste."

"It's the best buy," Miller added, "Yields sixty-two percent meat."

Atif filed this information away. "Pawnee is large, rich taste. Good for baking. Early harvest, right?" Miller nodded. "Cheyenne pecans. Small, light. Your best seller."

Atif knew the details but had not accumulated what Miller had: pecan clusters emerging in spring, catkins horrifyingly bright green. One cluster at a time, they were delicate, bewitching in their simplicity. All together, though, they were alien pods, breeding and unfolding overnight so that a single day later at budbreak the trees encroached on the pathways, hovering. They had to be thinned, cut and disposed of or used for grafting.

"Eighty years my family spends building a crop and then you come and swipe it?" Miller was a pecan farmer now or as of eight months ago, but who could tell the man he'd been before?

"You don't seem like farmer."

Nubit soured Miller's stomach, shame prickling his hairline. Atif understood in a few minutes what Miller had been sure of his whole life.

"Yeah? Well, you're too well spoken to be a thief," Miller said and quickly wishes he hadn't. Then, right after that he was annoyed because why shouldn't he say it? Was it wrong to offend the guy who was trying to rob you?

Miller had his father's Winchester still pointing somewhere between Atif's chest and neck, but Atif knew it was half-hearted. Instead of firing it, Miller found himself listening to Atif.

Atif hadn't told anyone anything, because mostly no one asked and mostly he didn't have the time to reflect or craft a story with any sort of resolution. His family had grown khadrawi dates and first he'd dreamed of importing them, but they were too dark, high quality but unsuitable for long journeys.

He could almost recall their sweetness, the slight saltiness in each bite, the ragged interior where the pit hid. "Basrah Province. You know it?" Atif said. Miller shook his head, too embarrassed at his own ignorance to find only anger at this intruder. He could not point to this man's hometown, possibly could not identify the country in a blank map of the Middle East. "I moved to Houston. South Gessner Road?"

Miller's gun seemed to ask for more so Atif hurried with the facts. "Michigan, Massachusetts, Houston. The place where we go now, the Iraqis. RIAC. Refugee and Immigrant Assistance Center. You take English classes and maybe, like my cousin, find a job as janitor assistant or dishwasher."

Atif patted his hair down at the sides, crossed an ankle over his knee. "He takes two buses and the Metro at five in the morning to wash all the plates at Rice University. You know it?"

Miller said he did. Atif's posture was perfect, like the women at the yoga studio near Miller's old apartment. He could barely recall the feeling of his mat, having the time between classes to do something as indulgent as breathing deeply or going for a run. Had he been a scholar or just always en route to this life in this field?

"How'd you … get here?" Miller cleared his throat, tried to picture Atif in his natural environment, but instead imagined them both as bears in Russia, fume-high and whirling.

Atif clicked his tongue on his front teeth. "I was engineer."

His English was good, but not good enough to insert the article before engineer. I was *an* engineer. What was I? Miller thought. A PhD candidate. An almost professor of pure mathematics. Intersection theory. Pullback of cycles. Suppose that X and Y be nonsingular projective varieties, and let $f : X \rightarrow Y$ be a morphism. Suppose that $Z \subset Y$ is a closed subvariety. Suppose he never became anything other than what he was now. What was that, exactly?

"And then?" Miller prodded.

"And then …." Atif paused, unsure if he should tell him or keep the scene in his own mind. "I see my wife and children murdered and come here to clean the floors of a pharmacy."

Atif could not see Miller's face, his eyes watery. In the end, Miller had pushed the morphine, watched the stillness ripple over his father's chest, his beard bright white against his ashy skin. What had Atif seen? How had he survived?

"This is your farm?" Atif asked, anxious to keep Miller talking. Miller opened his mouth to explain, his grandfather's, then father's, not his, now his. What did it matter? "I smell something."

Miller sniffed. "Chicory burning. Keeps the insects away."

"I thought maybe it was the pecans." Atif's chest rose and dipped fast, his eyes on the gun, which did not interest him and then the trees, which did. In the past weeks he'd been prowling, there often seemed more trees than sky, and he found it comforting to be surrounded by such old growth. Deep sandy loam soil, he'd learned, good for drainage and steady crops. That's what Miller's farm had. Deep sandy loam soil, he repeated the phrase in his head now as some foreign lullaby. "You know," Atif admitted, "I never eat them."

"Ate them?"

"Ate them."

Miller sighed "Wait. You're stealing this stuff, my livelihood here and you haven't ever had a pecan?" Was that his Texas accent returning? *Pee-kahn*. Would he let it creep in or keep it at bay like unwanted pounds? "Pecan pie? At Thanksgiving ...." He stopped himself. "Where is the rest of your ... family?"

Atif threaded his fingers together, nesting his hands together on one knee. "My father is back there." He gestured as though Iraq was somewhere in back of the house. "My mother in Fort Worth with my sister. My brother is dead." Atif inhaled loudly. His stomach rumbled audibly. "Where is *yours*?" He checked the farmhouse as though they might be there, in overalls or aprons, pie ready for them.

Miller cradled the shotgun. "I don't have any." It was the first time he had said this aloud, the night shrugging onto his shoulders, infiltrating the words so that the sentence felt suspended in air.

"There's a girl in the house?"

Miller nodded, swiveled his gaze to take in the small farmhouse. No, she wasn't by the screen door but no doubt holed up on the settee happy in her insomniac spread – cereal and bad TV. Miller realized that Luna would never be entertaining missionaries or living out some fantasy because the life she had right now was it already: high school boyfriend Miller LeCraw came back from up East and settled in where he should have been all along. They'd picked up right after the funeral without much talk of the woman he'd left behind in Boston, the baby they'd almost had. "She's a...girlfriend I guess. She hasn't ever left this town."

Atif nodded. "Most women I know were like that. Now they won't leave whatever place they come to." He paused. "So...pie." Atif slid his hands over his belly, keeping them where Miller was able to see them, and reached in for something.

Miller went on, watching. "I never really liked pecan pie. Too sweet. But. Still. You should try it at least once."

In a couple of months it would be Thanksgiving. His first without his father, and he'd bake a pie, spiraling the Pawnee pecans out from the middle in a snail coil, and later hide a Wichita in the steamed Christmas fruit cake the way his mother had done for luck. Miller had a vision of Atif eating the cake in late December on a holiday that wasn't his, maybe cracking a tooth on the baked nut.

"It's not a weapon," Atif said as he reached into his pocket. He removed a small parcel wrapped in brown waxed paper and held it out to Miller.

Miller took it without asking what it was and found two cookies. He handed one back, shifted the shotgun around from the crook of one arm to the other, slinging it across his back while he considered the cookie in front of his mouth.

"Kleicha," Atif said. "There's a friend of a friend, in Nickerson?" Nickerson was thirty miles away. Had Atif walked from there?

"Kleicha." Miller said the word back to him, trying to replicate the accent.

"National cookie. This one ... dates. Kleichat tamur." Miller nodded. He could picture it. The earthy dates mixed with smashed pecans, the discarded ones. "There is another one. With nuts and sugar. Kleichat joz."

"It's really good," Miller said. He wished for more and then felt greedy. Could Atif write as well as he spoke? Would he give out the recipe? Could Miller manage to replicate them?

When Atif shook his legs out, trying to warm them, he kicked over a coffee tin. The contents rattled but didn't spill.

"I apologize," Atif said and it was unclear to Miller if he meant for knocking over the tin or being here or attempting to rob him but he nodded anyway.

"Open it up," Miller ducked his chin toward the can.

Atif crouched down, wondering just for a moment if the insides would explode in his face, but then pried off the plastic cover. Inside, a pigpile of pecans.

"I made them myself," Miller said. "You dredge the nuts in egg white and then roll them in cinnamon and sugar or chili powder if you want a kick and bake it on low for a long time."

Luna had come into the kitchen in the middle of this batch, been revolted by the stick of egg white on Miller's fingers. She didn't want him in the house, just out in the field where she could see him but not have talk, just receive her texts. Each day it seemed he'd come in from work and find a new bathmat or trinket they didn't need marring the farmhouse. By the front door, a planter shaped like a cat, with herbs growing out of the skull that Luna thought was sweet but Miller found lurid, or by the stove a utensil pot one of her friends had made from bottle caps. Avant garde, Luna had said, rhyming avant with ant which Miller hated and then hated himself for being bothered by her pronunciation.

Miller felt discomfort just knowing Luna was in his house, rearranging the sheets his father used as tablecloths, trying to weed out whatever she considered dated, even if it was perfectly functional. She'd gone through the bookshelf, boxing up worn paperbacks, the spy novels his mother had liked, tool manuals and machinery warranties long-expired. When Luna had gone to her sister's, Miller had re-shelved each one. *The Book of Useful Plants*, which had been his grandmother's. *Qualities of the Modern Farmer* published in 1928, the pine green spine preserved by old linoleum floor tape. Miller hadn't done more than look at his father's name printed on the inside cover. His father's handwriting was jagged, he'd left school in sixth grade. Look, he'd pointed a finger over the faded pencil to show Luna. She'd shrugged.

Miller squinted to find her in one of the tall windows. He would have to ask her to leave in the morning. Possibly she was already packing in there. There wasn't much; she had only an overnight bag and hairspray, toothbrush, a mess of magazines too old to keep at the dentist office where she worked.

"Tell me something," Atif said and stood up without asking permission. "Will you press charges against me?"

Miller opened his mouth to answer but the sound of pecans dropping to the ground in great torrents stopped him. Truck tires rolled onto the ground popping the fallen nuts, sharp cracks firing into the air.

Miller grabbed his gun but Atif was faster, running toward the sound, toward the pick-up that nosed right onto the tree roots. Atif yelled at the intruders in English, and then in what Miller assumed to be Arabic, flailed his arms, to signal to Miller.

Miller aimed his shotgun but didn't fire until the truck started up, reversing quickly, lights sweeping as the tires belch over fallen pecans.

Out of breath, Atif jogged back to meet Miller. "They are gone. Americans, I think. Texans, maybe."

Miller tried to absorb what Atif had done, watched Atif's face for regret but saw only that he was thin, the cold settling onto his skin after his sprint. Miller took a fabric remnant, ugly, maroon, from his pocket. His father had a bin of scraps, this one long enough to be used as a scarf. "You look cold."

Atif took the fabric and wrapped it around his shoulders. "I have nothing."

Miller didn't know if Atif meant to reassure that he was unarmed, or still cold, or just saying in general.

They stood there, shaking slightly from the surprise invasion.

Blue but mute police lights flickered out at the property's edge. Atif's fingers worried the scarf ends as he tried to separate stray bits of fabric, his eye on the first trickle of morning pink way off to the east.

"Stay here?" Miller asked. Atif nodded.

Miller headed to the driveway where the police car stopped, and Atif could see the officer's elbow on the rolled-down window.

This was it. Atif stood there accepting his fate. He would be reported and jailed and Miller would use the empty pillowcase for its original purpose, forgetting about Atif entirely. Atif reached into his pocket, pulled out a Wichita pecan, rolled it in his palm, smelling it through the tough skin. He imagined keeping this same pecan forever, in a jail cell or on bedside table he didn't own.

Miller jogged back, the shotgun uncomfortable on his back.

"It's not easy, you know," Miller said once he was in front of Atif. The police car's lights swiveled across the front porch, the field, and out onto the road that lead back to town. Miller's voice was angry now, determined. "Shaking trees and sweeping. See there? The brush is dense. It cuts you sometimes."

Miller paced, his overpriced hiking boots worn at the heel and loosely laced, worn now as farm boots. "And the irrigation system's faulty. You have to check it four times. And that's just these two tracts. You know I only found out two weeks ago we have another twenty acres? Down past the house there's twenty goddamned acres of irrigated Bermuda grass we used to lease. It's like there's a manual for my life somewhere and I don't have it."

Atif listened, nodding as though it all made sense, as though he had always planned on being a pecan farmer, figured on finding Miller and starting a farm store, shipping boxes his sister would decorate with old symbols and pecans of varying sizes.

This much became clear. Miller would not shoot Atif. Atif would not steal the pecans. Each man guarded the pecans or the fields or each other. They stayed there through the night, taking turns on the cold folding chair, rising up and sitting back down like fume-inhaling bears, clumsy-pawed and sad, something impossible to recognize in the dark.

Emily Franklin is the author of a novel, *Liner Notes* and a story collection, *The Girls' Almanac*. She is also the author of sixteen young adult books including *Last Night at the Circle Cinema*, selected by the American Association of Jewish Libraries as a Sydney Taylor Notable Book for 2016, a Junior Library Guild Selection, and an ALAN Pick. Her work has been been featured on National Public Radio and in the *New York Times, Boston Globe, Monkeybicycle, Word Riot*, DIAGRAM, *Mississippi Review, Carve Magazine*, and *Post Road* among other places. She was longlisted for the 2015 Sunday Times EFG Award, the largest short story award in the world. She lives outside of Boston with her husband and four children and is at work completing a new novel and another story collection.

A Bad Year for Gnats

Rhett DeVane

It's a bad year for gnats.

Like the year my daddy was born, to hear Mama tell it.

But they're both gone now, and it's just me and my daddy's two old calico cats, Goodness and Mercy. From that Bible verse: "… and goodness and mercy will follow you all the days of your life …." Psalms, I think.

Daddy always led a parade of devout animal fans wherever he went. Dogs. Cats. Squirrels. Even a baby raccoon he once found abandoned in the woodshed. The last senile hound died two years back.

Goodness and Mercy follow me now.

Mama passed three months ago. Gabe and I split up two weeks later and I escaped, from him, from the city. I moved the cats to this little excuse for a house. Ain't much, but it's mine. Room enough on the front porch for one rocker. Maybe two, someday if I get past the hurt and fear.

I drag the rocking chair to a leaf-shadowed part of the yard. Early mosquitoes—small, but bloodthirsty—seek the sweet spots I missed with repellant. Every critter has to eat.

Never mind the skeeters or the dang gnats. The pollen's stopped raining down yellow gold and the days stretch longer. Not much spring left. I lift my nose to catch the faint scent from fading honeysuckle blooms. Summer is bearing down, ready to scorch this part of the Deep South. At least the magnolia blossoms will take over soon, with their lemony perfume.

The porch rocker hasn't been refinished since Daddy, then Mama, died. "Time to dust off your lazy bones," Daddy always said about projects requiring sweat and strain.

The chair has been in my father's family for over seventy years. Held together by pegs, glue, and paint. Should take an ax to it. Commit it to the junk heap. Or use it for kindling.

But I won't.

I stand, judging the old rocker. The woven seat and back need refreshing by someone with skill. I circle the chair, chewing a torn cuticle until it pearls blood. Broken cane splits stick out like my own unruly hair. Cut it myself. No way to afford the hairdresser at nearly thirty bucks.

Two hundred and fifty dollars give or take, for the new cane job. I checked around. No way to afford that either. Divorce and starting over take a lot out of a girl's pocketbook. I use a screwdriver to poke the jagged splits beneath intact sections of the weave.

Except for the caned back and seat, Daddy and my grandfather built this chair. Only thing Daddy kept of his father's. Never met the old man. Both of my daddy's folks died when I was too little to remember. *Hardscrabble*, the way Mama described Granddaddy, *with an edge of mean his own daddy beat into him.* He and Daddy never got along, not from the start.

I overheard Mama tell my aunt that Daddy was a colicky baby, sickly. The infant's constant crying didn't sit well with his father. Granddaddy called him "Nat," not on account of his middle name being Nathanial, but because he thought his son annoying, like the gnats that were so bad that year.

This chair, one faded black and white photo, and a gravestone are the sum total of granddaddy's print on this earth, other than my daddy.

Now the chair belongs to me.

I puff one bumbling gnat and a wisp of damp hair away from my eyes. My armpits already stink.

This job will be my doing, or undoing.

My daddy spent hours refinishing the dang collection of spindles and flats, every three years or so when the paint started to shingle. I should let it sit and age ungracefully.

But I won't.

Last time I helped repaint it—two years before his bad heart sent him to glory—I asked Daddy, "Why not take it to one of those dip and strip places? Would be much easier."

Something flickered in his rheumy eyes. A flash of anger, sadness, then gone. "Some tasks are better done by your own hands, my angel girlie," he answered. "Paint covers a lot of sin."

Girlie. Me near fifty and he still called me girlie. The *sin* reference eludes me.

My initials, AGP for Angel Grace Ponder, show on one arm. I may look like an angel—petite, blonde wild curls, blue eyes—but I seldom feel like one. Grace doesn't describe me either. I can trip over air.

The loop of the P is not as deep as the other letters. I carved them into the wood when I was a young teen, full of self-importance. Daddy caught me, mid-P, and scolded. Didn't yell. Just painted over the spot.

He never spanked me. Never raised his voice. Not once. I can't count how many times he sat me down in this rocker before I grew up and flew the family coop. "Gave me a good talking to," as he said. Mama told me he couldn't abide hitting his only young'un. Besides, the disappointment on his face was enough to keep me in line.

I shove the chair and it pitches back and forth, back and forth. One rocker rail is a couple of inches shorter and ragged at the blunted tip. Paint drapes several tooth mark ridges. A puppy—can't recall which one, as we were forever taking in strays—chewed the end. Daddy shoed him away. Kept that scruffy mutt until he was old, then dead.

The vintage electric sander, rescued from Daddy's shop, compromises the top dark green layer and uncovers brown, navy, cottage red, brown again. I stop noting the colors. Chips of paint rain onto the leaves.

Nothing fazes the gnats. They tickle the fine hairs on my nape. Buzz in my ears. They use the sweat beading my upper lip as a drinking pool. I slide the power tool until my hands throb with the vibration. A couple of aspirins tonight, for sure.

On the second day, I drag the rocker to what I now mentally refer to as "the killing spot." Goodness and Mercy pad behind me and take up their posts nearby on a rusty bench swing. That project will have to wait until the fall. Chair first. I'll have to put in the vegetable garden soon if I want tomatoes that don't taste like red nothing.

So much to do on the dilapidated house. Have to get busy and find a job. Somewhere. Not like Atlanta, where I could pick up part-time work with little effort. The meager cash left from the sale of my parents' house won't last long.

I start on the rocker rails with coarse sandpaper, move to fine, then extra fine. Tiny flecks of paint fog the air and glitter the tops of my tennis shoes. Glad I'm wearing safety goggles, actually old scratched sunglasses, like Daddy taught me. The gnats slip beneath the lenses.

Four hours later. My hands, forearms, and shoulders cramp.

Day three. Showdown at the killing spot. Goodness and Mercy laze in the spackled shade, commenting when I cuss. I could stop now. Slather on a sleek sheen of polyurethane. Call the finish Shabby Chic. Popular these days.

But I won't.

The wood has to be under here somewhere. I catch glimpses of it beneath what I hope is the final layer.

Black. Who paints a porch rocker black?

I sand. Scrape. Sand some more. One section on the right armrest defies me. I will see the bare wood here if it takes until the coming of the next ice age, until they pry the gnarly steel wool from my curled fingers, or until I draw my last, gnat-filled breath, whichever comes first.

Daddy always layered this spot with extra paint. Why?

That's the shame about parents and kids. By the time I am old enough and want to take the time to ask the right questions, they are already gone. Like, what made him move to this backwoods corner of north Florida after he left the Army? People only come here if they're hiding or running, or both. How did Mama feel the first time he kissed her? And how had Daddy gotten the curved scar on his temple? Actually, I did ask him one time. He said he'd had it since he was a little boy.

I smell so gamey, the gnats should shy away. I should stop now. Paint over the spot.

But I won't.

Day four. It rains. Dang.

Day five. I attack the chair arm. I swat gnats. Probably eat a few. Southern protein snack. Tiny shards of the holdout layer cling like a dark grudge. I bear down with a tool I fashion from an old plastic frosting spatula.

The paint gives up.

I drop the tool. Stare at the stain. Rusty brown fans out in droplets from the center. Doesn't take a crime scene investigator to ferret this one. Goodness and Mercy twirl at my feet, bumping my shins. The spit dries in my mouth. I crumble to a cross-legged sit.

Paint covers a lot of sin.

Gnats ski on my tears.

Careful to glob a thick coat on that one armrest, I sweep the brush over the cleaned wood. A deep purple, my favorite. The color of spirit. Maybe the exact color I'll see before glory. A gnat lands on the wet gloss. I slather over him.

It's a bad year for gnats.

Rhett DeVane is the author of six published mainstream fiction novels: *The Madhatter's Guide to Chocolate, Up the Devil's Belly, Mama's Comfort Food, Cathead Crazy, Suicide Supper Club,* and *Secondhand Sister.* She is the coauthor of two novels: *Evenings on Dark Island* with Larry Rock and *Accidental Ambition* with Robert W. McKnight. She also authored middle grade fantasy, *Elsbeth and Sim* and *Dig Within,* the first two books in the "Tales from The Emerald Mountains" series. *Suicide Supper Club* received the 2014 President's Award from the Florida Authors and Publishers Association.

Rhett is a Florida native, originally from Chattahoochee. Her hometown, a small North Florida berg with a state mental institution on the main drag, serves as the colorful setting for her Southern fiction series. For the past thirty-plus years, Rhett has made her home in Tallahassee, located in Florida's Big Bend area, where she splits her time between her dental hygiene practice and writing fiction.

THE CATERER

David James Poissant

The husband was not my husband, but I would make him mine. I did not feel sorry for the wife because he did not feel sorry for the wife. She had, after all, let herself get fat. I was not fat. I was tall and leggy and lean. I had a stomach you could scrape spoons across and make music. The wife had also let herself get old. She had gone as far as to turn fifty. The husband was fifty, but he was a *young* fifty. I was twenty-five, which any woman will tell you is a man's favorite age.

The husband had a mustache that rode his lip like some furry Amazonian caterpillar. It tickled when we kissed and tasted like whatever he'd eaten. If he'd had his head between my legs, his mustache tasted like me. I'd say I hated the taste, but that wouldn't be true. I came to adore it, to look forward to it the way those tattooed with frequency come to relish the pain.

Sometimes, when we fucked, the husband pressed his mouth hard to mine. Those times, the mustache bristled more than tickled. Mornings, my mouth wore a rash like red pepper.

Our first fuck was nothing like this. The husband was a gentle lover. He did not do a thing without asking permission. He was quiet when he came and together we cleaned up the coat closet floor. Outside, his wife asked whether anyone had seen Gerald. We snickered, we hid. We hid in the closet a long, long time. We held one another, waiting for the open door.

We met at a party the husband held in his home. The husband was an Atlanta CEO, his guests business partners and employees, men mostly. Each man was accompanied by a woman ten years younger and a hundred pounds lighter than himself. I was one of eight girls who navigated the

3,000 square foot apartment balancing a silver platter piled with shrimp. I should not even have been there that night, wouldn't have been had Melinda not called in sick, had I not needed the $15.00 an hour I earned serving food for a midlevel catering company who cut costs watering down drinks and shorting their clients on anything tough to keep track of: pounds of pasta, quarts of strawberries, ice by the bucketful.

The party was Christmas-themed. In place of our usual uniform accented by bowtie and maroon cummerbund, we wore red sashes and sprigs of holly pinned to our shirts. All night, the leaves dug like tiny tridents into my chest.

Guests, too, dressed idiotically. Otherwise beautiful women brandished elf ears, felt antlers, and the gaudiest of holiday jewelry. Men's guts bulged red and green beneath sweater vests. A lone yarmulke bobbed in a sea of Santa hats.

The exception was the husband. He wore a dark suit, lightly pinstriped, and a black tie. His one concession to ornamentation was a small silver candy cane that hung like a question mark from his lapel. The wide woman at his side was wrapped like a Christmas present, her hair done up in festive, gold ringlets, face caked with blush. It was hard to imagine that this woman could be the man's wife. Sure, the man wasn't tops in the attractiveness department. Maybe he was a little old. Maybe a handful of waist spilled over his belt. And that mustache—unfashionable, perhaps. But. *But*. There was something exquisite about him, some indefinable quality, the way, in catering, you can tell, ten times out of eleven, which men will slip a dollar bill into the wineglass at the bar.

I could not predict what the husband might do for me, whether he might slip anything of his into anything of mine, but I had to find out. All evening, I orbited him. When I watched him, I was contented. When I drew near, I was warm.

The husband kept a hand on his wife's waist. He steered her through throngs of employees, introducing her to each but never settling in one place for more than a minute. He hovered, he spoke, he glided away. Hover and glide: It was a pattern with him, one I would come to recognize, one not peculiar to dinner parties.

When, finally, I approached, the husband plucked a shrimp from my tray without looking. Then, mid-chew, his eyes met mine. The shrimp's pink tail peeked out between his lips like an arrow's fletching, feathery, obscene. Slowly, he reached up, touched his face, and pulled the tail away. I held out a cupped hand and he dropped the shell in. I want to say that I trembled, but that's only memory's imagination. In truth, at the time, I did not recognize the man, his power or wealth. I only knew that a large, vaguely obese fellow in a Brooks Brother's suit had just dropped spitty seafood into my palm and that, when he had, his wife had noticed. Her eyelids fluttered. Her eyeballs bulged. Cupping the tail, making a hasty retreat, I felt—there is no other word for it—*alive*.

After the first guests left but before the crowd thinned, the husband found me. He took me by the elbow and guided me to a closet. I did not resist. I did not resist when he licked my neck. I did not resist when he cupped my breasts. And, when he asked, his hands like meat hooks on my thighs, it was all I could do to release a breathy *Yes*.

The husband had many homes. He kept a small apartment in Buckhead where we met Tuesday mornings and Fridays at 4:00. It was not an apartment the wife knew about. No name graced the mail slot. No number adorned the door.

Inside, the walls were white, the thermostat set to 70°. The main room boasted one couch, one coffee table, and two shaggy plants. Arriving was like stepping into a doctor's office. In the bedroom, blank walls rose to meet a ceiling white and bare as a beach. Except for the bed, a four-poster tucked into blue linens, the room remained vacant. I asked to decorate only once. The husband sighed and shook his head. "Of course not," he said.

In my most paranoid moments, I wondered whether there were others, girls like me he brought to our room. I wondered whether he had apartments all over the city.

The husband only laughed. "You think I have time for two of you?" he said. He licked his lips. He ran his hands up and down my legs.

The husband could not be relied upon to be on time, and sometimes he could not be relied upon to show up. He would have to work late or he would forget. Hours I'd wait, watching the walls. I learned to bring newspapers, books. Or I'd fall asleep and wake to his hand on my hip, teeth on my neck.

The husband always showered after sex. He took short showers in hot water and scrubbed until he smelled like himself, then dried himself and dabbed his wrists with whatever cologne he'd put on that morning. Dressed, he pulled a tiny comb from his pocket, ran it several times through his mustache, zipped the teeth across his collar with a flourish and returned the comb to his pocket.

"I feel like a new man," the husband would say. Or, "Clean as a whistle." Or, "Yessiree, Bob, now that's what I call clean."

The husband did not kiss me or come close before he left, and he always left first. I left once he was safely away. Understand: There was no prenup. He could not afford to be caught, no matter what.

And what will you think of me when I say that, sometimes, I would not wash? Will you trust me once I tell you that, times, I did not shower for days? Whatever this makes me, I was happiest smelling like him.

The husband bought me dresses and bracelets, bags and jackets, shoes and scarves. He bought me a piano and a Pekingese, a temperamental puffball, butter-yellow with a white belly. I named the dog after the husband. "Gerald, off the sofa," I'd yell, then watch the dog rise and run. This felt liberating, always.

The husband bought me pen sets. The husband bought me paintings. The husband bought me bakeware and a stove that would wet the pants of master chefs.

The husband bought me a fish tank and had it filled with tropical fish.

If a fish died, I had only to call a number and, within hours, Randy arrived. Randy's van featured a portrait of a goldfish in profile, across which had been stenciled, in blue curlicue: *Water you waiting for? Call* Randy's Fish and Aquarium Emporium *today!* Wielding a green, long-handled net, Randy deftly removed the corpse. He filled vials, ran tests, raised eyedroppers over the tank and squirted green streams into the water. He siphoned water from the tank into an orange bucket, then tipped gallons of distilled water into the aquarium. "Recycling bin?" Randy said, ankle-deep in plastic jugs. Each time, feeling guilty, I shook my head, and, each time, Randy sighed, then left, taking the empty containers with him to some better, landfill-free place.

The husband bought me things he would never see, for he never set foot in my house. "Come," I begged. "Come once. Just to meet Gerald. Just to see the fish. Just to admire the Cassatt by the bed." But the husband was nothing doing.

The husband bought me everything but a ring.

After the first year, I asked when the husband was leaving the wife. The husband said I talked too much about the wife, said he was sick of discussing the wife, that he mustn't hear the word *wife* again. *One more time*, he said. But that was all he said: *One more time.*

The first time was an accident. The husband meant to punch past my face. Aiming for drywall, his fist caught my ear, which rang for days.

The husband was sorry. He worried. His worst fear was that I would be afraid of him. Everyone, he said, in business, in life, was afraid of him. He needed me not to be afraid of him. I wasn't, but I let him think I might be.

The husband bought me a car, a Mazda RX-7 with extra cup holders and a sound system that made you think the singer was in the backseat. When I could not afford the car insurance, the husband paid for that too.

The husband loved lemurs. He loved them the way he loved whatever he could not have, something I know a thing or two about. This is the condition of all collectors, love born of lack.

The husband acquired whatever he wanted: An early Van Gogh, a journal penned by Miguel de Cervantes, the molars of an Aztec prince. The teeth, pocked and pitted with cavities, he lined up in a humidor alongside the cigar from Fidel Castro. When it came to *lack*, the husband lacked only a lemur.

"Why a monkey?" I asked.

"Lemurs are not monkeys," the husband said. "Say it with me."

"Not monkeys," I said.

"Not monkeys," the husband said.

Lemurs, the husband said, were prosimians, apes' ancestors, and Madagascar the only place in the world they were found. Madagascar was an island and its own country.

"Like Australia," I said.

"Australia's a continent," the husband said. "Madagascar's an island off the coast of Africa. Jungles, mostly. Very beautiful. But the lemurs they keep to themselves."

"Lemur hogs," I said.

The husband had hoped for years to have one smuggled from a zoo. In the end, it was easier to have one smuggled off the island. When he told me, already a lemur was in route, stowed away below deck on a cruise ship. I pictured the lemur crossing the Atlantic, its little hands gripping the bars of a steel cage, its belly retching with seasickness. Because I did not know what lemurs looked like, I pictured a monkey.

The thing that arrived looked nothing like a monkey. The thing that arrived looked like a raccoon, an underfed raccoon with a pointy nose and a tail that wouldn't quit. The lemur wore a raccoon's dark mask. Stripes like black bracelets banded his tail. His hands, though: The lemur's hands were human. Five fingers, opposable thumbs.

The husband had commissioned an enclosure that now filled the secret apartment's front room. The walls were Plexiglas for optimum viewability. Branches bolted to the terrarium's sides bridged the space between. Ropes hung from the roof. A hideaway rose from one of the branches.

The kitchen—which had persisted without appliances—now housed a refrigerator stocked with fruits, nuts, and tan bags labeled CHOW.

I couldn't imagine where it all came from. As with so many things—the car found parked in the driveway, packages waiting on my front steps—the cage, and the lemur it held, had simply *appeared*. Tuesday, the apartment was as it had always been. Friday, the apartment was half lemur playground.

That evening, the husband and I did not fuck. We sat side by side on the husband's couch and watched the lemur. From his branch, the lemur watched us back. He sat on his haunches, hands on his knees. He wore his black mask like a little bandito.

The husband held grapes, but each time he stood, each time he approached the cage and the easy-access trapdoor that unhinged for feeding, the lemur scampered up the branch and into his narrow, domed shelter.

The following Tuesday, the hideaway was gone. The lemur sat on the floor of the enclosure. He held his tail in his hands the way, in pictures, a Swiss guard holds his lance at the mouth of the Vatican.

"This is why I wanted a *zoo* lemur," the husband said. His left hand was bandaged. Five stitches held the end of one eyebrow in place.

"He's scared," I said.

"Little fucker," the husband said.

"Give him back his house," I said.

"He has to learn," the husband said.

The next day we were to meet, I arrived early. The lemur was on his side on the floor of the cage, an arm outstretched. The fingers of his hand curled and uncurled in spasms. His long toes twitched. His stomach, swollen and white, rose in successive bursts before deflating. When I crossed the room, his eyes did not follow me.

I knelt and tapped the Plexiglas. The lemur did not move. Tiny bugs crawled in and out of his eyes. He blinked. I ran.

I don't know if the door closed behind me. I don't know whether the husband arrived within minutes or hours of my departure, or if he'd planned to come at all, whether he knew what I'd find, or not. Whether he wanted me to see.

That night, Gerald—dog Gerald—sat in my lap and whined when I cried. The husband would have called me ridiculous, crying over a creature I'd known for a handful of hours. But seeing an animal like that, weak, broken on the floor of a cage, tells you everything you need to know about its owner. I had accepted that the husband was imperfect. I had come to understand that he could be unkind. But I had not known that he could be cruel.

When we met next, the cage was gone. The square of carpet had been replaced, the room returned to its original configuration of plants, table, and couch. The refrigerator was empty. It was as though there had never been a lemur.

When the husband arrived, he moved through the room and directly to the bed. He did not say a word. He took me in his arms. I fought the urge to shudder.

For our second anniversary, the husband and I took a vacation. We had never vacationed before. Outside of the apartment, beyond our two trysts each week, we had not spent time together the way that lovers spend time together. Never in public. Never by daylight below a blue sky.

Together, I imagined, we would walk on the beach. We would have dinner at long tables with other couples, and I would tell anyone who asked that I was his wife. I would tell stories about our home in the Hamptons and our children, Doug with his love of Little League and Meg with her passion for finger-paints. Meg had begun first grade that fall. She was nervous but made the transition beautifully. My husband was up for two awards with the company. He would retire soon, whereupon we would sell the house in the Hamptons and move to Madagascar. Even now, workers waited to break ground on our ten tropical acres, but my husband, I would admit, was very particular. He couldn't decide between two houses and three. "If he doesn't make up his mind soon," I would say, "the mansions will never be ready by summer."

We would take separate flights and meet in St. Lucia, the southernmost U.S. Virgin Island. In Atlanta, December was icy and cold, but in the Caribbean it would be luscious, warm. The brochures promised water and sunshine and sand.

Except that, once we reached the resort, the husband would not leave the room.

"Everything we need is here," the husband said. "Bathtub, bed, bar." The bed was soft, the tub a small pool. The wet bar was stocked with every mixer and drink imaginable. A wine rack cradled two-dozen bottles.

Beyond the window, the tide, coming in, licked the shore.

"Let's sail," I said.

The husband said, "Later."

"Let's swim," I said.

The husband said, "I have a paralyzing fear of sharks."

"Let's tan," I said.

But the husband could not return with a tan. "She thinks I'm in Salt Lake," the husband said, "and the rest of the week in Denver."

The husband was not stupid. He lied well and might have told the wife that he had business here, or in Florida, anywhere one might return from with a tan. He was being difficult on purpose, and so I would be too. I would not spend my days in our room and nothing but fuck him.

That evening, a bellhop brought us dinner. At the center of his cart rode a vase and a single white rose. Lids were lifted from two silver trays revealing thick steaks in their own juice puddles. They were gorgeous cuts, their presentation superior to anything we did where I worked.

You're maybe wondering why, when I had the husband, I still carried trays and submitted myself to the minor abuses of catering. And I answer: The husband gave me gifts, but he did not cover my rent. He did not buy my groceries or pay the electric bill. Many times he offered me money, wide, manila envelopes stuffed with rubber-banded bundles of cash. And, each time, I gave them back. I was a girlfriend, a lover, a mistress if you must. But to take his money, that might have made me something else.

That night, I stared at my steak. I was hungry. I said I was not.

"Try it," the husband said. Already he had swallowed two forkfuls. I cut into my piece. The center was warm and red, a perfect mid-rare.

"I can't eat this," I said. "It's bloody."

The husband said, "That's how you like it."

I couldn't argue but did.

"How would you know?" I said. "How would you know how I like it?" Had we ever been out? Had we ever shared a meal? Had we ever shared more than two hours at a time in a cramped apartment reserved only for lovemaking?

No, the husband said, we had not. This did not seem to bother him. Quickly, he dispatched his steak and then mine.

That night, when his fingers found my side, I rolled away. I waited for more, ready for him to try to talk me into it, but, within minutes, he was snoring.

Our last night on the island, the husband conceded to dinner out. I picked a Hibachi joint I knew he would hate, the kind of place where they cook the food while you watch, where they do tricks with onions and cutlery. We took our seats at a high U-shaped counter alongside other guests. We faced a long, silver cooktop and sipped hot tea and read menus that assigned our birth years to animals.

An islander dressed in Japanese garb, or the restaurant's idea of Japanese garb, appeared at our table and spun eggs on the stovetop. One at a time, he lifted the spinning eggs into the air on the end of a spatula and flipped them into his tall, white chef's hat. With each egg, our group cheered.

The husband was not having fun. I was not having fun. I said, "Isn't this fun?" The husband grimaced.

A few minutes in, the man to my left introduced himself. He was young and thin. He was attractive in a fussy, glasses-wearing kind of way. Before long, we flirted, openly, loudly.

"Where are you staying?" the man asked.

The husband leaned close and whispered something I could not hear.

"Oh," the young man said. "I'm sorry." He looked at the husband, searched his face. He asked, "Is this your father?"

The husband took me by the arm. He pulled me from the table and out of the restaurant and onto the street. He pulled me down the sidewalk and into a cab. He pulled me along the beach, through the resort, and into our room.

The second time was not an accident, just as, certainly, the first time had not been an accident. There would be no third time. That night, I purchased a plane ticket I could not afford and flew home.

Without the husband, I didn't know who to be. Tuesdays found me checking my watch, as though there was still an appointed hour, as though there was still somewhere to be. Nights, I drove past the building. Sometimes, I parked. When I parked, I watched the rectangle where white curtains hid our room. I watched for shadows. I watched for other women.

I watched for him.

By spring, my fish were imperiled. Green algae climbed the tank walls and choked the filters with mossy tendrils. I called Randy, who rushed to my house just as he had when the husband and I were whatever we were. An hour later, the fish swam, happy in fresh water.

"I was paid to come if you called," Randy said. "But this will be the last time."

It shouldn't have surprised me, but it did, that even this contingency had been accounted for, that I had been closed like a business deal in the same detached, efficient manner that had made the husband a very rich man.

"How is he?" I asked.

Randy shrugged, and I gathered that he had been told what to say and what not to. He spun his long-handled fish net like a gun about to be holstered.

"Recycling?" he said.

I shook my head. Randy nodded. He gathered his gallons and left.

I sold the paintings, the jewelry, the car. I kept the piano. I kept the dog. They reminded me of the husband, but that was okay. I did not mean to forget him entirely. He would be with me, always, a thumbprint caught in wet paint.

And then, one day, *her*. I saw her at a wedding reception, the wife.

That afternoon, I had been relegated to the carving station. It was not my specialty, but the butcher took long smoke breaks, and I was the only server who could work the chopping block.

I stood rending ribbons of golden fat from meat when I spotted the wife in line. I surveyed the room to be sure that he was not with her, and then I took my time, carving carefully, deliberately, until wedding guests grew impatient. Slowly, I moved meat from board to plate. I hoped that the line might go on forever, that the wife might never reach me, but, soon, she was there, standing before me, dish raised like an offering plate.

I did not look up.

"How do you like your prime rib?" I asked. "Rare? Well-done?"

"Either's fine," the wife said, and her voice was so quiet I wanted to cry. I looked up. The wife smiled. She was not as fat as I remembered, and neither was her makeup too bright or too thick. Her hair had been stripped of its highlights and had turned a somber, muted gray, the color of putty. She looked dignified, classy.

What I felt, seeing her, made my hands shake. I worried that I would drop the knife. I lowered a pile of slices onto the plate.

Right then, I wanted to tell her that I was sorry. I wanted to tell her that she was my only regret. I wanted to admit, seeing her, that I knew now what I had been.

Instead, I said, "You'll find condiments at your table."

The wife thanked me and walked on. She joined a group of women at another table. They spoke and nodded and smiled and laughed and were beautiful together the way all women are beautiful among people they love.

David James Poissant is the author of *The Heaven of Animals: Stories* (Simon & Schuster, 2014), longlisted for the PEN/Robert W. Bingham Prize, winner of the GLCA New Writers Award and a Florida Book Award, and a finalist for the L.A. Times Book Prize. His stories and essays have appeared in *The Atlantic Monthly*, *The Chicago Tribune*, *Glimmer Train*, *The New York Times*, *One Story*, *Playboy*, *Ploughshares*, and in several anthologies. He teaches in the MFA program at the University of Central Florida and lives in Orlando with his wife and daughters.

Pink Moon

Pat Spears

Norman tries willing his belly full but when he fails he can no longer hold off going for his one meal of the day. Because he hates waking mornings with nothing in his stomach, his habit is to wait until midnight before walking the six blocks to the bus terminal from where he stays in an alley at Ninth and Springdale. Frigid gusts of wind suck at the frayed lapels of the overcoat he took last winter from the public library on a day just as cold, and if stealing is a sin then sleeping cold is a thousand times more so.

The dry heat inside the terminal sticks to his face like wet fingers to ice and the smell of greasy food twists his gut, reminding him of the smell of freshly torched bodies. He stands at the counter and nods to the waitress he's come to know as Shirley. Her dark eyes are dull buttons pressed into her dough-like face and any warmth she might have once had has long ago eroded, leaving in its wake a fatigued shell of a woman, not unlike those he'd seen hurriedly escorted along the shattered streets of Iraq.

He orders coffee and the house special, dry tuna on yesterday's white bread with a side of crumbled potato chips. Shirley slides a cup toward him, spilling coffee that puddles like oil on the counter. He bites his tongue, screaming profanities inside his head, then pleads with her for a top off.

"Sure, anything for music land's prince charming." Her voice is thick with contempt and her thin, ruby-red mouth twists into near-permanent sarcasm.

"Now now, sweetheart, don't be unnecessarily naughty." He pushes the empty cup across the counter. "Make a teeny-tiny slip-up behind that counter and you and I become neighbors." He mocks her, measuring his index finger to his thumb while flashing his best *have a good life* smile.

Her sneer vanishes as if he'd slammed her pudgy face behind a heavy door and she hisses through gapped teeth. "Drop dead, freak. I ain't like you." Her expression is that of the fearful old women huddled in vacant doorways, their swollen ankles crossed, their knees spread, and their possessions clutched to bloated stomachs. He wishes for the simple pleasure of despising Shirley, but instead he settles for filling his pocket with tiny tubs of cream and packages of hardened sugar over her silent protest.

Norman crosses the terminal and takes a seat at a booth near the video arcade. He forces himself to eat slowly, putting the sandwich back down onto the thick, chipped plate after each measured bite. Caressing the coffee cup between his palms, he sips the heavily sweetened white liquid and it warms and soothes him like he believed Sarah's breast milk nurtured and comforted her fretful son.

He met Sarah last spring, after a winter of bargaining sex in exchange for a warm apartment with full cupboards and racks of good domestic wines. When he tired of the owner's possessiveness, he drifted southward, following the promise of sun and sanity. He'd traveled no further than Tallahassee where he first saw Sarah, sitting alone on a park bench beneath the ghostly glow of a pre-dawn streetlight. She invited him to sit and they shared a smoke, and he came to know her as a near-prefect replica of his own loneliness.

Sarah took him in, never complaining that he spent his summer days writing bad poetry at the university's air conditioned library, and when he asked her why not, she leaned against him and quietly said, "Good doesn't always need to come with half the rent. I like that you don't hit on me and that you make my little boy smile."

Although there was no mention of the baby's father, he believes that Sarah was never a woman whose child had a father she couldn't name. Evenings, when the summer's heat had relaxed its suffocating hold, he, Sarah, and the child took slow walks along cool, tree-lined streets, stopping to buy double strawberry ice cream cones. On one such walk, Sarah said, "Walking from the shade into the sunlight is like letting go. Yet nothing ever feels free enough to be love."

They walked on in silence and he too felt mostly empty.

When he and Sarah got high, she sometimes cried, and he'd hold her, stroking her ordinary brown hair that smelled of the fried foods she served to college students at one of several near-campus bars. In times like these, he knew only to say to her that which his mother had promised. "For now you're caught beneath the dark side of the moon," he whispered, placing his arm around Sarah's thin shoulders. "You're due a pink moon. Any time now, I think."

"Norman, do you really believe in the magic of a pink moon?"

He answered Sarah in the same hopeful way his mother had when promising him the same.

He stayed with Sarah and her son until the notion that if not poetry, then maybe song lyrics. He kissed her and the boy good-bye and made his way to Nashville, where his songs have so far failed to catch on.

He chooses to believe that it was his mother's faith that led her to deposit him with an already burdened aunt, explaining only that her ticket drove an SUV with barely room for two. She yelled back that he was to expect a bus ticket. He went daily to the rural mailbox, but the ticket never came; only a single birthday card the year he turned twelve that had arrived two years and three months late.

He hitchhiked to Galveston only to learn that she'd left the SUV man for one driving a big-assed Buick with California plates. He spent the balance of the year walking Galveston, searching for such a Buick, and by the time he accepted the futility of his search, Rita had blown in and he had forfeited his welcome back with his aunt.

Norman puts the last of the sandwich back onto the plate, distracting his hunger by watching bumpy-faced soldiers clad in olive-drab uniforms prowl among flashing video screens, noisily killing electronic enemies, and he's sure these boys have yet to see combat. He imagines that their games too are distractions from hunger, but not his hunger. Their hunger is fed by dreams of sweet, wet reunions at the end of long bus rides.

After Galveston, he'd worn the same uniform, motivated by the promise of three squares and a roof, and there was the assurance of money to pursue his dream of college. He served two tours in Iraq, his dream still intact, until in a fit of mutual passion he shared a shower with his platoon sergeant, and instead of perks and privileges he earned a dishonorable discharge.

A man leans across the table, catching Norman by surprise, and the intruder says something about the place being overrun with holiday cheer. He holds a cup of coffee in one hand and the tuna special in the other. The thick cup clatters against the coffee flooded saucer he holds in a small trembling hand.

"No," Norman says.

"Fuck you, Cinderella," the boy-man says, turning away.

"No, no, it's okay. Sit, if you want." Norman motions toward the vacant seat.

The man places a tattered copy of *To Kill a Mockingbird* on the table and slides onto the ripped plastic seat across from Norman. He doesn't bother to remove a black kit cap, but greedily takes up the tuna sandwich, wolfing it down like an abandoned dog. When he's stuffed the last morsel of food into his mouth and slurped the remaining coffee from the saucer, he deftly sweeps crumbs from the table into his palm and with a pink, wet tongue, he licks them from a nasty palm. When he's done, he runs his hands along the legs of his baggy trousers. He has yet to speak, having carefully avoided eye contact.

Still Norman says, "A wonderful book, pity there weren't more."

The man's face flashes a cornered look and he reaches for the book and opens it to a tattered page three-quarters of the way into the book.

"I mean ... only that there are no more books from her," Norman stammers, an embarrassment left over from his childhood.

The man runs a quick finger down the left-hand page, stopping at a middle paragraph, his gaze moving rapidly back and forth across the page.

Norman steals glances at the man, deciding that he's in his early twenties. He has beautifully shaped hands spoiled by dirty nails, bitten back into ragged cuticles. He's dressed in the multiple layers of oversized clothing common to the streets, and he looks all together like a small black capped chickadee, ruffled against a cold night. Norman tries to imagine what the tiny man might look like after a hot bath, shampoo and shave. He pictures him dressed in white trousers and a loose-fitting white silk shirt, and barefoot.

Norman brushes at a soiled spot on the sleeve of his coat, wondering what the stranger notices about him. He wishes he'd washed up earlier and worn the cleaner shirt stuffed in the pocket of his overcoat. He would have wet down his too long hair and combed it straight back, even though he doesn't think of the style as flattering with his oblong shaped face. He remembers the many taunts of "horse-face" from classmates and the way they'd imitated whinnying sounds.

Over the noise of the crowded bus terminal, Norman hears Shirley calling out an order for a double cheeseburger and fries. How simple his taste has become, and he imagines the immense comfort he'd derive from a greasy burger, even with the artificial yellow cheese he once detested.

The slender man coughs several times into the sleeve of his coat, his cheeks flushed pink, and he's begun to sweat. He looks in the direction of the window at the front of the terminal. "Goddamn, it's snowing again. I hate the bitching cold." He shoves his hands into the side pockets of his jacket and lifts his narrow shoulders, shuddering.

"I'm Norman. And down in Macon, Georgia, where I come from, I prayed for just one snowy Christmas. Had I only known." He risks a slight smile.

The small man stares with watery eyes that give away nothing and then he says, "Fuck you Norman Bates and your goddamn snowy Christmas." He clutches the book to his chest, as though preparing to leave.

The man's surprising rudeness stings Norman and he stands, placing the last of the bread crust into the pocket of his overcoat. "For the birds in the park. Oh, yes, I feed the birds. Why wouldn't I?" Needlessly shamed by the man, Norman steps away from the table.

"Fair Norman, Sir, please wait. I am your servant, Sidney Who-Gives-a-Fuck. I apologize and beg of you to stay. It is, after all, the season of good will."

Uncertain as to why, maybe only that the man's pleading echoes his loss, Norman turns back. The man is standing next to the table, his body swept into a courtly bow.

"You have a loud, unnecessarily vulgar mouth." Norman crams his hand into his coat pocket, fingering the last of the loose change there. The accent is southern Appalachian, Norman decides, and although he despises Sidney's crudeness, he's captivated by his voice. How could such beautiful resonance pass through the mouth of a tiny man with a chipped front tooth?

"Yeah I do, Norm. Loud is hereditary and vulgar is acquired, the result of extensive travels through my less than serene life."

"Yes, well, I'm going for a donut." His stuttering worsens under stress.

"Sure thing, Norm, make mine jelly filled, if you've got extra on you."

"All right, but don't call me Norm. I hate superficial familiarity, and in a bus terminal for Christsakes."

"Relax, my generous man. Here now, gone tomorrow. Sinking ships passing and all that bullshit."

Norman forgives Sidney his tangled cliché and even his cheap theatrics. He walks across the terminal to the counter and orders donuts, fearful of spending his last dollar. He can always set aside his song writing and work the corner he's come to think of as wishful Washington and never Lincoln. If good fortune eludes him, he can easily hook up with some aged queen who'll buy his favor for an evening.

While a limp eighties tune plays from the juke in the arcade, Norman sits, watching as Sidney squeezes thick cherry jelly through the hole in the doughnut. He licks the jelly playfully, squeezes the doughnut, licking again and again until the doughnut shell grows limp. He wraps the spent shell in a napkin and tucks it inside his jacket pocket.

"For the birds, right Norman?" Sidney pushes back against the seat and he smiles with a sweetness that causes Norman to overlook the chipped tooth. "Don't know about you, but I hate waking to my guts romping and stomping. Reminds me too much of home."

"West Virginia?" Norman offers.

Sidney frowns as though bested at some unfamiliar game. "Now I remember where I've seen you. You work the first floor bathroom at the main library."

"If it's any of your business, I go to the library, but I go there to write." He doubts Sidney would understand the sense of kinship he derives from the quiet proximity of other library patrons.

"You write?" Sidney drops the meanness as quickly as he'd picked it up.

"Yes, I've written poetry until recently."

Sidney looks at him like a true believer and Norman relaxes a bit.

"Most recently, I'm trying my hand at writing lyrics…it's like writing poetry, but set to music without actually knowing how to write music." He giggles shamefully, diverting Sidney's penetrating gaze.

He'd duped himself into leaving Sarah and the boy on the chance that he might write hit songs. He's daydreamed about flying her and the boy first-class to the Grammy awards where he would stand on stage and include a tearful Sarah among those he thanked in a rambling speech that expressed a liar's deeply felt gratitude to loving parents. He wouldn't thank the father his mother had laughed and named "Tom, Dick or Harry Fucker." He'd laughed at her remark too, although he hadn't felt to.

"Shit, Norm. You don't look nothing like a poet." His tone changes like playful sex turned ugly.

"And you don't look like a reader," Norman glances down at the open book and Sidney slowly nods, his blue eyes deeply sad.

"You're right, Norm. I can't read what I'd know to write." He caresses the book, the weak smile playing at the corners of his mouth doing nothing to brighten his eyes.

Norman looks away and aches to take back his part in their hurtful exchange. He doesn't have a single poem to offer in defense of his claim. What little he wrote, he left with sweet Sarah who promised to read daily to her boy in the hope that some day he too, would grow up to write great poetry. He liked that she'd pretended.

"If you're going to someday read a book, you've made an excellent choice." He thinks about offering to teach Sidney to read, but nobody stays around that long.

Sidney leans across the table, his face as innocent as a sugar cookie. "Did the one-armed colored dude really buy it, like in that old black and white movie?"

"If by that you mean was he falsely convicted? Yes, he was and yes, he died."

"Poor dumb bastard. He should've fucked the lying cracker bitch." Sidney pounds the table with a tiny fist, sending a spoon clattering to the floor.

In spite of his better judgment, Norman wants to embrace the tiny loud-mouth carrying a tattered book he can't read, but the momentary good he feels is shaken by the noticeable anger of the four men seated at a nearby table. Their hateful stares signal that they too have heard Sidney's ill considered remark. Norman is no bigot, but he wishes these men would return to their earlier lambasting of welfare mothers and their bastard babies.

Sidney has pushed to the front of the seat and now he leans across the table, the book clutched in his hands. "Would've settled things with them rednecks, right Norm?"

"No, I don't agree." Although he thinks Sidney means only to balance the scales of injustice, Norman fears the electricity that has begun to surge from the next table.

"Look, a man died and he got nothing for his trouble."

"I know, but he was a better man."

"You think good matters?"

"I think it has to."

He and Sidney continue to sit in the warmth of the bus terminal until most of those having destinations have boarded buses, leaving the station to an assemblage of men, women and children crowded along a dimly lighted corridor. Norman nods to a couple of old panhandlers he knows only as Mr. George and Ms. Chattahoochee Babe. She insists on being addressed as *Ms.*, laughing in the crazy way she has, claiming her share of entitlement to women's liberation.

At the dreaded sound of batons slapping the leather-gloved palms of three security guards, the homeless slowly rise, gathering sleeping children and meager possession. Except for a girl who bargains sex for a longer stay, they shuffle through the station door and into a Christmas Eve night fresh with snow.

"Say, Norm babe, you got a number where we might get in out of the cold?" Sidney winks. "I'm new in town without a proper reservation."

Norman thinks about touching Sidney's slender hand. "I can offer you an all-weather crate at the end of a nearby alley."

"Meaning your box can accommodate two cock suckers?" Sidney grins, again showing the chipped tooth.

Sidney's boorishness disturbs Norman and he thinks about withdrawing his offer until Sidney says, "Pardon my rudeness, my dear man. Please consider me as your grateful crate-guest for what's left of this beautiful Christmas Eve." He tenderly picks up the book and places it in one of the many pockets inside his jacket, gingerly patting it down.

From the bus terminal they walk the six blocks, straight into the teeth of a frigid wind.

"My castle, Sir Sidney." Norman blushes, lifts a loose corner of the blue tarp that serves as door to the two refrigerator-sized, heavy-duty cartons he's duct taped together and covered with a larger tarp for better insulation, and steps back.

Sidney ducks through the opening and pushes to one end, making room for Norman who squats to light a candle. Its glow flickers orange, their shadows dancing against the cardboard walls, illumining the art of home Norman has drawn with colorful magic markers: a double bed covered with pastel pillow shams and comforter, two deep seated maroon colored recliners, plasma TV/stereo, an apartment-sized refrigerator, microwave, and a flaming log fireplace, all on the interior walls of the crate.

"Whoa! Crate-man art." Sidney's huge baritone voice blasts against the flimsy walls of the crate. "You're fucking Michelangelo."

Norman laughs and picks up a marker, expanding a chair into a loveseat on the wall opposite the fireplace. "Remodeling is such a breeze," he says with an artistic flare. "Let's cozy up near the fire."

They sit on the cold, bare floor of the crate, sharing a reefer Sidney retrieved from the hem of his jacket sleeve. He wants Norman to know that he had a life before the streets. "But when Father Roy got done with me, I'd lost all interest in seventh grade. When the entire world took his side, I started drifting, staying wherever I could." Sidney pauses, his arms folded across his chest, his small hands slipped beneath his arm pits, rocking back and forth in a hypnotic rhythm. "The one after Father Roy gave me a safer place to stay and all the peanut butter I could eat. It was my favorite, the crunchy kind." Sidney shivers and Norman reaches to hold him.

"I know," he whispers, "then the price of peanut butter went sky high."

Sidney slips Norman's embrace. "Jesus Christ, Norm, don't go and bum out on me. Think of the streets as an education with no reading required." Sidney's laugher rings hollow, but Norman manages a quick smile, recognizing Sidney's need for such terrible lies.

"We're only temporarily caught on the dark side of the moon." Why does he choose now to return to his old religion? He has declared belief in a pink moon to be heresy, like bad poetry and lyrics without moving chords.

"Shit, Norm, you're balancing on a razor's edge with that kind of bullshit." Sidney shifts, moving away from Norman. "I'm going for a cold one." Sidney pantomimes. "What can I get you, blues boy?"

"Amaretto please, Sidney."

"And just what the hell would that be?" A twisted grin lights up his round, sweet face.

"It's an almond-flavored liqueur made from the pits of apricots."

"Damned if you ain't the fucking internet."

They have perfunctory sex, although Norman would have preferred tenderness. He studies Sidney's face in the candlelight and imagines a longer, sweeter moment with him someplace truly warm. He moves closer, pushing against Sidney for added heat, grateful not to be alone. Closing his eyes, he silently vows to teach Sidney to read if he should decide to stay around.

Norman's mind drifts into that murky state between reality and dreamland, only to be awakened by animal-like noises from the street end of the alley, and the air inside the crate electrifies with their fear.

Although Norman knows the approaching avengers of decency won't be fooled by silence, he whispers that they are to hold still and pinches out the candle's flickering light. Sidney takes Norman's face between his palms and kisses him fully on the mouth, arousing in Norman the intimacy he'd hoped for earlier.

"Just a little something for your trouble, Norm baby," Sidney says in a jerky voice, trembling with his fear.

There's a blinding light and the side of the crate opposite the fireplace caves in. Norman tries to stand and when he does the skin across his right cheekbone rips open and he tastes blood on the raw pulpy flesh of his bottom lip. He gropes in the darkness for Sidney before his left arm twists in the strong hands of one of the men he remembers from the bus terminal. When his arm cracks and a white pain races along its length, he looses all will to resist, collapsing to the floor of the crate.

Norman manages a weak response to the woman's voice calling to him from behind the glow of a flashlight. She slips on protective gloves before offering to drive him in her patrol car to the nearest emergency room that treats charity cases. In a deep southern drawl, she claims to have only seen the four men run from the alley and drive away in a black F-250 king cab, too late at any chance of apprehending them.

Hours later, he leaves the hospital with his arm in a wrist to shoulder cast and twenty- five stitches across his right cheek. The young female intern advises that he should stay indoors and keep warm. Norman pulls the coat tightly across his chest and laughs.

The young woman's failure to appreciate his humor is tattooed on her pale face for a brief moment before she turns her newly acquired skills to the next case, and Norman imagines her lack of humor is fueled by the notion that his world is one of choice.

"Hell yeah. This is America, not some sand pile oozing black gold like mother fucking Iraq," he shouts in passing to a bundled form cuddled against a federal building. His only explanation for having done so is simple insanity.

Christmas snow is falling lightly on his shoulders and above the deserted street, in a piece of sky exposed between tall buildings, a sliver of moon floats overhead. He pulls his coat together against the icy winds, walking the twenty blocks to the alley entrance at Ninth and Springdale where he learns that Mr. George has moved on south without Ms. Chattahoochee Babe. The bearer of the news speculates that since she got pneumonia the cold has been too much and she put herself back in the squirrel cage.

Norman can't remember seeing one without the other. He shifts his broken arm inside his coat, the empty sleeve flapping in the wind like a tattered sail.

The man bows his head, buries his hands under his arm pits and shivers hard. There is a half-empty bottle of Night Train among the man's belongings and Norman wonders again how the four men knew which alley dwellers to torment.

Grief for the old couple lodges in Norman's chest like busted stones as he hurries along Springdale. He needs to learn Sidney's fate.

Inside the bus terminal, he brushes snow from the coat and spots Shirley.

"Hey, Shirl, did you miss me?"

"Don't come in here acting like we know each other." A blurry-eyed Shirley stands and steps to the counter. "If we did, you'd know already my name ain't Shirley. It's Mavis. This here name tag belonged to her before she got fired for being too old and slow."

"Darling, by any name, your rejection is breaking my heart." He exaggerates his best effeminate gestures.

She studies the empty sleeve of his coat. "That there empty arm hole don't bode well for you. Neither do them cuts and bruises on that pretty face you're so proud of. What happened?"

"How sweet of you to notice, but I would have thought you'd know exactly what happened." He takes a seat opposite her. "Then let's just say there was a small difference of opinion on the nature of man's greatest pleasure."

She steps back, putting space between them. "If you ain't ordering then you can't sit at the counter." Her words are harsh, but her face seems softer.

"The little guy I left here with, has he been back in?"

"You're joking, right? Do I look like I care enough to notice?" She glances toward a booth in the back corner where the night supervisor sprawls across the table from a young waitress.

"Listen, you cross-eyed old cow, tell me what you know before I go back there and tell that fat fuck that you're my long lost mom's secret lover."

"Your kind's disgusting. Unfit to be around normal people."

"Yeah, maybe so, but you fucking know I'll do it."

"All right, all right, don't get your panty-hose in a wad. But you didn't hear it from me." She squints at him through crippled glasses, an unhinged leg held to the frame with a twisted bread tie.

Norman nods and takes the cup of coffee she slides across the counter.

"Some rough looking guys left out soon after you two freaks."

He drains the lukewarm coffee and pushes the cup across the table. She refills the cup, out of habit more than any sense of generosity, he thinks.

"They came back later bragging they'd put one fag in the hospital. The other got away in the ruckus."

"Has he been here looking for me?"

"Am I so in love that I'd keep tabs? I ain't the department of missing persons."

"No darling, you're Mary Magdalene and I'm Jesus Christ."

She steps away from the counter, covers her open mouth with the back of her hand. He drains the last of the coffee, fills his pockets with packages of sugar and tubs of cream, and walks from the terminal.

He sits on the curb beneath the streetlight and, turning his face into a fully arrived Christmas day, his attention is drawn to a lone black capped chickadee. He takes the bread crust from his pocket, tosses into the snow, and the bird fluffs its feathers, hops about, peeking at the bread until it's gone, then flies away.

Staring along the quiet street, he remembers his momma's pitiful advise that in a flood, he should snag the nearest floating log. He chooses to believe that under the right circumstances he could have cared for Sidney-Who-Gives A Fuck, and he believes that by Sidney's crude measure, they'd each gotten something for their troubles.

Norman goes to stand in the alley, sprinkled in wet, dirty snow, and assesses the damage to the crates. With more duct tape stolen from the hardware at Elm and 7th, he can make it a home once again. Maybe he'll add a third crate, just in case. When he's readied the crate-home he has in mind, he'll return to the terminal tonight at his usual time.

Pat Spears's second novel, *It's Not Like I Knew Her*, was released by Twisted Road Publications in July 2016. Her debut novel, *Dream Chaser*, was released in 2014. She has twice received honorable mention in the Lorian Hemingway Short Story Competition; first in 2013 for her story "Stranger At My Door" and again in 2015 for her story "Free Ride". Her short stories have appeared in numerous journals, including the *North American Review, Appalachian Heritage, Seven Hills Review,* and anthologies titled *Law and Disorder* from Main Street Rag, *Bridges and Borders* from Jane's Stories Press and *Saints and Sinners: New Fiction from the Festival 2012.* Her short story "Whelping" was a finalist for the Rash Award and appears in the 2014 issue of *Broad River Review.* She is a sixth generation Floridian and lives in Tallahassee, Florida.

Mom's Mustang

Sheila Stuewe

When I turned three, I began sleepwalking. I moved from room to room, talking about my Crissy doll with her adjustable auburn hair. Some nights, I sat on the couch and sang, "Jesus Loves Me." When I awoke, I had no memory of having nudged my older sister, Elise, awake to ask her if I could listen to her new Beatles album *Let It Be*. The pediatrician assured Mom my subconscious would simmer down once I started going through puberty. It didn't. My midnight strolls seemed harmless, until one night when I was in sixth grade, my mother found me sitting on the back porch after midnight talking to George, our dog. I have no idea what I was doing outside. Maybe I was hoping she'd bring home my favorite, sausage and peppers, from her Italian dinner with Albert. The next day, on Mom's insistence, David, the man she had been dating for two years, installed chain door guards near the top of the front and back doors, high enough so I couldn't reach them. Before she went to bed each night, Mom was supposed to secure the chains to keep me safe.

A week later, I unlocked the back door after school with the key dangling from purple yarn around my neck. I picked up the flower arrangement the florist had left on the porch and placed it on the kitchen table. Holding the tiny envelope in my hand, I called Mom at her office from our one phone that hung on the dining room wall adjacent to the kitchen. "The florist delivered another dozen roses," I said.

"Who sent them?" Mom asked.

I opened the card and said, "John."

"What a surprise."

"Who's he?"

"Last week he took me to a Blackhawks game. He owns a small steel company. If he popped the question, I'd never have to work again."

During my parent's fifteen-year marriage, my mother had never watched hockey, baseball, or football with my father, even when he was sober. Mom liked Broadway musicals and opera and Ed Sullivan on Sunday nights. But since Mom had begun managing a luxury high-rise rental building near Lake Shore Drive last winter, she never passed up invitations, especially from men who wore pinstriped suits, owned companies, and drove Porsches.

"Please stay home tonight." I stood with my hands on my hips, the phone cradled under my chin.

"I can't. Jack's taking me to the best steak house in town—Gene and Georgetti. I'll bring home a doggy bag."

I lowered my shoulder and let the phone drop to the floor. I didn't want to pick it up, but I did. When I lifted it back to my ear, Mom said, "I think I'm going to start with lobster bisque soup and I'll order a filet with creamed spinach for my entree."

"We were supposed to go for pizza tonight," I said. "All the Tupperware is empty."

Elise, three years older than me, would have figured out something to make, but she had to stay after high school that Friday night for a basketball game. She always made sure I wrote out my spelling words twenty times on Thursday nights, and for weekday dinners, she heated up the chicken, spaghetti, meatloaf, or stuffed peppers Mom had cooked on her one day off and packed in plastic containers.

"There's a Banquet fried chicken dinner in the freezer—your favorite," Mom said. "But be careful when you light the pilot."

Elise refused to turn on the twenty-year-old oven by herself since she didn't know how fast the gas would escape. Instead, I'd strike a match, hold it over the hole at the base of the range, and shout, "Now." Then she'd press down on the switch and slide the knob to the appropriate temperature. I'd only scorched the hair off of my right arm twice in the past six months. It hadn't hurt, but it had stunk like campfire and skunk mixed together.

Somehow my subconscious knew to avoid the oven while I slept—but not the freezer. Once at one a.m., Elise found me sitting at the kitchen table eating strawberry ice cream out of the carton. I never put myself in danger during my nocturnal strolls, not even when I'd gone out on the porch with George.

Although my mother was celebrating her fortieth birthday, she still looked like she had when she won Chicago's *Miss Photoflash Contest* twenty years earlier—her auburn hair wavy and long like my Crissy doll's, her eyes azure blue, her lashes long, her skin pale. She could have dated immediately after the divorce—instead she waited two years, a self-imposed penance for breaking her sacred vow. She started out slowly, with only David. But when she began working downtown, where she was surrounded by wealthy potential husbands, she changed. During the week leading up to her special day, she'd received six-and-a-half-dozen roses from seven boyfriends.

After the one from John—the third arrangement—arrived, I hung a cheat sheet on the back of my bedroom door to keep track of each man's flowers:

Harry: Half yellow, no vase, they came in a box

Ron: A dozen red, really nice ones, cut glass vase

John: Twelve pink with lots of baby's breath

Later I added:

Albert: A dozen white for purity. (Albert was Catholic and lived with his mother.)

Frank: Green vase, red roses, twelve, small petals.

Doc: Huge red roses. Their scent filled the house.

When Harry, Ron, John, Albert, Frank, Doc, or David picked her up, I made sure to place the man-of-the-evening's bouquet in the living room, hoping each had a cold so he couldn't detect the rest of the flowers in our house. David's roses were a deep burgundy color with thick long bulbs surrounded by exotic greens and baby's breath, similar to the ones he'd given her the prior year when he was her first and sole boyfriend. A month before Mom's thirty-ninth birthday, he'd taught her how to steer, brake, and parallel park while driving the bumper cars at Kiddyland. When David took Mom to get her license at the Department of Motor Vehicles, one of his delivery men parked a used 1967 Ford Mustang with a bright yellow body and a black vinyl top in front of the house.

As they returned home, I was watching from the beveled glass front door. David opened the Mustang door and handed her the keys. Mom jumped up and down, laughing, screaming. She circled the car, sliding her fingers along its sleek lines and its trademark rear end scoop, dusting off the headlights with a tissue, checking the gas cap to make sure it was on tight. She kicked the tires before she sank into the black leather bucket seat. Sticking the key in the ignition, she waved for me to join her. I ran outside and crawled into the back. She adjusted the rear view mirror as David sat on the passenger side. Mom drove us around the block, yelling at everyone who was on the sidewalk, "I finally have my own car."

After she parked, she ran up the stairs. She took the spare front door key out of the vase on top of the bookshelf in the foyer. Reaching for David's hand, she said, "I want you to have this. You're welcome any time."

They started kissing, so I left the room. A few minutes later, Mom told me to go play with Michelle, my best friend, for an hour before dinner. Years later, I understood why.

That day David must have been sure she was his and only his. He must have thought driving, versus relying on the Chicago Transit Authority, would make it easier for her to get home from work. He didn't anticipate (nor did I) those wheels giving her the freedom to stay out past the hour when waiting on a street corner became unsafe.

A year later, David remained the only male voice I heard in the middle of the night from across the hall, panting and saying, "So tight. So good." Mom should've closed her bedroom door, but I usually slept soundly, even when I strolled. Had she kept it open so she could hear if I started ambling around? Luckily, I never sleepwalked when he was there.

Before Mom left for Gene and Georgetti, we established the evening's alibi. She instructed me to tell any man who called, especially David, she was at a Parents without Mates meeting. Other nights she "worked late" or "attended a PTA function." I often wrote the lie on the inside of my palm so I wouldn't forget it, as I did for the long Bible verses I had trouble learning for catechism class.

Later, David called from Bo's, the neighborhood pizzeria he owned. For two weeks, he rang at 7:00, 8:30, and 10:00 and asked, Where is the meeting? (*Mom didn't tell me.*) Who is she with? (*I don't know.*) Why isn't she home yet? (*I have no idea. She hasn't called.*) I said as little as possible so I didn't have to remember any more lies. Unless I wrote them down, I couldn't keep track of them. But I had to tell those tales to protect my mother. If she hadn't been beautiful—and convincing—she'd never have gotten away with her stories for almost a year. Plus I didn't mind telling David tales. Once when he brought over a pizza he asked why I was fat and Elise was skinny. What adult asks a twelve year old such a question? Secretly, I was hoping Mom would find someone else, someone who cared about me, too. Someone like Albert. When he picked Mom up, he always handed me a grocery bag filled with ice cream and fresh raspberries.

David's pizzeria was closed on Mondays, so that night belonged to him. For two years, he had picked up Mom and me every Monday night for dinner. (Elise didn't come with us—since she took honor classes, she always had homework.) The Monday after Mom's fortieth birthday was different. David didn't come to the door. He sat in his midnight blue Caprice Classic and honked like a spoiled brat. He had nothing to be upset about. Mom was ready to go if only he'd walk up the steps and ring the doorbell. I waited in the foyer, my stomach growling, anticipating something other than ground beef and chicken, something which hadn't spent days in plastic. Mom peeped through the living room's white sheers. "He has a lot of nerve sitting out there. That's no way to treat a lady," she said.

The longer he remained in the car, the harder he pressed on the horn. Instead of going outside and confronting David, Mom walked the opposite way. Was she heading to the kitchen? Maybe she was going to make dinner. She passed her room on the right and mine on the left, so I followed her. My hopes for having a meal alone with Mom were dashed when she turned into the bathroom to check her make-up. I stood in the doorway as she added another layer of mascara.

"I'm hungry," I said.

"Didn't you eat your peanut butter sandwich at lunch?"

"That was a long time ago."

She walked toward me, touched my cheek, and grabbed my hand. "Let's go. The best thing about eating out is that we won't have to do the dishes."

While we put on our coats, she added, "I hope he isn't grumpy through dinner."

She locked the door behind us. I ran to the car while she sauntered down the front steps of our rented bungalow. I got in the back seat. She paused for David to open her door. He didn't even look in her direction. He stared ahead. Something was wrong, but I didn't know what. If only she had turned around, gone up the stairs, latched the new chain, and made me dinner—but there was nothing in the refrigerator.

David didn't utter a word during the twenty-minute drive. Not once did he turn his head toward Mom. He listened to Hank Williams sing his greatest hits including "Long Gone Lonesome Blues," "My Son Calls Another Man Daddy," and "Cold, Cold Heart." He'd played the same cassette six months earlier. During that ride, I'd overheard him tell my mother his ex-wife wouldn't let him see his daughters even though he had finally paid his late child support payments.

When we arrived at Jackson's Steaks and Seafood, the same restaurant we went to each Monday, he pulled into a parking place, threw open his door, got out, and slammed it shut. He rushed ahead.

"Did he see the other roses?" I asked.

"Of course not," Mom said. "He must've had a fight with his ex-wife."

"He's mad at you."

Mom stopped. She grabbed my chin and said, "One more word and I'll wash your mouth out with soap." She turned, raised her coat collar, and raced to the door.

I had to run to keep up with her. Pursing my lips, I kept everything I needed to say from spilling out. Even though she didn't want to believe it, David had to be suspicious Mom had other men in her life. How could he not know? She never was home, and all those roses. I watched as she darted forward, dazed, refusing to accept she might not have fooled him.

The hostess delivered his drink—J&B Scotch on the rocks with a splash of water—before we reached the table. Mom asked for her usual, a Dewar's Scotch old fashioned. As we opened our menus, David lifted his empty glass and requested a refill. He proceeded to order the same thing he did every week—a very well done New York strip steak, a baked potato with butter, no sour cream, and soup, no salad. He turned his chair away from us, smoked a Camel, and stared out the floor-to-ceiling window at the back of the restaurant. Mom slid the vase with pink carnations from the middle of the table closer to her and asked me, "How was school?"

"I got a 90% on my math test," I replied.

Mom lifted the vase and smelled the flowers. She said, "I was never good with numbers."

She didn't look at David or watch him gulp down his drink. I did. After his third Scotch, I wondered if he'd be able to drive us home. He had never ordered more than two before. David wasn't a drunk like my father. The year before the divorce, Dad had wrapped his Rambler around an elm tree. Watching David chug down his Scotch made me worry about the ride home. I didn't want to land in the hospital for two weeks like Dad had.

Even after his fifth Scotch, David didn't slur his words. He got louder—"Where's the waitress? I need another drink." Each time he put down his glass, the Coke in mine swayed back and forth, almost, yet not quite spilling over. I pushed back my chair, tapped Mom's knee, and signaled her by raising my fist to my ear. *Come on Mom—go to the pay phone. Call someone to pick us up.* Instead, she lifted her glass and sipped her old fashioned, and pushed the flowers toward me. Her eyes drifted around the room, not looking at me, and ignoring all the Scotch David was drinking as she had Dad's alcohol consumption for fifteen years.

"Why are you wearing red?" David asked, scuffling with his chair, moving it so there was barely an inch between him and my mother. Smoke poured out the sides of his mouth. His face flush, his ear, too. I watch him and waited—for what I didn't know. As his charred steak was placed in front of him, he said, "I've told you I don't want you wearing red. Red is for hussies."

I put my elbows on the table and covered my face with my hands.

"You know red is one of my favorite colors," Mom said. "For my birthday you gave me a matching red hat and this blouse along with those beautiful roses. I thought you liked red."

I wanted to get up and lock myself in the ladies room. Yet I couldn't leave her alone with him. I don't know what David was complaining about—Mom's red silk blouse had long sleeves and a tie at the neck—it wasn't sexy. I sat on the edge of my chair, my knee pulsing up and down. David had never before called her names. He must have found out about the other men. Of course he was mad. She no longer cooked his favorite homemade pot roast on Wednesdays. She didn't press his shirts or stop by the pizzeria to pick us up a large with mushrooms and green peppers. Yes, he still came by in the middle of the night once a week, but had he ever snuck over when she wasn't there to find her bed empty? She should never have given him a key.

David pointed at me. "If I had known she was going to purchase something that color, I would've never trusted her to buy your present." Mom didn't respond. I wanted to kick her under the table. She should have stuck up for my choices. A few weeks ago, David had handed me a hundred dollars to buy Mom something she would never buy for herself. So I chose a hat she had tried on at Lord and Taylor and a blouse to match. When Mom wore it, she looked like Ingrid Bergman in the last scene of *Casablanca*. Mom wasn't plain like my classmates' mothers—she could have been a movie star. And David should have been more like Rick, the movie's club owner, and stepped away graciously.

I had put my first piece of salmon in my mouth when David asked Mom, "Where were you Saturday night? I called you at 11:30."

Mom smiled at David. I wrung my hands. She raised her glass and took a sip. My eyes opened wider—I couldn't blink. I'd talked to him twice that night, but if I'd answered the phone at 11:30, I had to have been asleep. I checked my hands for notes, but I must have scrubbed off the ink.

"I was on my way home from a meeting," Mom said.

"Sheila told me she had no idea where you were or what time you were coming home," he said. He stuck out his chin, leaned forward, and waited for my mother to answer.

Mom turned to me and said, "Is this true?"

I shrugged. I didn't know what to say. Had he misinterpreted my cryptic responses? A week earlier, Ron had called after ten and I answered in my sleep and told him Mom was dining at La Tour with Harry. The ringing of the phone became part of my dream. I carried on conversations, having no memory of what I said until Mom's boyfriends filled her in later.

David lit another cigarette and took a drag. He exhaled, aiming smoke rings over Mom's head. The fumes formed a gray halo over her auburn hair. I leaned to my left trying to locate some air he hadn't contaminated with his Camels. I put down my fork and took a drink. Even my Coke tasted like burning leaves.

"I could've been asleep." I said.

It didn't matter what I'd said. No one has meetings every evening. What forty-year-old mother goes on dates five nights a week or gets seven bouquets? Who tells so many lies and doesn't get caught?

Leaving his steak untouched, David stood, hurled a hundred dollar bill on the table, and said, "Let's go." He knocked over his water glass. He scowled at Mom as if she'd made him do it. He clenched his fists. Although I'd seen him yell at his pizzeria cooks when they went outside for a cigarette break and let four pizzas burn, that Monday was the first time I worried he might hit my mother. Those five Scotches brought out a side of him I didn't want to know. When my father drank, he turned melancholy, and the only thing he balled up were tissues. Dad never raised a hand to my mother, my sister, or me.

I wiped my mouth with the napkin, stood, and put on my coat. Mom stayed seated at the table. That was Mom's way. She was determined not to react to David leaving the table. Even if she wasn't in control, she made you think she was by not acknowledging what was happening around her. After he flung open the front door, she slid back her chair, picked up her purse, stood, and wiped the crumbs from her lap. She grabbed her coat, hung her purse on her left arm, and walked toward the entrance. Mom believed everything happened according to God's will. I knew God wanted her to call a cab and use the twenty dollars she kept in her purse for emergencies. Still I hoped David wasn't as drunk as Dad had been after my cousin's wedding reception when he'd sideswiped ten cars.

No words were spoken on the ride home. Donna Fargo didn't blare from the radio—no Tammy Wynette or Conway Twitty. David raced sixty miles per hour through red lights and stop signs. The Chicago wind whipped about the car and whistled around the windows. When he stopped at a busy intersection, I lurched forward, hitting my head against my mother's seat. Mom stared straight ahead. I watched her reflection in the window, her face expressionless. Was she willing us to our destination? Or was she pleading her case to

God? She needed to develop a plan to get David to calm down. But it didn't seem possible. David was gripping the steering wheel so tight the veins on his hands looked ready to break through the skin. Mom reached over and touched his wrist. He batted her away and raised his arm. I sucked in air, holding it—waiting. He turned to her, shook his head, and placed his hand back on the steering wheel. I exhaled.

I buckled my seatbelt, trying to protect myself from another sudden stop. I silently prayed, *Dear Jesus, please get us home safely. I promise to do the dishes every night for at least a week. I really want to live. I'm only twelve, and I'm a good girl.* I closed my eyes when we reached Fifty-Ninth Street—only three more miles. I repeated *please Jesus please Jesus please Jesus* over and over until we pulled in front of our house.

As soon as he turned off the engine, I jumped out, ran up the stairs, unlocked the front door, and headed to my bedroom, pulling the door shut behind me. I didn't want to hear David calling my mother *whore, slut, bitch* as they walked down the hall to the kitchen. Yes, she was dating too many men, but she was still my mother. She had kept food on the table even when Dad gambled away his paycheck. Since the divorce, she'd paid the rent and utilities with no help from my father; she bought us new shoes each September and stayed home if we were sick. Until that year, she had rarely gone out in the evening. But how could she resist all those fancy restaurants after years of trying to figure out ways to feed a family for days with a pound of hamburger?

David's voice roared from the kitchen, "You better say your prayers, you two-timing whore, because you're going home to meet your maker."

I jumped off my bed and opened my door.

"Put the gun away," Mom said. She didn't shout or plead. She held her tone steady. David kept a gun under the driver's seat of his car in case someone tried to rob him on his daily restaurant deposit runs to the bank. *Please Jesus.* Leaning on my doorway, I crossed my arms and held tight to my core. *Please please please.*

Elise, who had been studying for a French test in her bedroom upstairs, ran past the kitchen down the long, narrow hallway to my room. "He has a gun pointed at her head," she whispered. "We have to do something."

In the dining room, a few feet from the gun the phone hung, inaccessible. The burn of my half-digested soup and salad jolted into my mouth. I swallowed hard and rushed to my bedroom window. It was only a five-foot drop to the pavement.

"What if I jump out the window?" I said. "I can run next door and ask Sue to call the police."

"Just use the front door. He's looking the other way," Elise said. "Go on now. Run. I'll be your look out."

"Let's open the window wide enough for you to leap out if the gun goes off," I said. We raised the sash as far as it would go. Cold fall air filled the room. Elise grabbed a sweater out of my drawer and pointed toward the foyer, "Get out of here."

I didn't want to leave her, yet I needed to get out of the house and away from the gun. Elise must have known that. I tip-toed to the front door, watching behind me. PO5-1313, the number for the police, kept repeating in my thoughts. Elise was right; he couldn't see me unless he took his eyes off my mother and leaned out the kitchen doorway. There was no chance of it happening while he kept screaming, calling her names—some I'd never heard. I dashed to our front door, turned the knob slowly, opened the door, and slipped outside, shutting the door behind me. I sprinted down the steps and to our neighbor's house. I rang the doorbell. I banged on the door. I pounded on the window. What was taking Sue so long? She was almost seventy; she had to be home. Finally, she answered the door, out of breath and dressed in her evening muu-muu.

"David has a gun pointed at Mom's head. Call the police!"

"I'm not getting involved," she said. "I don't want him coming after me."

I didn't have time to argue, so I rushed past the startled old biddy, picked up the receiver, and put my finger in the rotary dial. My hand shook. I dialed an eight instead of a seven. I got the "O" correct, but the five became a four, since I didn't swing the dial back far enough. I couldn't get those seven digits right. After the fourth try, I put my finger in the "0" and waited.

"Operator."

"I need the police."

"I'll connect you."

"Chicago Police Department—may I have your address please?"

I gave it and said, "My mother's boyfriend is pointing a gun at her in our kitchen."

"Is there an adult I can speak with?"

"Sue, she wants to talk to you."

Sue sat in her rocker, arms across her chest, shaking her head no. Couldn't she see I needed help?

"My neighbor is too afraid to come to the phone."

The operator assured me the police were on their way. Sue's doorbell rang, and Elise walked into the living room, her face pale, her eyes darting around, as if unable to focus.

"Did he shoot her?" I shouted. I didn't need to know anything else.

"No, but she screamed for us to get out of the house. I think he's about to pull the trigger."

Elise fell on her knees in front of the couch, her hands folded, her neck bent downward—she prayed out loud, "Please God, don't let him shoot Mom." I paced in front of the windows. I couldn't do anything to stop David, so I opened the front door and listened. I didn't care if I was letting in the cold air. I had to hear the shot.

David had spent thirty dollars on bumper car tickets last summer so Mom could gain the confidence to drive. He'd bought her the Mustang, and now he wanted to destroy her because he wasn't the only man in her life.

As four squad cars approached, red lights flashing, no sirens, Elise and I ran outside. Two policemen leapt up the front steps. Two went to the right side of the house and two headed to the left. I have no idea where the other two went. They moved so fast.

"The front door is locked," one officer said.

Sue had a spare key in a cabinet near her front door. I took it to him.

"Honey, get inside. You have no shoes on," he said. "You must be freezing."

Up until that point I hadn't felt the cold. I had been engulfed in a whirlwind of escalating rage. If only it had been a dream, then I'd wake up tomorrow and this night wouldn't even be a memory. I began to shiver. I pressed myself up against Elise. She wrapped her right arm around my shoulders and stroked my hair with her left. She kept repeating, "I promise, I'll take care of you." How could she? She was only a freshman in high school.

Flanked by two policemen, Mom sprinted from the backyard. Elise and I clung to her, weaving our arms around her. The police escorted David in handcuffs out the front door and down the steps. They pushed him into one of the cars. I let go of Mom. Everything I'd eaten that evening came spilling out of me onto the sidewalk. One of the policemen handed me his handkerchief and rubbed my back. He told me to go inside and lie down, but I couldn't move from my mother's side.

The police sergeant, who had arrived moments earlier in a blue sedan, informed Mom she would need to go to the station to file a complaint. Shoulders slumped, she walked up the steps to the house to get her coat and purse. I asked the sergeant to walk with me to the kitchen, where he watched as I looked through every drawer and cabinet, in the refrigerator, and behind the garbage can.

"Honey," he said, "the police took the gun."

I don't know why I thought it would still be there.

Mom assured Elise and me she would be home soon. After she left, Elise called her best friend, while I sat in the kitchen and ate a half-gallon of vanilla ice cream. Its cold creaminess slid down my throat, coating my stomach.

When the sergeant dropped Mom off two hours later, I heard her close the door and thread the chain into the lock. She walked into my bedroom, kissed me on the forehead, and said, "Sweet Dreams." She didn't speak a word about what had happened. She didn't assure me David was in jail. After she turned off my light, she ran bath water. Her drawer creaked when she took out her flannel nightgown. Her sheets rustled when she got into bed. Finally, I could hear long, deep breaths, and I knew she was sleeping. Too afraid to close my eyes, I stared at the glow from the streetlight peeking around the edge of my curtain.

The doorbell rang. 2:00 a.m. I jumped out of bed and hurried to the door, pressing my face to the glass to see who was there. The light from the end of his Camel put a red-toned shadow around David's eyes. Was I dreaming? Sleep walking? How had he gotten out of jail so soon? This couldn't be real. I pressed my nose closer to the glass and cupped my hands around the rim of my eyes to block the reflection from the light coming from the hall.

"Go away," I shouted.

"Get your mother," he said.

Mom came up from behind me and unlatched the chain.

"Should I call the police?" I asked.

"He won't hurt me," she said.

I didn't believe her. She turned me around and pushed me into the living room before opening the door.

But she didn't let him in. Standing with cold air rushing in around her, she listened to his pleas for forgiveness. She said nothing.

"Mom, I want to go to sleep. Please tell him to leave."

I could barely hear him when he whispered, "I love you. Give me another try."

"I'll think about it," she said as she closed the door.

"Mom."

She threaded the chain guard and turned to me. "He's gone," she said. "Are you happy now?"

I wanted to slap her and tell her to wake up. If only she could emerge from her stupor. She wasn't the mother who had taken us to church each Sunday, made lasagna for Saturday dinner, and insisted we say our prayers together before bed. During the past year, she'd acted like a boy-crazy sixteen-year-old. But the men she dated weren't harmless, pimple-faced boys. Did she crave male attention after spending a decade and a half married to my father, who reeked of whisky and beer? Did she fear if she passed on a potential suitor, she'd miss out on the perfect mate? When she picked out a hat, she tried on a wide assortment to see which one accentuated the nuances of her cheekbones, her eyes, her pale complexion—was she using the same technique to find a man? But why couldn't she have dated one man at a time? Was she worried, at forty that her looks would soon wane?

The next morning, Mom sat at the kitchen table, sipping hot tea.

"Would you like me to make you some pancakes for breakfast?" she asked.

"Cereal is fine," I said. "My stomach is still upset." I grabbed the gallon of milk from the refrigerator and Frosted Flakes off the counter.

I ate slowly. Mom told me to take a jacket to school since it might rain later. She didn't say one word about the gun, how she got away from David, or if she'd been surprised to see the police.

When I rose to leave for school, she reminded me, as she had done many times before, not to tell anyone our family secrets. I walked out the front door, my books cradled in my arms. Like the divorce and Dad's drinking, Mom wanted last night to go into the taboo file, forever sealed in a manila envelope, placed at the back of a steel drawer—unchallenged, unspoken, neatly packed away, never to be examined.

On my walk to school, I kept glancing over my shoulder, certain everyone in our neighborhood must know. They had to have seen the red lights flashing. How could they have missed the squad cars blocking the street? Even though none of our neighbors had come outside to watch, they must have looked out their windows. Our pastor, who lived down the street, smiled and said hello as he passed by me. The Italian man next door, who hardly spoke any English, stood watering his flowers; he didn't say anything. It was as if no one had seen the eight policeman running in different directions, not even Dwight, who sat behind me in school. His house stood kitty-corner from ours. Not one of my classmates had seen anything. It was as if nothing had happened.

That afternoon as I walked up our front stairs, Sue held up the neighborhood newspaper and yelled, "Look at page fifteen."

I went inside, placed it on the kitchen table, and peeled back the pages. I hurried past grocery store ads and high school sports results. The mechanic on Sixty-Third Street was running a special on oil changes. The Colony movie theater was showing *Benji*. Over the past weekend, St. Gall's had raised two thousand dollars at their rummage sale. But where was Mom? Finally, on the second to last page I saw her name. I leaned in close to read it. Only four sentences long, it didn't say I had called the police. Why wasn't it on the front page? Why was the story of David trying to kill my mother next to articles about stolen cars and bikes?

I took out my scissors and cut it out for current events class. I didn't want Mom to forbid me from exposing that evening's details, so I threw the rest of the paper in the garbage.

The next day, as soon as we put away our sixth grade spelling books, I raised my hand and started bobbing it up and down. I yelled out, "Ooh-ooh-ooooh."

I kept waving until Mr. Himmelmann pointed at me and said, "You must have a good one today."

I tripped on one of my shoelaces as I made my way to the front of the class. I didn't fall. Most of the kids laughed. I did, too. It made me feel less anxious. Once at the front of the classroom, I cleared my throat, rubbed my wet palms on my shirt, put my shoulders back, and said, "The title of my article is 'Man Arrested after Threatening Woman,' from *The Southtown Economist.*"

Mr Himmelmann interrupted. "Sheila, you know the rules. The articles must be about something that impacts the world we live in, and it needs to be published in either the *Chicago Tribune* or the *Sun-Times.*"

I walked over to his desk and in a calm, even tone said, "This happened at my house. I know it's not from the *Tribune*, but I have to talk about it. Please don't tell me I can't." I didn't wait for him to give me permission.

My classmates stared at me the whole time I spoke. No one shuffled papers or coughed, no passing notes, no spit balls. I suggested if something like this happened to them they connect with the operator immediately and not waste time trying to dial those seven digits. I didn't mention David had come back later that night; I didn't think anyone would believe me.

Not one person had a question or comment. As I walked back to my desk, Michelle had tears on her cheeks. I sat down, looked forward, and breathed.

For the remainder of the day, hardly anyone talked to me. They didn't know what to say. No one had held a gun to their mother's head. Michelle hugged me. Mr. Himmelmann took me in the hall and asked how I was doing. I told him I was fine. I wasn't fine. I was terrified of David. I knew how to call the police, but what if he came back to kill us and I couldn't get to a phone?

During the weeks that followed, I slept fitfully, waking when the floors of our old house moaned and when my mother flushed the toilet in the middle of the night. I didn't sleep walk.

A month later, Mom stood in front of the bathroom mirror etching her eyebrows dark brown while she readied herself for David's arraignment. She had gone to the beauty salon the night before and had slept with a silk scarf wrapped around her head. No longer dating numerous men, she focused on two: Doc, the chiropractor, and Ron, the married man.

Her hips swayed as she walked down our front steps in her navy suit, three-inch pumps and a low-cut white blouse. She must have wanted David to yearn for what he'd miss in prison. I watched from the front porch as she hiked up her skirt and slid behind the Mustang's steering wheel. She put on her sunglasses and started the car. I waved. She didn't roll down the window or shout, "Goodbye." The wind might have loosened the curls piled on top of her head. Instead she honked twice and pulled away.

I closed the front door and paced the hallway. That afternoon I took out a new quart of butter pecan ice cream. While I shoveled in spoonful after spoonful until it was all gone, I prayed, "Dear God, please make the judge sentence David to twenty years in a downstate prison."

Hours later when I heard the key turn in the lock, I ran to the door and asked, "How did it go?"

"Fine."

Fine? Before I could ask about David, she hurried to her room and shut the door. A few minutes later, she appeared, wearing a terry cloth robe. Without saying a word, she headed to the kitchen, placed a frying pan on a burner, and made three hamburgers. We sat down to eat and she inquired about Elise's and my day. We shrugged our shoulders and said, "Fine."

All day we had waited for her to tell us we were going to be safe. But she wasn't divulging anything.

After her third bite, Elise said, "How long will he be in prison?"

"I couldn't press charges."

"What?" Elise and I yelled.

"Only the Lord can condemn. The Gospel says, 'Judge not and ye shall not be judged.'"

Elise gagged on her food. I covered my face with my napkin. I couldn't look at her. Mom hadn't been to church in a year. Now she was quoting scripture. Forks clashed against plates, spoons scraped serving dishes. No one spoke. Mom finished her dinner, excused herself, took a bath, and went to sleep. Elise and I cleaned the kitchen.

"We're not safe," Elise said. "David still has a key."

"He could kill us in the middle of the night. We wouldn't even wake up," I said.

"Her midlife crisis better stop or we might not make it to college."

"I'm afraid."

"Me, too."

Mom never called a locksmith to re-key the front door even after I came home from school the following week and the living room's television stand stood empty. I looked behind the couch, under the coffee table, and in back of the bookcase for the TV. It was the only thing in the house other than the red hat and blouse David had given my mother. So, I checked her closet. I was relieved he hadn't taken her birthday present.

Over the next few weeks, I ate only ice cream because I threw up everything else. Before I turned off my light each night, I built a barricade of books, dolls, and chairs against my bedroom door.

Two months later, I walked into my mother's room as she brushed her hair. I asked, "Why didn't you put him away?"

"He didn't want to hurt me," she said.

"What about me?"

"What do you mean?" Mom asked, her brow bent, her eyes narrow.

"How do you think I felt when he was holding a gun to your head in the kitchen? What if he shot you, where would Elise and I go?"

"I never thought of it that way."

She got up, walked to the bathroom, washed her hands, and dabbed on some concealer below her eye. Mom was finished talking about it. I, on the other hand, told anyone who would listen—my Girl

Scout troop, my Sunday school class, my choir director, and everyone in the choir.

The next Saturday morning, I took George for a walk. Heading back up our street, I didn't see the Mustang. So I ran inside to ask Mom where she had parked it.

"It's in front of the house," she said without looking. Then she ran out the front door.

"Who would want it?" she asked. "It's got bald tires. The odometer hit eighty thousand miles last week."

I shrugged. A few minutes after she called the police, the doorbell rang. The sergeant, who had waited with me in the kitchen while I made sure the gun wasn't there, waved as I unlocked the door. He had parked where the Mustang once stood.

"Honey, do you mind if I come in? I need to talk to your mother," the sergeant said.

I led him into the living room and called down the hall for Mom.

She walked into the room, extending her hand to shake his, "So nice to see you again."

"I'm concerned about your car," he said.

She motioned for him to sit down. I plopped down next to her on the couch. He ruffled through some notes on his clipboard. "A '67 Mustang was found in St. Gall's parking lot. The car had been doused with gasoline and set on fire. Words were spray painted in red on the charred exterior."

"What words?"

"I can't say them in front of the child. Also the driver's side door had a bullet hole. Was it there before the car was taken?"

Mom's eyes widened. Her shoulders slumped forward.

"No," she said. Her hands shook. She sat on them so the policeman wouldn't notice. But her shoulders began to tremble; she could no longer hide behind her controlled exterior. I moved closer to her. We leaned into each other—scared.

"Do you think this is related to the domestic disturbance call we responded to a couple of months ago?"

Mom looked toward the front door and said, "I don't know."

"Ma'am, I'm going to talk to the man we took into custody that night, but since you didn't press charges, I can't arrest him unless we can prove he stole your car, which isn't going to be easy. But I want to stress you and your children aren't safe here."

I looked at Mom and hoped she was listening.

It took those words for Mom to realize she should've pressed charges against David. Growing up believing God would provide, she thought God had told all those men who sent flowers on her birthday to ask her out so someday one of them would pay the rent or buy her a house. For almost a year she had been dream-walking, searching for a CEO or a senior vice president, maybe even a millionaire—someone more financially secure than David. Yet she was unwilling to give him up. Did she love him or did she simply feel obligation because he'd bought her the Mustang? That car gave her freedom she'd never known before. She didn't have to rely on the bus or a friend. She finally could go anywhere she wanted to without any constraints. Yet she was still insecure. My guess is she needed David as a backup plan.

After the policeman left, Mom called Doc. That weekend we moved out to the suburbs and lived with him. I wasn't allowed to tell anyone our address or give out our phone number, even to my best friend Michelle. I don't know what the sergeant said to David, but we never saw David again.

Mom started cooking dinner at the new house, even though she still went to work downtown. Doc bought her a used, powder-blue, four-door Cadillac de Ville sedan. He told her she looked elegant behind the wheel. One evening before he arrived home, she said to me, "I feel like an octogenarian on my way to church when I drive that boxy thing. It has no pick-up. Plus I'm over forty, not dead."

A car means freedom, especially a first car. I bet she still longed for her Mustang with its sleek lines, bucket seats, and V-8 engine. When she had pressed down on its accelerator and looked at herself in her rearview mirror, she saw herself as young and uninhibited, sunglasses on, auburn hair flying in the wind, going from zero to sixty miles per hour in less than eight seconds.

Sheila Grace Stuewe grew up in Chicago, earned an MBA in Nashville and has been trying to find a home ever since. After decades of manipulating numbers, she came to her senses and earned an MFA in Creative Nonfiction from Vermont College of Fine Arts. Her essay "Residual Value" essay won an Association of Writers and Writing Programs Intro Journals Prize for Nonfiction and was published in *Artful Dodge*. Her essays have also appeared in *Hunger Mountain*, *Hippocampus Magazine*, and *drafthorse*.

High Point

Gale Massey

Crazy streaks of yellow crashed against a purple sky and thunder rumbled overheard. Dory wanted to run outside and feel the crackle of electricity on her skin. Instead, she folded her arms across her chest and forced herself to pay attention as the high school counselor outlined her choices for the future. "There's the community college, the management program at the Waffle House." The woman yawned, not bothering to cover her mouth. "And there's the WalMart going up on Highway 9. They'll be hiring soon."

Wind whipped against the windows so hard that the kids eating lunch under the trees in the quad grabbed their trays and ran inside. The sky would split open soon but this was just an early season thunderstorm – hurricanes never bothered with the fifty thousand acres of withering Florida graze land, stumpy fields and dried-up ponds of Biggs County. The last thing her best friend, Lucy, said to her before she disappeared with a boy in a Mustang who she'd met at the Dairy Queen was, "Girl, get the hell out of here. There's nothing in this town but hard labor and dust. And that's if you're lucky, which you are not."

Sitting in the counselor's office now Dory considered her future; her contempt for textbooks, the too-sweet smell of syrup, her ambivalence regarding useful plastic objects. She stared out the window. "I don't know," she said and rain began pelting the window pane like dried moths.

The woman rose from her chair and said, "Think about it." She'd skipped Dory's past but that was nothing new. Her past made most people cringe. She'd been raised in a series of foster homes that by state regulations held two to a room, never more than three. There weren't many folks in town interested in adopting girls when boys could at least help with the livestock. Dory had survived ten social workers, a dozen roommates, and been shuffled around enough to know that home didn't mean anything more than a roof and a blanket, a place to sleep at night.

Outside in the hall a line of students stared dull-eyed at the green linoleum floor, all of them facing the same options.

She holed up in the library and searched the internet for some way to escape, anything that would get her out of Biggs County. The walls of the computer lab were lined with the usual posters; the Army, Air Force, Marines. Soldiers on mountaintops, soldiers in front of the U.S. flag, a group of soldiers (two were women) standing in front of a fighter jet. The caption claimed she could see the world.

Huh, she thought, I'd settle for seeing another state. She found the Army application page and printed it out.

She practiced running sprints on the long dirt driveway behind the Little League bleachers, a place that offered some privacy, and after two months she could do twenty push-ups, fifty sit-ups and run an eight-minute mile. She opened a bank account and began collecting everything listed on the Army's web site: shoe polish, black wool socks, tampons, a dozen pair of underpants, foot powder, and a cheap waterproof watch. Headlines were in the paper daily and on the news channels the house super kept on in the kitchen; the war in Iraq was gaining steam. Filling out the application, she skipped the part for the death benefit. She had wanted to write Lucy's name in that box but the rules were clear; only natural family could make a claim. She left it blank.

On her eighteenth birthday a pretty young social worker dropped by the house and gave Dory a file two inches thick. The mute girl, Larry or Laurie – no one knew exactly how to pronounce her name – watched from the kitchen table. She was only ten and her fingers were always sticky. When the social worker offered to go over the file with her, Dory told her no. She barely knew this one and what would be the point when she was getting booted out of the system anyway. Matriculation, they called it. Dory thought the word had a ring of sophistication. The mute girl turned back to her math homework, started drawing flowers in the margin of her workbook.

All the details Dory hadn't been allowed to see until now were stuck in that manila envelope, secured with a giant rubber band. By then she had a letter of acceptance from the Army and a copy of the Greyhound schedule. She took the file to her room, hers alone since Lucy left, and waited until the house was quiet to open it. From now on there wouldn't be anyone mucking around her business. That reality brought a new kind of loneliness, one that she hoped to handle like the adult she was becoming. There'd been a shift in her life, a great meridian dividing all that had come before and all the lay before her now. She saw herself as having been asleep, curled in a cocoon, and now emerging in a sense, with wings.

She squared the contents with what she'd been told: parents killed in a late night car wreck while she was home with the sitter. Dory flinched at that but then figured she hadn't really known them. She saw that she'd lived in seven foster homes but she only remembered the last three. She'd been that young. She checked the names of her closest relatives, knew her grandparents hadn't taken her in and saw now that they'd passed, too. There was another name there, one she'd never heard before. Jack Hastings. Who the hell was he? She'd never considered there might be someone. Maybe an uncle – he had her last name – and the idea unsettled her.

It started then. At school, she searched the faces of the other kids – in town, the people on the street. There was nothing about a Hastings in Biggs County on the internet. The phone book showed just one, at an address on Route 9. She tore the page out and tucked it in the manila folder. Self-consciousness shifted to suspicion that she couldn't shake off. People turned away when she stared for very long but she couldn't stop. She had blood somewhere. Anyone with a gap between their two front teeth or wide-set eyes might be a cousin. After a few weeks the idea cooled to a low simmer. That was a lifetime ago after all and a part of the old life that was falling away like a husk she was shedding. There was no reason to reach out now. She hid the manila folder under her bed, but pulled it out sometimes and read his name out loud. Jack Hastings – a thing left undone when most everything else felt complete.

The day after graduation she got some empty boxes from behind the grocery store and packed away the things of her youth: a thread-worn stuffed bear, most of her clothes, an old CD player, and folded the cardboard box flaps clockwise jamming the last one into place. Her life, tucked in three boxes.

The war was constantly on the news. It was beginning to ramp up and there were reports of scattered U.S. victories along with some American casualties. She wanted to contribute, maybe make a difference, be a part of something that big. It made her muscles tense just to think about it.

Her last night in foster care the house manager baked her a cake. After everyone had gone to bed, Dory went outside. Clouds hid the rising moon giving it a smoky glow and blanketing the stars. She went back inside, dialed the number for the Hastings listed in the phone book, and was startled when a woman answered on the third ring.

"Hello," Dory said. "I'm looking for Jack."

"He's in the barn," was the reply. "Who's calling?"

"Dory. Dory Hastings. We might be related.

Dory thought she might've hung up – and why wouldn't she, some stranger calling to claim a relation. She added, "It's important. His name was listed in my file."

"Huh," the woman said. "I wondered if you'd turn up someday."

Something hot turned in Dory's gut.

The woman sighed. "Hold on." Then said, "Let me get a pencil."

Dory's vision slanted white at the edges. She braced herself against the wall and tried to give the details in a steady voice.

"I'll let him know when he comes in," the woman said and hung up.

Dory crawled in bed sometime after midnight but sleep came hard. Noises startled her; the curtains shifting in the window, the sound of a toilet flushing. The wind grew during the night and she finally shut the window. Near morning she dozed off but her dreams were wild and tilting. A noise startled her awake, a quiet dream receded. She grasped at it, closed her eyes, and willed the hazy image back.

A man walked out of a morning fog toward her, his face obscured by the mist. She coaxed the next frame forward. A black mare, gray along the length of her nose and led by a simple leather cord, emerged from the fog to stand by the man's side. There were no words but when he extended his hand his meaning was clear. She reached out and took the lead from him, almost touched his skin, understanding at that moment that the figure was her father. She wanted him to lift his head, wanted to see his eyes beneath the brim of his hat. But the fog moved in, swelled up from the ground, curled around his arms and head until it reclaimed him totally. Only the horse's questioning eyes remained leaving Dory unguarded and assaulted by a longing that burned a fever down her spine. The horse backed into the fog, pulling the lead from Dory's fingers, and disappeared. Dory let a few hot tears roll from her eyes and stared at the ceiling, listening as the younger foster kids got ready to leave for their summer day camps. Through the window she watched them file out to the driveway, the mute girl in the front passenger seat, the van backing out of the driveway.

When they turned the corner at the end of the block Dory dressed and turned on the television.

The old wooden attic stairs folded down from the hallway ceiling. She picked her way up the rungs allowing her eyes to adjust to the darkness and the light slanting through the air vents. Dust particles lifted and floated. Boxes jammed every corner, unclaimed lives of state wards. But none of them belonged to Lucy, she hadn't left a thing behind. The attic was filled to the point of sagging but Dory found one last nook, swept aside a small universe of cob-webs and claimed it as her own. She carried her boxes up the stairs into the attic wondering all the while if she would ever return to claim them. No one ever did. When she was done she lifted the ladder up into the ceiling, bending it back into its resting place until it snapped shut.

A quiet thrill passed along her skin. If anyone had seen her just then they would have caught a smile on her face and a strange light in her eyes but Dory could make her face unreadable at will. She and Lucy had a game they use to play of reading each other's face. Lucy was a natural but Dory eventually matched her. It was a skill that came in useful, especially after Lucy was gone because in foster care, a place where the future mirrored the past like a flat highway, outward displays of joy sparked nothing but jealousy. Dory enjoyed the small thrill for a moment, then thought of Lucy. She'd phoned one time. Dory shifted her face, molded it to its blank mask.

In her room she packed her gear into an old gray duffel bag and listened to the television warnings of a tropical storm forming in the gulf, an entity with a name all its own and twenty-four hour coverage. Finally, Biggs County was in its trajectory. She turned the television off and took one last look around. In the mirror she saw a reflection that pleased her enough. She'd grown two inches in the last year, her baby fat fallen away. The walls were bare now; her teenage boy band posters thrown out, bed made. There was no indication of who might have lived there save for the pink trim on the matching bedspreads.

She scribbled a farewell note and stuck it to the refrigerator with a magnet. She swung the duffel bag over her shoulder, the weight of it knocking her into a wall, straightened and squeezed through the doorway.

The bus to Missouri was scheduled for one-thirty. Dory would miss the hurricane but that's all she'd miss. By then the Greyhound would have got her out of this grimy two-horse town and she'd shake off the dust of Biggs County forever.

The bus station was a two mile hike through town. Gusts from the outer bands of the storm slammed across the rooftops lifting loose shingles in intermittent blasts. Dirt whipped at her pants leg and at her face. A plastic grocery bag blew aimlessly down the street and a witless brown mutt chased after it until it snagged in a bush. The duffle caught in the wind and she spun with it to keep from falling.

At the station she dropped the bag at the counter and bought a ticket to Ft. Leonard, Missouri, and saw she had three hours to kill. She found a bench out of the wind. Nobody seemed to notice her sitting there, caught up as they were coming and going, so when a cowboy stepped out of a beat-up pickup and walked toward her, she paid attention. His jeans were rough and worn but there were fresh creases on his sleeve. His belt buckle was bigger than a fist and his cowboy boots had seen a few decades of mud and muck.

She'd seen this man in town, the boots, the belt buckle, on Saturdays when country folks came to town and shopped. He stopped at the end of her bench and stared at her duffel bag but looked away when she caught his eye. He just stood there, his big hands jammed in his pockets.

She debated if it was him. A lady waited for him in a beat up pick-up and Dory wondered if she was the one who had answered the phone. They looked exactly like what she'd expected, yet all she felt was a heat building in her chest. Crap, she thought, why had she called? There was nothing he could say now. He cleared his throat and stared at the ground.

"Are you Jack?" she finally asked.

He nodded at her duffel bag. "We got those for Christmas when we were little."

"Who?"

"Me and your dad."

Dory looked at the beat up gray bag. She'd always had it, never considered where it came from.

"I guess it could've been my Dad's."

"It was. They don't make 'em like that anymore." The wind lifted his ball cap but he caught it and held it to his head. He reached out his hand, said, "Jack Hastings. That's Sadie, in the truck. She's the one you spoke to other night."

She stood to shake his hand, her mind suddenly clattering with too many words, but, "Dory," was all she said.

He looked over at the truck. "She says you're leaving."

"Boot camp." Dory fingered the strap of the duffle.

"Where abouts?"

"Missouri."

"That's a long way off."

"Nothing but dust for me in Biggs County," she said remembering Lucy's goodbye.

A bus pulled into the station, its brakes whooshing, its doors crashing open. Fifty disoriented passengers spilled on to the platform. Dory and Jack waited while the crowd rushed past like a spooked school of minnows. Wind whistled between the buses. He seemed an illusion standing there flatfooted and solid.

"I got to go," she said and grabbed her bag.

"That's not your bus." It wasn't a question. "And there's something that needs said." The wind plastered his shirt to his belly.

She held the duffel against her chest. It seemed a door banged inside her head, wild on its hinges.

He stared at the wall behind her. "I was sixteen and never knew someone to die. My folks never mentioned your Daddy again. They let the state take you and after that I didn't think much about things."

"I guess I know that," she said.

He looked toward his truck and lowered his voice. "I don't feel good about it."

Dory stepped away from the sheltering wall and turned her face to the wind and let it cool the heat gathering behind her eyes.

"Anyway," he said, "Your folks, they're all buried on a rise in the back pasture. You can come visit anytime you want. The farm is all I got left of them."

She turned toward him and he fixed his eyes on her at last.

She said, "You could've had more."

He rubbed the back of his neck and nodded. "I see that now."

It wasn't enough, not by a long shot. The old grief hit her hard and there was nothing for it. She turned toward the bus.

"Your bus won't be here for a couple hours. I want to show you something." He reached for her duffle and she let him, watched him walk away with it; throw it in the back of the truck.

"I don't owe you anything," she said, meaning forgiveness.

"No, you sure don't." He hesitated and Dory wondered if the words had hurt him but then he said, "One hour is all I need."

Sadie scooted to the middle and made room for Dory. They headed down Main, past the high school and the courthouse, the five blocks of storefronts. The Dairy Queen across from the high school had been boarded up overnight. A caution light blinked at the vacant intersection where Main narrowed into a county road and its faded blacktop sloped into ditches of weeds and dank water.

Sadie told Dory that she hadn't had time to clean the house up for company, she hoped she understood.

"Don't like cleaning much, myself," Dory said. When the woman fell quiet Dory wondered if that might've been taken as an insult. After ten minutes Jack turned left onto a gravel road and bounced through a few potholes.

"The county doesn't maintain private roads," Sadie said. Dory grimaced and held tight to the door to keep from banging against the woman.

Jack slowed down some and cracked that Florida had to be the only state in the country where a thirty foot rise above sea level could earn the name High Point.

Calves slept folded into the deep grass, their mothers grazing nearby with their backs to the wind.

She'd never been this far out of town before and the old house was unfamiliar.

"You were born in that room," Jack said and pointed to a high window.

Beyond the house on a distant rise was an old oak tree surrounded by a sagging wrought iron fence. Dory guessed it was the family cemetery and shivered at how close the graves were to the house. An old staircase was just inside the front door.

Jack explained that her dad's room was the first on the left upstairs and excused himself to the barn.

Sadie shrugged and headed to the kitchen. "He always runs off to the barn when he doesn't know what to say. You know how men are."

Dory nodded like she understood. She gripped the banister and took the first steps slowly. The wooden steps creaked beneath her feet. Her heart was a wing in her chest. She turned the knob, pushed open the door.

The room was dim, lit by a single window on the far side. A dresser, a bedside table, a desk, and a bed covered with a worn quilt. There was a poster from the 1973 Biggs County Fair tacked to the wall and next to that a blue ribbon from the junior bull riding competition. A Stetson hung on the high post of the headboard. She picked it up, saw the thin line of a sweat stain inside the headband, and the unexpected proof of existence made her heart trip. She set it on her head anyway and looked in the mirror over the dresser, thought she saw a resemblance.

A scattering of photographs lined the top of the dresser and she searched them for faces she might recognize. An old man and woman stood next to a tractor, stiff and frowning. A faded clipping from an old newspaper was taped to the mirror; her father as a boy riding a jet-black horse in a Fourth of July parade. In another, he is a young man standing on the courthouse steps with his arm around a startled looking girl of maybe sixteen years. The girl wears a yellow dress and the shadow from his hat falls across her body.

A snapshot sitting in a small wood frame behind the others caught her eye. She pulled it out and sat with it on the edge of the narrow boy's bed. Whoever took the picture had snapped it too soon, catching the brothers off guard. They aren't looking at the camera but at the child in their arms. Dory, maybe two years old. Her father, standing a foot taller than Jack, is handing her to his little brother. But Jack seems unsure of what to do and stands there with his palms facing out as if to guard against her swinging fists.

She stood the picture on the nightstand and picked the quilt up off the bed, pressing the cloth to her face and hoping for some human scent, some memory of that lost birthright. The quilt smelled only of musty cotton, but Dory wrapped it around her body and sat on the bed. She closed her eyes and waited for that ancient longing, sharp enough to take her breath, to pass.

When it passed she shuffled to the bathroom, turned on the tap and splashed water on her face and went downstairs. Sadie looked up from a game of solitaire she was playing on the kitchen table and told Dory to help herself to some coffee.

Jack appeared beyond the back door screen, lit a cigarette, saw her and motioned over his shoulder.

"I kept her all these years," he said.

She stepped outside and looked beyond him to where the old black mare waited by the barn, a leather lead around her neck.

The horse looked strangely misshapen but then Dory understood she was pregnant.

"She's my best brood mare," he said.

Dory touched the wide dusty space between the mare's eyes, thought she saw exhaustion in the way she dropped her head.

"Has she had many?" she asked.

"A few, it's all she does though. She's a good mama." He stroked the mare's side, offered Dory the lead. "Stick around and you can help raise this one."

"I don't know anything about horses," she said, thinking about her bus, due to leave in two hours.

The mare shook her big head and Dory stepped backwards. Jack yanked the lead and pulled the horse's head level. "Don't let her spook you. She's easy to control once you learn how."

He walked the mare in a circle to settle her down.

It never occurred to her he might ask her to stay.

The horse tripped slightly but didn't go down, her big belly swayed like flood water.

Stay, she thought to herself. Her mind flashed forward in a panicky zigzag. Bales of hay were stacked just inside the small barn. The house must've been a hundred years old. Her family had worked this land for generations yet she felt nothing tying her to this spot. She felt more connected to the little mute girl drawing flowers on her homework, to Lucy who'd never sent even a single postcard.

Jack walked the mare to where Dory stood and the horse stamped its foot on the ground. "She's just testing you," he said. "We got this big house. You could have your dad's old room."

Sadie appeared at the back door, the truck keys in her hand. "Yeah, stay. Give yourself a chance at a normal life."

The mare dropped its head and Dory read that as exhaustion. Her legs felt like useless sandbags but all she needed was that one first step, the rest would follow and momentum would take her away from here. She made her way to the truck. "I already signed the papers," she said, latching on to the one thing she knew to be true.

The trip to Missouri took thirty-one hours, long enough for Dory to reconsider the wisdom of her choice. The further she got from Biggs County the more she thought about her uncle's offer. A place to live, raise horses, maybe have a normal life. That's probably what generations of Hastings had done and what for? Shouldn't she at least try? Leave Biggs County and see some of the world? Becoming a soldier meant she'd serve something greater than herself, her small town, her broken family.

It was midnight when she stepped off the bus. She was directed to a single story building constructed out of plywood. Inside the dark barracks Dory found an empty cot, dropped her duffel bag beside it, and fell asleep under a thin blanket.

Days were filled with long lines and waiting, paperwork and vaccinations. At night the barracks were full of young women and a lot of yammering about the lack of locker space. Within a few weeks Dory got some cards in the mail; one from the mute girl at the foster home and one from the high school principal. Already, they considered her a hero and she had just graduated boot camp. She wrote them back, as her staff sergeant ordered, saying thanks for the letters but not much more.

In three months Dory was promoted to E-1 and scheduled to deploy. It was exciting; the seriousness of purpose, being a part of the war and even though her assignment would keep her behind the lines, she would participate in rebuilding Iraq's bombed-out infrastructure. This is how it feels to matter she told herself, what it means to be a soldier.

Before she shipped out she bought a postcard from the commissary and addressed it to Jack. She found it hard to know what to say. She'd found some comfort in thinking about the effort he'd made that last day – he and Sadie had watched from the truck until her bus pulled away – but didn't know quite how to put it. Instead she wrote that she was okay, that Army life was fine, and that she was going on a deployment. She signed it, Love Dory, and hoped that those two words meant more than the small effort it took to write them.

When she stepped off the plane she was instantly thankful for the last minute purchase of sunglasses from the commissary. The desert light pounded against her eyes. If Biggs County was empty and lifeless the oceans of sand in Iraq made it seem like an oasis. What surprised her most that first week was seeing a few bone-thin milk cows chewing on hay inside a rickety fence at the edge of a small village, and a small boy on a horse at the side of the road waiting for her convoy to pass. She hadn't expected any animals here and wondered how much longer they would survive in a war zone where food and water were scarce.

The Army brought in ten by eight hot and airless tin trailers for the women, four to each one. It was like living in a hot can of soup but everything in the Army was temporary and she could tolerate anything for awhile.

After supper the showers were off-limits to the men for one hour but there was scarce water left by then. Most days she and the other female soldiers took baths from a bucket, washing what they could reach then dumping the rest over their heads. They helped each other with that, laughing at what relief a little water brought to the heat. There was a shortage of tampons, none were available in the commissary, but Dory had brought a six-month supply. She traded them for things like 8-Hour energy drinks and Advil which she'd forgotten to buy at the commissary back home.

The workdays were long, eighteen-hours at times, distributing building materials across the region. They began before sunrise, and if it was a long ride, ended after midnight. Dory rode in the back hanging her legs off the tailgate, watching the horizon, staring closely at the edge of the road for any suspicious looking debris, her M4 tight in her left hand. She rode with PFC Ross in a two-ton truck, usually in a convoy of four trucks. Leaving base was hard, especially with stories of IED's coming in daily, but PFC Ross always managed to get his truck last in line, where they were less likely to get blown up.

She took it for granted that he was following a prescribed order from headquarters until one morning the driver in the first truck stopped at the edge of the base, got out and came up to PFC Ross' window shouting, "Get the fuck out front and lead for once for fuck's sake."

That day Dory saw three dead hajjis on the side of the road. PFC Ross yelled back to her that they'd been caught setting up a daisy chain IED. They'd been shot on site by two SPCs who were still with the bodies, poking though their gear. That's when the commander started posting a rotation for the order of the trucks.

In chow line she overheard an SPC bugging out over killing the hajji, "I've killed three times since the last time I got fucked. My nuts are going to fall off. What the hell they bring bitches here if we aren't allowed to screw them?" The guys noticed her standing behind them, laughed but looked away.

Dory took her tray back to the trailer. The others were still out. She ate what she could and left the rest for later. When she got to the shower there was a soldier sitting outside. "Just precaution," he said when she walked past him to the entrance, but she noticed his M4 was tucked by the door, just inside the shadows.

The next morning at mail call she heard her name. It was from Jack, forwarded from Missouri and postmarked months ago. Inside the envelope she felt the stiff thickness of a photograph and tore it open. The foal had arrived, a colt all legs and eyes, and Dory wondered if the sting she felt was homesickness. On the back he'd written that she could name this one. The first word she thought was Stetson and it made her smile. She'd write soon and let them know. She folded the photograph into the envelope and stuck it inside her flak-jacket.

Leaving the base was scary. In the back of the truck she drank energy drinks to shake off the sleepless nights, kept energy drinks in her kit. The drives got longer. Sometimes eighty kilometers and back, in the small convoy on narrow roads that shifting sands covered over nearly every night. She kept her water bottle filled, kept an eye on the thermometer. It could get to a hundred and twenty Fahrenheit in the back of that truck. That day, they left before daybreak and Dory rode with a new PFC, she didn't get his name but thought it was the same guy who'd been outside the latrine. She hung her legs out the back, picked at her cuticles, bit a fingernail that had been bugging her and spit it out. When they got outside the gate she brought her M4 to her chest and tucked her legs up inside the truck. They rode for an hour, her truck in the lead position for the third time that week. She cussed her luck, checked the distant hills, and kept a close eye on the side of the road, watched for anything that might be planted metal.

The sky turned to gun metal then the sun rose on the craggy hillside fracturing the mountaintop and bursting across the open valley. Something beneath the second truck's front wheel glistened and a different kind of light, a spit of fire, shot up from the ground. Her truck tipped forward in a hail of sand and fire. A boot hit her in the chest. Dory was on the ground in a cloud of black smoke. She moved forward, toward the screaming, but a second blast hushed the world. She stared face up wondering at the columns of black smoke rising from the ground. And the quiet, how was it that the world was suddenly so quiet? She closed her eyes and waited for the sky to clear, but it was darkness that descended, swifter than a wing.

When she came to she was on the ground and leaning against a burning tire, unable to move save for her eyelids and then only slightly. Her body felt like fire. It was only a few minutes, though it felt like hours, before the PFC got to her side. She wished she'd got his name. His eyes widened. "Can you hear me?" he mouthed and she understood that she could not. A wave of terror such as she had only known in childhood nightmares washed across her brain, a terror that was soon relieved by another black wave brought on by whatever the PFC injected in her arm.

It was impossible to believe but a boy and a horse walked out of the smoke, black silhouettes against the graying sky. They came toward her and the boy dropped off the back of the horse. He touched her forehead.

They lifted her then, the boy and the PFC, draped her over the mare's back. The PFC explaining that he'd get her e-vac'd right away.

The horse was large and sturdy as she lay against its spine. It smelled musty and sweaty and reminded Dory of home. But what was home? This smell, this smell was home.

She was surprised at how the horse stood there so calmly when so much of the world was on fire. She moved and shifted and sat up, shocked that she could, shocked that the pain was passing. It had to be the morphine. But it was all right, the pain was a distant rumble.

The horse took a step and it felt like wave rolling beneath her body. The sun was a gray ball of light on the smoldering horizon. The desert – an ocean washing her home.

Gale Massey's stories have appeared in the *Tampa Bay Times,* the *St. Petersburg Times, Sabal Volume 7, Seven Hills Review Volume 16, Halfway Down the Stairs,* and *Blue Crow.* "The Train Runner" was nominated for a Pushcart Prize. Gale is the author of *Grief: reminders for healing.*

The Man Who Liked 1959

Jane St. Clair

The day that started it all, the day that Noah found the box springs, began the usual way. He woke up when he felt like waking up, ate what he felt like eating (three cans of Mountain Dew guaranteed to shrink your dick), messed around the World of Warcraft, checked Facebook, and then walked to the town dump. The way was familiar to him—as was every brick, every crack in the sidewalk—everything in the little town of Altoon, Ohio.

Noah waved at a neighbor pushing an ugly baby in its stroller, he nodded at the farmers drinking coffee in the Checkerboard Cafe, and he greeted Officer Cronkite smoking in his patrol car. They all ignored him because they did not think Noah Evening Dove was trustworthy. It was true he had grown up in Altoon, but it was also true he had left town and gone to Cincinnati or some other goddamn place like that, and that was not trustworthy. Why the hell would he leave Altoon when everyone knows you got all you need right here.

Noah arrived at the town dump, and as usual he ran his eyes over the day's assortment, looking for a toaster-oven in a half-assed way. Suddenly his eyes rested on a glittering form of iron squares. The object was beautiful. It had a solid rectangular frame of heavy iron that went the length and breadth of it, sealing and protecting its more delicate twirling innards. The top and bottom of the springs were an elaborate crisscross of iron strips, as if Rembrandt had designed a chain-link fence. The two sturdy but intricate frames were more than up to the job of shielding the coils of iron arranged between them. These pretty symmetrical curls were made of heavy gauge wire, beautifully tangled like silver hair frozen in stone on the statue of a goddess. Noah stretched out on the box springs to test the delicacy and perfection of its design. The steel mattress caressed him and followed the undulation of his legs and back and head, exquisitely and perfectly lifting and supporting his entire form like a thousand little clouds. The box springs were a triumph of form and function, and like all objects designed without superficiality or wasted effort, the box springs were simply beautiful. They could've been put on a museum wall, but that would be a moral error, for such a thing so perfectly designed is meant to be used, just as a darter fish is meant to swim.

People stared at Noah as he dragged the box springs down Main Street but he didn't really care. He knew he already had a reputation as the town crank because he lived alone in an empty house he had inherited from his Grandmother Hightower.

The box spring was so heavy that Noah was sweating as he dragged it through town. It had sharp edges and Noah cut himself several times on its crisscross and coils. It was especially hard to drag it up the flight of stairs in his grandmother's house.

All that effort was worthwhile, for that night with his air mattress resting on top of the box springs, Noah slept with the angels. His grandmother came to him in a dream so that in the morning he woke up inspired. When he got to the dump, a gleam of aluminum caught his eye. It was a serendipity that could only mean his mission was from the gods. The flash of metal was bright like a morning star --steadfast, round, glowing and guiding him toward it like Venus guiding a sailor at sea. Then he took in the entire object itself -- a chair with strong, never-fail thick metal legs that went into a loop around its back. The back and seat of the chair were thick plastic. To compare this sturdy right stuff with today's plastic would be like comparing gauzy rayon to yesterday's hemp cloth. This plastic was a washable optimistic white with blue and red boomerangs that promised a magic future of space flights into new frontiers.

As he carried it back to Grandmother Hightower's, people hardly paid attention to him. The box springs had broken them down, and now the farmers sitting in the Checkerboard Café just stared at him without comment. They had already decided that Noah Evening Dove was just a damn fool maniac.

Within a week, Noah had a stand for TV dinner trays, a classic Ozzie and Harriet easy chair, a boomerang-shaped coffee table, a set of turquoise aluminum tumblers, and a lamp featuring Roy Rogers on Trigger. He also had a new set of life rules. From now on, everything he ate or used would have to be made before or during 1959. He would only watch television shows broadcast from that time. He would find a 1959 newspaper every day on the internet that corresponded to the same day in the present. What amazed Noah was how easy it was to leave the present time, which was the end of the world anyway, according to the Mayans, fundamental Christians, and anyone who believed in Ron Paul and the gold standard.

Noah's mission put a smile on his face all day long. It bestowed purpose and meaning to his life. He had a spring in his step and a twinkle in his eye, none of which the people of Altoon trusted. The farmers in the Checkerboard and his neighbors on Hightower Street mumbled against such cheerfulness. It wasn't healthy, someone who wanted to live in the past, someone who wanted to rebel against the 1960s and hippies. It was a bad influence on young people.

That afternoon Noah's only friend came over to visit. Annoying Muriel had a key to his house and an obnoxious way of making herself at home. When they first met, Noah believed Muriel had Asperger Syndrome, but on further reflection, he changed his mind and diagnosed her instead with Inherited Dorkiness, a condition that condemned her to the lowest rung of Altoon High School's social ladder, a rung he shared with her.

Muriel was always brusque, and that day was no exception.

"Where's the TV?" she asked, without first saying hello.

"I threw it out," Noah answered.

"Where's the Wii?"

"Threw it out."

"How come there's no food in the refrigerator?"

"I threw it out," Noah said, which technically was not true. While there was no food in his fridge, the freezer compartment had a plentitude of Swanson TV dinners, a neat stack of these colorful cartons taunting Technicolor food divided precisely in little gray plastic trays, circa 1959.

"What's wrong with you anyway? Now there's nothing to do," Muriel grumbled as she packed up her Queen Elizabeth purse and reached for her coat. Muriel always wore a long black coat that looked like drapery. The coat made her look like a bulging triangular teepee with a head balanced on top of it.

"Where did you get that crap-table?" Muriel asked.

"It's a TV dinner table."

"But you don't have a TV."

"I got it at the dump," Noah said.

"Figures," Muriel said as she tried to pull herself up from the Ozzie chair. "You're such a loser."

Muriel was having trouble pulling herself up. It would be no mean feat for all 250 pounds of her to get out of that chair, especially because she had sunk into its broken folds. She was stuck in the back end of it, like a semi-truck with its tires spinning in mud.

"Everyone's talking about how weird you are," Muriel said, trying to pull herself up with both arms. She kept rolling back into the mire. Noah engaged her hands, affixing hers to his as if he were a tow truck with chains.

"Everyone thinks you're weird," she repeated.

"I should care," Noah said.

"You take me for granted," Muriel said, slamming the door.

After Muriel left, Noah cooked a frozen dinner in the oven of his stove, having thrown out his microwave because they weren't introduced until 1967. Now he settled into his Ozzie chair to enjoy turkey with dressing tucked under it like a Thanksgiving surprise. Other treasures on the little gray tray were peas with little orange carrots cut like Vegas dice and a cherry cobbler in lipstick red. What a yummy dinner, Noah thought as he switched on a black and white version of "The Perry Mason Show" on his computer. Tonight's story involved Paul Drake and Perry staking out a client's house, and it called for them to shield Della Street just in the nick of time from the bad guy's evil gun. Della Street in her efficient helpfulness and consistent good temperament was Noah's ideal woman. Why hadn't Perry married her years ago? That night he slept like a baby on the box springs, dreaming of Della Street.

The next morning Noah read the news from the day that corresponded to the present. Elvis Presley was at Fort Hood, getting his hair cut for the Army, and quipping, "Hair today, gone tomorrow." Noah surfed over to a 1959 Life Magazine feature about Africa written by Ernest Hemingway. Ernest Hemingway was more like people today, Noah decided. Ernest Hemingway's life was always better than everyone else's, and then he shot himself.

Noah spent the morning watching "My Fair Lady," and found himself humming all the songs from it as he scrubbed his kitchen cabinets with Spic and Span. Then another glorious inspiration came to him. Someday he would serve this community as Altoon's mailman. He would sing snappy little tunes like "On the Street Where You Live" as he tripped through the various neighborhoods, bringing people together with his predictable cheerfulness.

"Good morning, Mr. Noah -- oh my, you're not bringing me more bills?" a friendly neighbor would say as he handed her a stash of letters and packages.

"Yes, there are bills, my dear, but there's also a letter from your daughter," he would answer.

"Thank you, Mr. Noah, you always make my day. You always make every day special for me just by being you."

Noah pictured himself in his green mailperson's shirt, khaki pants, and black Santa Claus boots with his big sack of mail flung across his back, dancing down the blocks, petting every toddler and kissing every dog. What a beautiful vision it was, and even his cereal was cheerful in agreement. Snap, crackle, pop.

Perhaps it was the 1950s food with its overload of carbohydrates that was making Noah so happy all the time. The daily menu of macaroni and cheese with green Jell-O for dessert, Chef Boyardee

184 The Man Who Liked 1959

spaghetti and meatballs, La Choy Chinese food swinging American-style followed by a plumped-up Twinkie for dessert made for a happy belly. Or perhaps it was the upbeat shows he was watching --one Rogers and Hammerstein musical after another -- Oklahoma, South Pacific, Gigi and Carousel. Noah always woke up with a song in his heart, and he had come to believe in romantic love, truth, justice and the American Way. He felt cooperative toward all of humankind and at the same time, he felt mighty. There was nothing he could not do because he had high hopes --he was a rubber tree plant who knew that any problem could go kerplunk.

That morning like every morning Noah could think only of what a beautiful morning it was, a morning when everything is coming up roses. The war was over, the good old US of A had won, and he was happy in a little house in the suburbs. He felt as if sun beams were radiating out of his hands. To celebrate his morning joy, Noah planted stick trees in front of his house. They were just sticks now, but someday they would be spreading chestnut trees and thick oaks, filled with mockingbirds and squirrels with puffed-up chestfuls of acorns. Just then Muriel came up the walk.

"You need to get a job or something," she said.

"I plan to become a mailman," Noah replied. "It's the ideal profession. I will get to know everyone in the neighborhood. I will promote cohesion and cooperation."

"Are those freaking flamingoes?"

Muriel was staring at his two-dimensional bird statues. Noah thought his pink flamingos brought cheer and diversity and color to the barren areas between the new trees.

"God, they're awful," Muriel said. "You're so stuck in retro. Everyone thinks you're weird."

"Why are you such a grumpy pants?" Noah asked as they went inside the house.

His Magnavox Hi-Fi was just finishing Connie Francis' "My Happiness" and then the place started to rock.

"What's that shit?" Muriel asked.

"Buddy Holly and the Crickets."

Muriel opened the refrigerator.

"Damn it, Noah, you used to be interesting-nuts," she said to its empty shelves. "Now you're just plain nuts."

"I'm sorry," Noah said in a voice he hoped sounded like Rock Hudson talking to Doris Day in the pink telephone scene from "Pillow Talk."

"I'm sorry," he went on, "but I found something in 1959, something real and vital to me, something that makes my life worth living. And I intend to stay in 1959 as long as I need to."

"You are scary," Muriel said. "You are fucking scaring me. I'm out of here."

She covered herself in her black drapery and walked toward the front door. Muriel did not walk like a normal person. She had thick legs that were so fat they rubbed together at the thighs, so she walked with her legs apart like a statue mounted on tree stumps thumping like stilts that made the floor shake. She got to the door, hesitated, and then turned back toward Noah.

"You want to go the mall?" she asked.

That was a big concession on Muriel's part. She was not the kind of person to give up anything. Like the Perry Como song about immovable objects meeting up with irresistible forces, sometimes something's got to give, but it's never Muriel. Noah had to acknowledge her big concession.

"Sure," he said. "Let's rumble."

"Oh for Crissake," Muriel said.

The radio in Muriel's truck was set to a rap station, and now the whispery voice of the singer with obscene notions of women and society, shot into the air like poisonous darts. Noah had been so happy all morning, whistling a happy tune, planting rubber tree plants, enjoying the bright golden haze of a beautiful morning. Now he closed his eyes in horror, and when he opened them, he saw a gigantic Girl with the Dragon Tattoo billboard, her metal piercings like cold medieval armor, her black mourning clothing, her hard little face that would never nurture anyone or anything.

The billboard was right outside Heritage Hills Mall, a covered world to itself, a coliseum of pointless games, a temple to the gods of materialism. Aggressive strangers stood outside the stores, putting toothpick samples of chicken at his face, spraying him with cologne, asking him to quit smoking by going green, demanding what cellphone plan he used, and imploring him to sit and relax in jumpy mechanical massage chairs. Noah felt surrounded by multi-tasking people, glitzy chandeliers, shining floors, glass escalators, and one store window after another screaming, "Look at me, look at me."

"I have to leave," he said to Muriel.

"Let's get something to eat," Muriel said. "You'll feel better if you eat."

As they walked toward the Food Court, the smells of Cinnabon, fried beef, chocolate, and Chinese food mixed together, a discordant and jarring orchestra playing five songs at once.

It was amid all this cacophony that Noah saw the girl of his dreams.

She was coming out of Barnes and Noble. Her curly blond hair was done up in a perky, beribboned ponytail that swayed with a wiggle when she walked. She looked fetching but wholesome in a saucy plaid pleated skirt, red cable sweater, and polished saddle shoes. When she cast her eyes down like the little girl on a Mary Jane candy wrapper, he knew he had found her and that now that he had found her, he would never let her go.

But she was disappearing so quickly in the profusion of stores and people that he could barely make out her perky little ponytail and Betty Boop bangs.

Muriel grabbed his arm, like a mother dog trying to pull a poky little puppy back on course.

"She's a fake-out," Muriel growled. "She's one of those girls who used to be Goth. I know the type — trying to look innocent like a Japanese whore in a Catholic girl's sailor suit. You don't get it. You've been crazy too long."

But Noah was lost in the magic of some enchanted evening, and caught up in the overwhelming feeling that if he let her go, all of his life he would live all alone. Could her name be Maria? Maria, Maria, Maria, Maria, Maria. If her name is Maria, then he'll never stop saying Maria. To call what it was happening to Noah "love at first sight" would be a diminishment of its intensity and importance. It was love, passion, obsession, and it was Cyrano, Romeo, Mr. Darcy, and all of them springing from his heart full-grown. To say he had never felt this way before was to say he had never breathed or lived or been Noah before. It was that important.

Now he watched as she tripped over a little iron chair in the Food Court, hurling it into its matching French ice cream table.

"I'm so sorry," she said to the chair, and then she turned it back upright.

"Space cadet," said Muriel.

But to Noah, her apology to the chair was too good to be true. You're just too good to be true, and I can't take my eyes off you.

After apologizing to the chair, this earth angel entered a glass elevator, and suddenly she was enclosed in it like Snow White in her coffin. Then she disappeared noiselessly, carried away from him by the same diabolical force that had taken his parents and beloved grandmother.

"I have to find her," Noah said.

"Oh for crissake," Muriel said.

"I have to find her," Noah was lunging forward on the second floor railing, watching the lovely apparition depart through the elevator doors and disappear into the crowd below him. He could not tell which direction she was pursuing. He ran to the elevator, pushing the down button over and over, frantically like a mad man. Bang! Bang! Bang! He kept banging his hand against the elevator button.

"Are you crazy?" Muriel said.

Noah was panting, hyperventilating, he could not breathe. He had no air, no life without her. Heaven had given him a glimpse of paradise, and he felt like a dying man left with a memory of a life-offering moment of light that cruelly had been tamped out.

"Noah, for crissake," Muriel said. "You're going to have another fucking asthma attack."

"I ... have ... told ... you ... not ... to ... use ... that ... language ... in ... my ... presence...." but he could not complete his sentence. His throat had shut down. He could not breathe.

Muriel reached into his pants pocket to retrieve his inhaler.

"She's gone," Muriel said, sticking the inhalator into his face. "We couldn't find her if we tried, so get a grip."

Noah was bent over, hyperventilating, shaking and burning up. He knew Muriel's assessment was correct. The woman of his dreams could have entered any number of the hundreds of stores in Heritage Hills Mall. She could have exited through any number of the doors that lead to the outside world. Even if his intuition told him she would enter Charming Charlie's instead of Ann Taylor Loft, he knew he could not find her - not that day anyway. Suddenly he stood up as tall as the Duke riding high in his saddle toward a Western sunset, as indomitable as Audie Murphy before a battalion of Nazis, and as resolute as Bogey in the rain.

"I will find her," Noah said. "I will find her if it takes every breath of my life."

"Let's get a gelato," Muriel said.

It was just like Muriel to think of food at the turning point of his life. It was just like Muriel to ruin his moment with thoughts of gelato.

"I'm in love for the first time," Noah said, "and you're not going to ruin it."

And that much was true. All the songs he had merely been humming now made sense to him. Embrace me, my sweet embraceable, you. Come on-a my house. There was love all around and he had just never heard it singing before.

"What time is it?" he said.

"Three o'clock," Muriel replied.

"What day is it?"

"Tuesday."

His mind made a million calculations about how he would find her. Fate would not be so unkind as to pull aside its dark curtain and reveal his goddess only to snatch her away from him. Fate would bring her to him. He would come back tomorrow at three o'clock, he would come back next Tuesday at three clock. He would haunt this environs until the goddess reappeared.

"We'll come back tomorrow," Noah said.

"No way. I have Accountancy class tomorrow," Muriel said.

"You don't understand…"

"Forget about it."

"I will buy myself a car."

Muriel was ordering a large strawberry gelato with chocolate sprinkles.

"It's true then," she said to him. "It's true you have no life."

The next week Muriel was nowhere to be seen, so Noah went shopping for a car. It had to be vintage 1959, and he had his heart set on a Cadillac Eldorado with gigantic chrome trim and a hood ornament with stream-lined wings on the side of Mercury's head, suggestive of effortless flight into the dawning space age. Since he had less than $8,000 in the bank, Noah figured he may have to settle for a Chevy Bel Air or Ford Fairlane. He looked relentlessly but could find no acceptable automobile in Altoon. The only thing to do was to go into Cincinnati and search the larger dealers there, but he had no way of getting into the city. The desperate hour came upon him and he was forced to ask Muriel.

"No way," was her flat answer.

"Come on, you're never busy," Noah said.

"I won't do it."

"Why not?"

"It's skank."

"Pretty please."

On some level Muriel knew that if she drove Noah to Cincinnati, he would indeed buy some crazy 50-year-old automobile that he would use to find the girl from Heritage Hills Mall. And once he found her, it was game over. Once there were two of them in 1959, there would be no stopping them and this madness would go on forever. There is strength in numbers and shared psychoses.

"Muriel, so help me God, I will find her. If I have to take it a taxi cab to Cincinnati," Noah said.

"Take a taxi then, but I won't do it. It's too skank."

Two more days passed, days of misery, days of darkness. Noah stayed home and played sad 1950s love songs on his Magnavox. *Heartbreak Hotel. The Man Who Got Away. One for My Baby, One for the Road.* He drank martinis the way Dean Martin did. He watched Twilight Zone and considered trying to reach her in some alternate overlapping reality. Love had taken him to the height and breadth of his soul, and love had lifted him out of the commonplace and into the rare, but just as suddenly love had plunged him into the dark night of his soul. He could not eat, he could not sleep, and his face broke out in pustules.

When he came downstairs on the third morning of his depression, Muriel was sitting on his couch. She was wearing her black coat and jingling her keys in her hands.

"I decided to take you," she said.

They walked in silence down his grandmother's sidewalk to Muriel's black pickup truck. He did not press his luck by asking Muriel why she changed her mind. He already knew why. He was her only friend, and she no doubt had gotten lonely.

"What's that crap you're wearing?" Muriel asked.

"Madras plaid," Noah said.

"I meant your smell."

"Old Spice."

"It's making me sick," Muriel said, rolling down her window to let in fresh air.

It was a Friday morning and the mall was mostly empty. In its gaudy style the mall was enthusiastically endorsing the concepts of Mother's Day and buying things for the occasion in the same way the mall embraced Christmas, Valentine's Day, and even Presidents' Day as great times for sales and shopping. Every day was a good day for shopping at Heritage Hills Mall. Its cheerfulness and lack of cynicism about Mother's Day endeared the mall to Noah. Everything about the mall was endearing because here he would find his Dulcinea.

"What shall we look first?" Noah asked.

"As if I give a flying fuck," Muriel said.

Where would a princess of her royal beauty and majesty shop? Where would such an angel alight? Somewhere with magic and music. He thought of Barnes & Noble where he had first seen her. Noah began to walk fast towards Barnes and Noble.

Muriel assumed that Noah had spotted the girl again, a thought that filled her with dread. Why had she given in to him when she knew better? She could not move her trunk legs fast enough to keep up with him. As they were entering the bookstore, she could hear the aria from Madame Butterfly playing, as if some momentous climax was upon them. Muriel could not stand the thought that Noah was going to find this woman. She felt an anguish inside her, made worse by her knowledge that it was she who had enabled him to proceed with this tragedy.

It was then that Noah saw her, sitting sweetly in the bookstore's coffeehouse. She was wearing a pink blouse with a Peter Pan collar and pearls, and she look like a blooming flower among the dark green tables, tan walls and brown wood of the coffeehouse. She was huddled over a book.

"Excuse me — miss — Okay —" Noah was fumbling for words, but he had surprised himself for finding the courage to speak at all.

"I see you're reading 'Gidget.'"

"Oh Golly Gee, you mean — re-reading it," she smiled a wide smile and his world came tumbling down. He wanted to find a summer place right then and there. He hoped this ingénue had a drowsy chaperone when they traveled to this mystical summer place -- the place where they'd walk along the beach, and then succumbing to their mutual fantasies, tumble into the wet sands of ebb tide, and lock in an embrace that would last from here to eternity.

"I just love this book," his princess said. "I love just about everything from the 50s. To me, Della Street is a role model for all women, and Gidget is just a young Della Street. She's so kind and she's so loyal."

She looked into Noah's glazed face and mistook mesmerization for boredom.

"Oh, how I do go on and on," she said. "I'm ever so sorry."

Noah thought her voice was music.

"Please, don't stop talking - I love it," he said. "Can I buy you a soda?"

"Only if we can get two straws." And she giggled a Sandra Dee giggle that tripped and bubbled like a brook of bright waters tumbling over pastel rocks.

Noah caught himself reaching for her hand. Then he noticed Muriel lumbering toward him with a look of abject horror on her face.

"Nooooo," Muriel moaned, lumbering toward them.

If she didn't stop him, the two of them would be stuck in this time machine forever. All her efforts to save him would be undone that magical moment he touched her hand. Muriel pushed people aside and elbowed her way toward them. Muriel felt as if she were watching a huge chunk of solid rock break off a mountain top, and now it was in a free fall with tons of mass, and Noah about to be crushed underneath it.

"Don't do it," Muriel said.

"You're going to have to let me do the thinking for all of us," Noah said. "If I don't do this, I'll regret it forever. Maybe not today, maybe not tomorrow, but someday. You know that, and I know that, and so it must be done."

Noah turned to the girl in pink. She reached over and touched his hand.

Jane St. Clair grew up in Chicago and graduated from Northwestern University. She was worked for the TV Show "Sesame Street," and for the Louisville Courier-Journal as a reporter/photographer. She has published twenty-one children's books in Korea, over fifty children's short stories, as well as short fiction for adults in literary magazines such as *Clockwatch Review, Brain.Child, Rosebud, J Journal, Thema, 34th Parallel, descant, QWF, Clare, Thematic Magazine*, and others. She has won first place in The Writers Network contest, American Accolades, Hollywood's Next Success, and was the 2005 winner in television writing for Scriptapalooza.   She also placed in the 2015 Tom Howard/John Reid Essay Contest. *Walk Me to Midnight,* her first novel, was published in 2008 by Oak Tara Press. Jane now lives with her family in Tucson, Arizona.

Poker

Linda Dunlap

Despite the breeze from the overhead fan, the backs of Martha's legs stick like gum to the plastic chair. She shifts and leans to the right for a better look at the cards her husband Banks holds in his hands. When she spots a wild card and two kings, she knows it's time to begin.

"The school nurse called today. Raleigh has head lice again," she says. She leaves the words to hang in the air where they blink like caution lights. *Beware, danger lurks ahead.*

Banks drops his cards. He props his elbows on the table and pinches the bridge of his nose between two fingers. When he gives an exasperated sigh, Martha relaxes. Good, the words have done their job.

Easing back in her chair, she lifts her long hair, damp and heavy, off her neck. The heat in the room is stifling. She'd happily cut her hair, but Banks likes it long. By noon, the summer heat and humidity have drained the life from it. Having to rush and pick up daughter Elizabeth hadn't helped. Now, at this late hour in the day--almost eight-thirty--her makeup has faded, too. Her hated freckles have pushed through to the surface and taken over her cheeks again. She's a mess.

To take her mind off her disheveled looks, she lets her gaze drift around the room. A floor lamp stands near the card table. In a far corner of the room, a metal bin full of loose clothing melts back into the shadows.

When Banks, chewing on a thumbnail, picks up his cards again and fans them despairingly, Martha turns back to the table. She never knows whom she'll find playing poker with Banks. Tonight, by chance, she knows them all.

Malcolm, overweight and bearded since the last time she saw him, sits across the table from Banks. She knew Malcolm played poker, but is surprised he's here. When she had trouble finding tonight's card game,

Martha--against her better judgment—phoned his ex-wife, Darlene. Even after their divorce, Darlene manages to keep tabs on Malcolm--or so she thinks. *Eyes and ears of the world,* Banks calls her.

"Hold on a sec, Martha. I'm on the other line," Darlene had said. In an instant, she was back, anxious to confide. "Malcolm doesn't play poker anymore, but sure, I still know where a game is," she'd said. "There's one over in Pineland at the Snow White Laundry. You know, the one on Troutman Avenue run by the Philippines."

Martha is about to remark to Malcolm on his changed appearance since his divorce, then catches herself. She's not here in the back room of the laundry to evaluate appearances. She's here to take Banks home with her.

On her left, John, his dark oriental eyes shining like two slick coffee beans, sits next to Malcolm. She's never seen such eyes on a man before, or such smooth unblemished skin. She wonders if he shaves at all.

Luke, the one she knows the best, is opposite John. She hadn't reckoned on finding Luke here, would never have taken him for a poker player. He smiles jauntily across the table at her.

Enough time has elapsed now for her to go on. "That's twice this year the nurse has called about lice. You can well imagine the state I was in by the time Raleigh got home from school." She pauses and gives them sufficient time to well imagine, then paints in the details. "I grabbed the pinking shears and whacked off his hair clean down to the scalp."

Malcolm fumbles a card then scrambles to retrieve it. A blower comes on in the room and the pungent odor of cleaning fluid stirs the air.

When she and Elizabeth arrived earlier tonight, John answered her knock and let them in. Since he owns the laundry, she supposed this made him the host. When she didn't explain why she'd come, just marched straight over to the card table, he gave her a bewildered look. Murmuring a quiet greeting, he offered her a chair and then slid back into his own seat at the table. Bashful Malcolm nodded shyly and Luke had simply stared. His hair, the kind she'd always wanted to take a brush to, was tousled as though he'd just come in out of a windstorm. Since she'd last seen him, streaks of gray had mingled with the sandalwood color.

Now Martha dodges Luke's dusty blue eyes. The look he gave her when she began to speak was one that could make her hesitate and question her intent if she thought about it long enough, so she doesn't.

Upon their arrival Banks had glanced up, too. When he saw who it was, he'd merely ignored them and turned back to his cards. Of course, only he knows why they're here. This isn't the first time they've appeared at his poker game. He hates it, of course, but what is he to do? He knows he can't haul her out physically. He might like to, but he won't; neither will he explode in anger. She knows her husband well. It isn't in him to cause a ruckus. So he does the only thing he can. He ignores them with a wall of silence as thick and stubborn as a plate glass window. In the world where men reside, saving face writes the rules for some of them, but not for Banks. Peace at any cost is his philosophy--even if it means enduring embarrassment and humiliation.

Peace at any cost gives Martha a stomach ache. Tugging the chair John has found for her closer to the table, she settles herself more firmly at Banks' elbow.

It's John's turn to play. Martha watches as he skillfully peels a card from the pack, his thumb caressing the slick surface. His narrow eyes squint against smoke spiraling in lazy circles from the slender brown cigarette in his hand.

Banks draws and discards, keeping an ace and three sevens. He slides three crumpled bills toward the pot building in the center of the table. "I'll see that, raise you."

With the exception of Luke, who has not one discreet bone in his body and glances quizzically from her to Banks and back again, the men avoid looking at Banks and eye only her.

Martha isn't surprised that they're reluctant to look at Banks. She's come to expect it. In fact, she's learned to gauge her progress by how the other players behave toward her husband. It's only a matter of time before they'll glance his way. At first the looks will be hooded, sliding glances that don't hold and stick. But for now, they're only baffled and curious. What is she doing here? What's going on? They know something is amiss. They're just not sure what. Women don't appear for no reason and plop themselves down at poker tables to talk about head lice, of all things.

Gradually the tension in the room will rise and when it does, the men will begin to shift uncomfortably in their seats. When it hangs thick and heavy like something tangible between them, their sentiments will change. They'll look at Banks differently, boldly, with a question in their eyes.

It's not a man's place to reprimand another man's wife. That's the husband's job. When he doesn't do his job, his manhood is diminished. When the looks directed at him become clouded with anger and contempt, she'll know she's won again.

Martha leans forward and studies Banks' cards. She says, "Raleigh's head resembled a badly peeled onion. He positively refused to set foot outside until I took him into New Hope for the barber to even it up. At twelve years old, your son's become extremely vain, I'm afraid."

Dark-eyed John shifts in his chair. He scratches behind an ear and then the back of his head. When he sees Martha watching, he jerks his hand down and busies himself with his cards.

Am I making you nervous, John? I hope so. Yet she knows this will never do. This isn't about John. She lets her gaze drop. She has to stay focused. The trick is to pretend that Banks and she are alone. She pictures them lingering over a last glass of sweet tea at supper, letting their food settle before she puts the dishes in the sink. Outside, branches of the weeping willow brush against the kitchen window--*swoosh, swoosh*--a soft soothing sound announcing their special time of day.

But while John is easy to dismiss, Luke is a different story. When she lifts her eyes and finds him staring at her, she's blindsided by a blizzard of memories.

I brought you a bouquet, Martha said to her mother, presenting the purple flowers she'd picked from beside the front steps. Her mother stared at them, her face as still as marble. They're a present, Martha went on. For you. Finally in a voice so low she strained to hear, her mother whispered, they're dead now. Like a statue, Martha stood, holding the flowers out to her mother long after she'd disappeared into the bedroom and closed the door. She made it sound as if I'd meant to kill them, Martha thought. She opened her fist and the flowers spilled onto the carpet. A hollow ache stirred in her gut as she stared down at the ruined flowers. Her mother was right. They were dead.

Martha looks away, escaping Luke's gaze. That same hollow ache she felt then and the panic that followed is what brings her back to the poker games. What she can't do is let these men know the feeling exists, that it's still there. Oh God, please don't let my outside match my insides.

She is sinking into quicksand. Fear washes over her as she struggles. At the last second, her fingers close around a sturdy clump of dog fennels. She clings to the foul smelling weeds and hangs on. When her fingers grow weak and tired, she will let go. The struggle will end.

Martha sits up straight in her chair and takes a deep breath, filling her lungs with courage and determination. Shaking her head, she dashes such thoughts from her mind. What is she thinking? She's fine. She simply wasn't paying attention. She's allowed Luke to unsettle her. For a moment, she'd left her thoughts unguarded. When they're left to wander, they become dangerous. She'll have to be more attentive. She tries never to spend time thinking about what thinking can't change. Much of the pain and suffering of life, she believes, comes from wallowing in wishes and fantasies of things being other than what they are. Yet some things she's found she can change. She decided a long time ago that no matter what she had to do, she'd never let the fear win again.

After they were married, she and Banks lived for a short time with his dad, Arthur, while they saved for a home of their own. The land was already picked out and paid for. It lay behind the old cotton gin and ran along beside O'Malley's Creek to the fork. Although it was overrun with blackberry bushes and kudzu vines, they figured in two years they'd have the down payment and could start clearing the underbrush.

Arthur was a gentle man, a caring man, like his son, with no hidden agendas. He was kind and welcoming to Martha, until, that is, the evening she entered the kitchen to find him and Banks at the table. They sat with spoons poised over a carton of chocolate ice cream, moisture beading the sides like tiny teardrops. They were huddled so close together their heads seemed connected. When they finally saw her standing in the doorway, they seemed annoyed and put out with her. Arthur had turned back to Banks with a frown that seemed to ask, *have you ever noticed how your wife is tarnished goods? You understand that by choosing her, son, you've settled for second best.* Suddenly, once again, she was on the outside looking in.

With her face pressed against the windowpane, she'd watch the children play in the street while outside on the ledge Tallulah, their neighbor's inside cat, shivered in the bitter December wind. When Tallullah curled her spine against the window, Martha stroked the glass in circles, yearning to feel the soft kitten fur against her fingertips. But she glanced over her shoulder, poised and guarded, waiting for the hand to grip her arm and jerk her away from the window. "No! No! No!" her mother would scream. Upstairs, Martha would lie with her pillow over her head to muffle her sobs and wonder what was so terribly wrong with her that her mother could not love her.

Martha was about to turn away from her husband and father-in-law when Banks beckoned to her with a smile. She crossed the room and he pulled her close, her hip soft against his side while he and his dad finished their ice cream. She found herself wanting to explain, to make excuses, to defend herself as she always did when she wasn't wanted. I never have been a fool about chocolate ice cream, she'd wanted to say.

Now, in the sallow light of the laundry, she thinks how silly it was for her to still feel left out and afraid when she most certainly is not. That was a long time ago, things are different now. Besides, Banks' father has been so pleasant since then, she's convinced she imagined the whole thing.

Still, it never hurt to take precautions. Although she didn't know the least thing about selling shoes, she found a job at Connie's in the mall, in addition to her position as insurance clerk at the hospital. By the next June, she had them in their own double-wide on the lot at O'Malley's Creek. She likes to think she did it on her own, but can't deny the need to keep Banks to herself, a need that strutted around like a bull fighter swirling his red cape with his chest out, had fueled her ambition.

A whiff of cleaning astringent stirs the air and tickles her nose. She rests an index finger under her nose for a moment to ward off a sneeze.

For a long time after they were settled in their new home, she'd slide across to Banks' side of the bed at night. Careful not to squeak the springs, she'd align her body with his, close enough to feel his heat but not touching. Gradually, the aching space inside of her shrank like a tail light fading into the distant darkness until it closed into itself and disappeared.

Martha taps Banks on the shoulder to make sure he's paying attention. "I put the hair with the lice on the refrigerator shelf in a Tupperware bowl with the lid on tight so they can't escape into the Three Bean Salad. You can see them for yourself when you get home."

Wearily, he straightens his shoulders and rubs the back of his neck. His nails, rimmed with grime from the service station, stand out against the pale calloused skin on his fingers. He insists on biting them. Martha has to keep reminding him not to chew on them in front of people. A bandage on the little finger of his right hand is soiled and loose. Tuesday of last week, he dropped the crankcase out of a Honda. His finger bent clear back until the skin split on the underside. Martha rewraps it every night, soaking it first in a special green soap she keeps under the sink.

"Not that I thought you'd figure out why the lice were there especially if you came home and I wasn't there to explain."

She sees no reason to point out that he hadn't come home. Instead he'd come to the poker game.

Across the table, Luke glances at Martha, then at Elizabeth, who leans against her mother with her eyes fixed shyly on the floor. With the tip of her toe, Elizabeth traces circles in the fine patina of dust that covers the concrete floor. When Luke looks as if he's about to speak, Martha feels a moment of unease. The other men she can read like a book, but Luke is different. He's always had a knack for saying things that leave her speechless. When he merely sits drumming his fingertips on the tabletop, she relaxes and goes on. "I could have cried. Never will I forget the sight of Raleigh's lovely curls scattered on the dining room rug."

Silently Banks shuffles the cards. He'd lost the hand. Although Martha welcomed Luke's silence, when Banks doesn't speak, she bites her lip. It's all she can do to keep from screaming. *If only you'd let me inside with you, wherever you are, I wouldn't have to do the things I do.* But she knows Banks. That will get her nowhere. This way is better with her words like water dripping on stone. *Drip, drip, drip*—a steady force, wearing away.

Malcolm hunches over the table, his shoulders turned slightly away from her. Studying his cards, he tries to follow Banks' lead and act as if Martha isn't there. He makes a soft grunting sound, then catches it up short.

Malcolm's divorce was not an amicable one. Darlene had bragged to anyone who'd listen about the spiteful things she'd done to make him suffer. The duplex where he'd wound up didn't allow pets, so his German Shepherd Leo, whom he loved almost as much as he loved his children and more than he'd ever loved Darlene, stayed behind. Once she'd called and told Malcolm that Leo had just been run over by a car while Leo stood beside her making little panting noises at the sound of his master's voice on the phone. Darlene had giggled at how upset Malcolm was until he figured out the sounds on her end were his dog pining for him.

Martha pictures Darlene, her eyes outlined in a bold dramatic black that make her look shrewd and untrustworthy. Malcolm, who by nature is as nonthreatening and defenseless as a turnip, was no match for her. Martha imagines how the incident had sent him spiraling down the rabbit hole again. She fails to understand how a woman will go to such lengths to crush a man's spirit.

Elizabeth worms her head under her mother's arm. "C-can we go home now?" she asks. When Martha looks down, green eyes, pale as celery, gaze back at her. She pulls Elizabeth close and rests her cheek against the soft blonde hair.

Recently Elizabeth has developed a stutter, although she's always had trouble pronouncing her s's. At four, she'd lie flat on her stomach under the kitchen table and practice her snake sounds while Martha mixed hamburger for meatloaf in a wooden bowl overhead. When she said, "try social security," Elizabeth stared at her with round somber eyes. Banks is good about helping his daughter practice her big words. He laughs and says, "Those are monster words for a six-year-old, even one who doesn't get her tongue twisted the wrong way sometimes." Elizabeth still has to stop and think before she says words like seesaw and spaghetti.

Raleigh says the poker games cause his sister's stutter and he refuses to go to them anymore. Martha doesn't see the connection. After all, it's not his stutter, so how would he know? But she doesn't argue with him. Her son has always been like his father until recently when he's picked up the habit of talking back.

"Elizabeth can't say the words right because she gets nervous when you make Daddy feel bad in front of everybody," Raleigh said. Martha was in her bedroom dressing when her son had planted himself defiantly in the doorway.

She stood at the bureau and tilted her head in front of the mirror to catch the best light. *What about me?* She wanted to yell. *What about me?*

Behind Raleigh, a broad swath of light slanted through the hall window and bathed Martha's face in its soft glow. The warm light felt as if it cared for her. It protected her somehow from her son's brassy hard-edged words, words aimed at her with scorn and disdain.

All day her mother kept her inside. Together they'd washed down the walls, the windows. For hours her mother stood at the sink wringing her hands, listening for the voices. Martha leaned beside her and stared down at the water running over those hands, the fingers long and tapering, the little finger bent at a slight awkward angle where she'd caught it in a door jam. Cars whizzed past outside. A horn sounded. She never understood why she couldn't go outside and play. Then they came and took her away.

Ignoring Raleigh, she leaned close to the mirror and with the tip of her little finger dabbed lipstick on her bottom lip. Finally, when she didn't answer, Raleigh gave up. He turned and stormed out the door, slamming it with a smart *crack!* Sighing, she inspected her lips. She repaired the smear where her finger had slipped when she flinched. She congratulated herself that she'd never felt the need to explain herself to a child.

"C-can we?" Elizabeth asks again.

Martha loves the feel of her cheek resting on the crown of Elizabeth's head. She relishes like a keepsake the smell of baby shampoo that lingers in her daughter's curls. At night, when Martha finishes reading Elizabeth's bedtime stories, she begs her mother to curl up in bed with her. Martha would have liked the feel of her child cradled safely in her arms. But she always tells Elizabeth no. At some point, children have to learn to sleep through the night alone.

When Elizabeth first saw Banks at the poker table tonight, she pulled away from her mother and started toward him, but Martha drew her back. She hadn't brought Elizabeth along to visit with her father.

"May we?" Martha corrects Elizabeth. "Honestly, if I'm not battling vermin, I'm playing English teacher. To tell the truth, I think it's due to all the time you spend with that Barr child." She glances up. "The mind is never stimulated by Looney Tunes and World Championship Wrestling non-stop on a regular basis."

Malcolm hesitates, his hand in mid-air. Luke shakes his head while John's eyes widen. His brows arch into half-moons. "Huh?" His glance darts across the table at Banks, then quickly away. Martha smiles to herself, elated to see the tension in the room shift. In that one moment, it becomes Banks' fault that this woman is here in the middle of their card game, interrupting with this absurd conversation.

Poor Banks. To think that he has to come home to this every night of his life. Sweet Jesus! Why does he just sit there? If she were my wife, I'd tell her to get the hell out of here.

The first time Martha found the poker game in the back of Ben Phillip's Meat Market, Banks had done just that, a pulse in his temple throbbing like a drumbeat. He balled up his fist at her—something he'd never done before. Yet Martha had scarcely heard his shouts.

So this is what you do when you're not with me, she'd screamed inside. *You attach yourself to someone else and became a part of them instead.*

As Martha stood in the doorway amid the rich smell of blood and freshly butchered beef, she hit upon the idea, its power in its simplicity. As her plan fell into place, her churning rage disappeared. Pulling a chair from the corner of the room, she'd settled into it with an alarming ease. When Banks realized she was there to stay, he'd looked at her with something in his eyes as close to loathing as she'd ever seen in them. Then he'd shrugged his shoulders and dealt the cards.

Warily, each man at the table had picked up his cards as well.

He's one of you now, Martha thought. I am the outsider, the one who isn't good enough. But I'll make you turn away from him. When he's no longer a part of you, he'll be glad I'm still here. Watch me! I'll tear this circle of yours apart without so much as raising my voice.

With Raleigh leaning against her on one side and Elizabeth the other, Martha began her quiet commentary. "Your mother called the middle of the afternoon. They'll be over Sunday for dinner and you're not to mention the bruise above Uncle Pepper's right eye. He got drunk Saturday night on that cheap homebrew. It drove him so crazy he called your father a perfect turd right to his face. Well, you can imagine! Your father decked Uncle Pepper, who fell and cracked his head on the corner of the butcher-block table. Now he's got a shiner the size of a sixty-watt bulb."

As Martha went on and on, the men shifted in their chairs, eyed her across the table. Was she insane? They couldn't be sure. Yet strangely enough, only when their glances shifted and came to rest on Banks did they seem to finally understand that they weren't the trapped ones--Banks was. They could walk away anytime they chose. And one by one, they did.

Finally, only Banks remained at the table. He sat then, staring about him, the overhead lamp spotlighting the bright tail feathers of the wood ducks decorating the backs of the cards strewn loosely about. The men, their skin oddly bleached by the stark light, gathered jackets and coats to leave.

That was eight months ago and Martha has scouted out Banks' poker games ever since. He'd started out playing once a month. Now he was down to every other month. Soon she'd have that number to zero. Once she'd intruded on a game, you can be sure the men in that game never played with Banks again. "Not on your life! " she practically heard them mutter. Good Hope wasn't a large town--a nothing of a town, really. Pineland, the next town over, was even more of a nothing. How long would it take for word to spread?

Malcolm pushes his chair away from the table now. He checks his wristwatch as if he's late for an appointment. Turning, he keeps his head down. Once at the door, he looks back solemnly at Banks, then turns and disappears into the night.

John rises next. He collects ashtrays and half-empty drink glasses. Silently, he too fades from sight. The blower in the room roars to life, then halts abruptly. In seconds the air hangs heavy with the odor of cleaning solutions.

Martha digs in her handbag for her car keys. Elizabeth is drowsy: her eyelids droop. Martha glances at Banks, who sits alone at the table now. Luke has disappeared through a doorway marked MEN. Nursing his injured finger against his chest, Banks chews on a thumbnail. He looks as innocent and child-like as Elizabeth nodding beside him. Martha yearns to lean across the table and cradle his head against her breast.

Not too long ago, she'd have done that. She thinks of how quickly they've moved to a place where that's impossible. Time has not done this to them. What has happened? When they reach home, she'll be awash in tears while Banks sits in stony silence. Eventually he'll promise never again and the black emptiness inside of her will go away--at least for a time.

The sound of Luke clearing his throat catches Martha's attention. She turns to find him standing propped against the wall beside the clothes bin. She'd forgotten about him. He seems mellow, relaxed. The light in the room seems drawn to him. It settles in his hair and holds it for a moment in a special glow. She smiles. There was a time … She remembers the pink peacock tattooed on his left hip and wonders if it's still there. She supposes so; she's heard tattoos are permanent.

'Why, Martha," he says with a mocking smile. "If you'd wanted to play with us that bad, all you had to do was ask."

Martha feels a flush creep across her cheeks. The skin on her face pulls taut, stretches tightly across the bones. Trust Luke to lead you into quicksand and then step back on solid ground while he watches you sink—always when you least expect it. She realizes now that tonight when she arrived, what she'd thought was a hint of welcome in his jaunty smile, wasn't that at all.

She feels her fingers begin to slip and is so afraid. She can't hold on. She lets go of the dog fennel. Her keening scream is stopped by the quicksand that closes around her, cutting off her air.

Martha takes a deep breath, steadies herself against the table edge. She wonders what made her think of the peacock at all. That was such a long time ago and at a time when she was still naive enough to believe you couldn't pick who you'd fall in love with.

Rising briskly, she bustles Elizabeth toward the door. She marches past Luke, staring straight ahead, determined not to give him the satisfaction of seeing her cry.

No one had explained to her that her mother was sick, that nothing was wrong with Martha.

Banks stands now, jingling coins in his pants pocket. Martha knows he'll follow her home in his car, the beams from his headlamps rising in the darkness like search lights as he crests the hills behind her.

Elizabeth falls asleep on the front seat near the door. Even at this hour, almost ten, the air is heavy, sticky with heat. A faint sheen of sweat rims her upper lip like a shiny mustache. When Martha reaches to wipe it away, Elizabeth stirs and curls into herself.

Martha swallows hard. Her lips are dry, her tongue feels rough and scratchy like it does when she takes the pills Dr. Doyle prescribed. When she tells him she doesn't like how they make her feel, he comes from behind his desk to rest a hand on her shoulder. "You can't do this alone, Martha. You need to take the medication."

She moistens her lips with the tip of her tongue. The numbing kernel of panic begins inside her chest. *Just watch, I'll show you.*

It is so quiet and still in the car, Martha is tempted to rouse Elizabeth and point out how the street lamps turn the slash pines into a swaying rhythm of tall dark shadows. For a moment, she becomes disoriented, all turned around. Nothing looks familiar.

She rolls down the window. The swish of warm air laps her neck and stirs her hair. She reaches up to adjust the rear view mirror. Slowing the car, she stares into the reflection for the gleam of headlights behind her. In her ears, she hears the drum of her heartbeat. *Thump-thump! Thump-thump!* The aching space swells inside her, expands and grows larger. It presses, a hollow knot, crushing her heart.

The car creeps along, barely moving now at all. She leans close to the mirror and searches for a speck of light behind her. But only the lazy pattern of weaving shadows stretches into the darkness as far back as she can see. The damp air in the car stifles her breathing; she feels faint. The road in front of her becomes a blur. Martha pulls the car to the side of the road and rests her forehead against the steering wheel. She tries to think, tries to clear her head.

Finally, she lifts her head and gazes over at Elizabeth, a dark mute shadow on the seat beside her. In the heavy silence of the car, Martha seems to hear the soft lisping stutter of the s sounds. S-s-spaghetti, s-s-social s-s-security. The sounds wash over her, then recede, like waves lapping against a river bank. She is so tired, the fight drained out of her finally. Reaching for her handbag, she fumbles for the medicine bottle inside. She unscrews the lid and shakes two of the tiny green pills into her palm. She collects saliva on the back of her tongue. When she swallows, the pills go down easily. In a few minutes, she feels her heartbeat slow and the hollow knot inside her chest relax. She is surprised at the quiet that settles inside her. She's been afraid to give up fighting the fear, afraid if she does, she will sink into the quicksand. It will destroy her. Now, as she surrenders to it, she's relieved to find that it's simply a peaceful feeling that closes around her like a warm bath.

Pulling the car back onto the road, she keeps her eyes fastened on the white line in the middle of the highway. A light drizzle begins and she turns on the windshield wipers. As she watches them struggle in a strange rain dance on the glass, she makes a deal with herself. She promises herself that she won't glance into the rear view mirror, but will keep her eyes on the highway until she turns into their gravel drive with the two oleanders guarding its entrance. Then, when she stops and gazes into the mirror above her head, she is convinced she'll see the beams from Banks' car. They'll be so bright, they'll light up the landscape for miles around.

Elizabeth makes a faint whimpering sound, then falls quiet. Martha tells herself that the lights will be there when she finally allows herself to search for them. But on the off-chance that Banks is delayed, an accident perhaps that he's come up on in the dark, she'll carry Elizabeth inside. Without undressing her—just this once she'll let her sleep in her play clothes—she'll tuck her between the Pooh Bear sheets. And just this once, she'll do as her daughter has begged. Martha will climb into bed with her and curve, spoon-like, against her back. She'll hold Elizabeth cradled in her arms until she hears Banks pull into the driveway.

Linda L. Dunlap began a second career as a fiction writer in the late eighties after a successful career as a registered nurse. Her first story, "I'm Here, Mr. Sullivan," was published by Pencil Press Quarterly in 1987. Since then, she's had numerous short works published in literary and university presses across the country including *The Crescent Review*, *Florida Magazine*, *RE:AL*, *Timber Creek Review*, and *Savannah Literary Journal*. She was awarded artist's fellowship grants from the Florida Department of Cultural Affairs in 1996, in 2000 and again in 2010. Her short story, "Goldenrod" was nominated for a Pushcart Prize in 2010. A collection of her short stories entitled *Rail Walking And Other Stories* is for publication this Fall. Ms. Dunlap is a proud native of Georgia and lives now in Winter Park, Florida. She tries to write every single day.

Dream Location

Daryl Scroggins

I lived under some bushes in a highway cloverleaf for a couple of months, but a few days ago I sold the place. There's money in real estate.

Red-leafed bushes—red at the edges, green inside and down to the ground, and grouped thick to where it looked like a cave in there. I got in the hard way the first time. There was a man came out of a gas station that didn't like me asking his wife for change. He shoved me and I stepped up like I might bring it back and he whips out a pistol with a scope on it. I took off on a hard zigzag run, hit the bush wall down the way there and felt like I had shoved myself through a sieve.

I'm almost a white man, five feet nine inches, one hundred and forty pounds, brown, brown, and my name is Larry Wicks.

Anyway, I couldn't see much in the dark at night under there, but I wasn't in a big hurry to come out. I woke up later and still couldn't see anything except for a scratchy kind of light here and there, and I realized the sun was up.

When I went to push my hair back it felt like a busted wicker chair it was so full of twigs. I got them out and my eyes adjusted to where I could see the big amount of room I had to move around in. I guess bushes care mostly about their outsides, because they looked to have given up on doing anything branch or leaf-wise at the bottom. I could stand and walk just barely humped over, and whenever I snagged a little branch it broke off with a pop.

Something about the place made me want to just sit and daydream for awhile. I could hear traffic going by all around, but it was hushed-like and far away seeming. I dozed off and woke up again when I heard voices. There was two men picking up trash, must have been working off a DWI or something, and they had stopped to have a smoke. They were only three feet away from me and I could hear everything they said, but I may as well have been a bug on a high leaf for all they could tell about me being right there with them. One of them said, "Shit, here comes ass-hole in the van, hide the beer." A hand comes in under the bush edge and lets go of a six pack of longnecks with only two missing.

Well that right there was the start of my realizing that I was in a lucky place. That beer would have been hot even if they had gotten back to it later, so I didn't let it go to waste.

A little bit after they left a city streets truck pulled up onto the grass and I took a peek at what they were doing. A man got out, bent down and opened an iron flap on the ground there with a key. He reached in and made a twisting motion and water started spraying out under a row of sick-looking trees over in a median. I remember thinking then—well, all I need now is electricity. Didn't take long and I found it. While I was spying on my location I saw a kid working over at the gas station, blowing the drive off with an electric blower. He had it plugged in at the base of a big sign, in a plug box that sat up on a piece of conduit. On the other side of the sign there was another plug almost hidden by weeds all grown up around it. It wasn't three feet from a storm drain, and the pipe to it had to lead towards me because water's got to head to a low place.

I don't guess all of this is very interesting, so let me just say this: I had a waterbed and a TV down there the next day. I had some money I had rounded up before John Wayne went for his cannon the day before, and I don't mind investing if it's for the home. I got a good gray extension cord and a hose and things over at the home and garden center, and what I couldn't afford I pitched over the back fence of the garden section like I always do. I walked around and picked up my stuff, and headed over to a couple of neighborhood yard sales.

The real find, though, came a few hours before my shopping spree. I was exploring my new land under the bushes, and I noticed that everything sloped down toward the center of the island. When

I got close to the middle, the bushes gave way to a little forest of wild trees and vines. I figure an old creek bottom went through there before highway construction carved it up, and this was part of the old land. You can't see much of it from any of the roads that wrap all around, because it's down low and the bushes at the edges are all up high enough to block the view. I felt like a pioneer down in there. And then I saw a big concrete drain box they had dug up when the highway and a new drain system went in. It was a big concrete square, open at one end and big enough to almost stand up in. About ten feet in there are two pipe-joint holes in both sides, each about big around as a garbage can lid. But the pipes were gone. I figure they just didn't think it was worth the trouble to get a crane to lift out something you weren't going to be able to see anyway.

We're talking, I don't know, a hundred square feet or so—plenty of room compared to an old refrigerator box lined with dog-eat sofa cushions. So like I said, I rounded up some things. I made a wall and a real door at the front opening, and a window out of one of the pipe holes with some plexiglass. I used eight pieces to make it hard for somebody to break in. I did something artistic with the other pipe hole. I got some quick-set concrete and a bunch of bottles in different colors and stacked them in there with some concrete between them. Nice stained glass effect, and I also ran a dryer vent hose through there for my camp stove.

I liked it all fine. I even went to the "oops bin" at the home center for some cheap paint. Outside I used gray and brown and green, and the place was invisible after I did that. Inside I went with a kind of sky-blue with yellow accents. I like an open feeling, even if it's inside concrete. Got some pictures for the walls and made a little pantry for my canned goods.

Okay, now I'm getting to the important part, that has a lot to do with more good luck that lets you know just how important location can be. My property, I noticed, was close to several motels—the good kind that they call an "Inn" or "Suites." They don't know in a big motel who all is checked in, so I went for a visit once I had settled in. Morning is the best time. I whip a bathrobe out of my pack and put it on over my clothes, hide the pack behind some bushes and head for the lobby. I look right at whoever is behind the desk, nod at them, and head straight over to the muffins and milk and orange juice. That robe has some deep pockets.

I figure most of life is a question of how you are going to get three meals a day and a place to sleep. So that one free breakfast trick is a pretty good part of the whole thing. It's hard to run out of motels and places where the same kind of thing will work every time. Well, depending on what part of the country you're in. One thing that takes some work, though, is keeping yourself looking and smelling good enough to command respect. I know a lot of people who just can't understand that they have bum written all over them. They come out from under a boxwood hedge at the mall, all wall-eyed and smelling like vinegar and pencil shavings—and they wonder why security everywhere is kicking them in the ass all the way to the property line. They are usually the ones who never had to think, and then they had to and couldn't. It doesn't take long to slip into a drift, like a person blindfolded and spun around in a strange place. One month—job, big screen TV, sports utility vehicle with cell phone— and the next month a pissed-on seat at the bus station, waiting for the mission to open.

Turns out the motel was worth more than just free breakfast. While I was loading up on free stuff I saw a bunch of people going into a conference room down the hall, past a standing sign that said, "Simplify And Find The Inner Peace You Can Never Buy." A Dr. Bingham, the sign said, would explain all. I found a name tag in a garbage can from some other seminar, went around the corner and took the robe off and put the tag on. Sometimes these meetings are catered, and sometimes what you have to listen to is better than a Bible sermon that gets you a pile of dry pancakes in some church basement.

It took me a while to believe what I was hearing, but those people were talking about how much trouble it is to *have* so much. I'm always interested in excess that might be relieved in my vicinity. A person would whine for a minute about the trap of stock trading, and then his pager would buzz, and he'd whip out a cell phone and drop the whole scene like nobody was listening anyway. Dr. comb-over Bingham talked for a while about how much money a person could save by moving to a place that had a good public transportation system. "You don't *need* more than one car," he said. I don't think they were buying it, though. Bingham must have felt things slipping away too, because he started a bunch of handouts circulating, piles of information that has the kind of bulk to it that tends to make people think maybe they weren't foolish to pay for it.

When the catering carts were pushed in, everybody perked up and headed in that direction. I hung back with the good Doctor; I wasn't worried about the food, since it's at the end of everybody's picking at it that you can pile the rest into a bag and nobody cares. I looked at Bingham, then shook my head and turned away. "What," he said. I turned back and looked him straight in the eye. "You're not reaching them because they only want to *feel* like things are simpler— they don't really want to give anything up." So then Bingham gets defensive, like I knew he would, and he wants to know how I know so much about *his* area of expertise. I shrugged. "I am engaged in an experiment in simple living that is going to revolutionize the whole way the territory is presented and marketed," I told him. I always try to work in the word "marketing" around people like him. Bingham laughed and I laughed too. He waited for me to say more, but I knew to wait longer. "So this revolutionary idea," he says, "what's that all about?" He covers his mouth like he's trying to stifle a yawn. "Right," I said. "You figure I'm just going to blurt the whole thing out to one of my competitors." We both laughed again, and I waited for that little phrase I knew would come. "Seriously, though," he said.

I get all my ideas under the gun or I don't get them at all. So what I came up with surprised even me. "Urban dude ranch," I said. "What these people want is just to know that life *can* be simple if they decide to make it that way. Once they know that, once they *experience* it, well then they can go on with what they have been doing."

Bingham looked at me like he was thinking instead of looking, but it was time to finish his lecture, so he could—the way I read it—get in a hot tub with a drink. But he said he hoped we could share ideas about the "business."

I was loading roast beef into a Styrofoam container when Dr. Bingham eased up and slipped an arm around my shoulder. "I like to see a man who lets nothing go to waste," he said. I winked at him and said, "And I didn't even pay to get in here." That set him back for a second, and then a look of admiration came over him. I moved in quick while he was off balance. "How about a field trip to my lab," I said. He looked puzzled. "Lab?" I told him it was a place right in the middle of everything that I had set up as a point of guided departures into a wilderness hidden right under our noses. A staging area where, for a small fee, a person partially sick of luxury could safely hide and view the staggering surplus of goods and services that make the concept of "never pay retail" look like a con. Bingham gave up on trying to hide his emotions. He knew I was right about these people and he knew there was money in it. I already knew what I was going to say when he came out with the partnership idea. "I'm an all or nothing kind of a guy," I said. "I try to stay away from potential complications if I can. But I tell you what—I'll show you my set up for the two hundred dollar fee I plan to charge for excursions, and when you move on to, I don't know, Houston or somewhere, you'll have a good handle on the concept." He paid me out of his wallet right there and I led the way.

We were walking along the side of the highway, just a couple hundred feet from the motel, when I ducked into a favorite fold in the wall of bushes beside us. Bingham didn't know where I went. He stood looking around like I had been beamed up off the planet. I thought about just leaving him there and moving on—two hundred dollars up. But I started to feel sorry for the man, so I reached out, got him by the arm and pulled him in.

It was not until we were almost to the house that Dr. Bingham seemed to realize the danger he might be putting himself into. I know I wouldn't go following some person I had just met off into a place that may as well have been the middle of a jungle. But right when he was starting to get really fidgety, I pointed and said, "There it is." He squinted. "What? Where?" I walked over to the front door, unlocked it, reached in and turned the light on. "Good Lord," Bingham said. He was still standing there when I walked back out and handed him a cold beer.

I showed him around, and then I just let him sit and soak up the feel of the place. After a while I said, "You know, this is the closest thing there is to being invisible. You're in the middle of everything, hundreds of people passing you every minute of the day and night— and you can see them if you want but they can't see you. Even the IRS couldn't touch you here." That last comment is what did it for Dick Bingham. He didn't even start with the partner thing again. He made me an offer. I rubbed my neck long enough for him to up it twice, and then I said, "Hell, I guess there's room enough in this business for me to move on and scout out some other locations in another state." We went to a nearby bank and it was a done deal before dark.

I'm going to miss the place; there aren't many as perfectly situated as that one. But every highway interchange like it is a possible four-leaf clover. And I don't like all the complications of being tied down anyway. I have my liquid assets set up in an account I can wire into for equal quarterly distributions, so now I have a payday coming no matter what happens. Couple more deals like this and I won't have a care in the world.

Daryl Scroggins taught creative writing and literature for a number of years at The University of Texas at Dallas and The University of North Texas. He and his wife, Cindy, recently retired and moved to Marfa, Texas, where they pursue art and writing projects. His poems and short fiction have appeared in magazines and anthologies across the country, and his most recent book is *This Is Not the Way We Came In*, a collection of flash fiction and a flash novel.

The Watcher

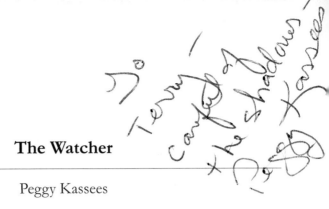

Peggy Kassees

Music vibrates through the club. The show is into the third set. He sashays on to the dance floor. Painted eyebrows, pasted smile, and barracuda eyes on alert, he searches. His hips gyrate to the music as he glides across polished hardwood, threads his way between twosomes, threesomes, and around those dancing alone.

A thrill runs from the slim six-inch blade strapped against his right ankle, up the length of his thigh, pauses in his groin, then whispers in his ear.

Hungry—

"I know," he acknowledges. His mind, as always, is in sync with the cold metal. "Wait—"

Need—

Arms raised high, his torso elongates. Cat-lean, each beat of the music creates an answering flex. He knows she'll be here. Lonely. Needy. Watching like he is for someone to take home. Stave off ennui. Silence the voices.

There—

Her bare feet twist and turn, narrow hips lift and rotate, not quite in rhythm with the musicians, but to her own song. One hand holds a half empty plastic cup of beer. The glass tilts, beer kisses the lip and eases down then up the other side with another sly embrace.

Thirsty—

He swipes his tongue across his parched mouth. She's not the one. Quick flicks moisten the crusted fever blister just under his nose. Cold steel pulses, and pushes against his shin, his belly. He arches his back, reaches for the ceiling, hands flashing with the disco-ball's reflections.

Want. Need—

"I know," he snaps, his voice loud to his own ears. A couple two-stepping over to the left glance at him. He smiles, but they notice his eyes, and back away. Air hitches in his chest. "Not them," he mumbles. "Not yet." One night he may follow them home. Wait until the lights are out. Sneak in. Play. But this dark night will be different. A first. A quiver races up his spine, catches in his throat and leaves in a moan. Pain and ecstasy – life and death. Air flows deep in his chest and out his mouth. Once again he licks his lips.

He raises hands that he caught sliding toward his boot. Fingers twitch, but he keeps them in the air, snaps in time to the music.

Now—

"No." Impatient, he snipes at the length of steel. Frustration mixes with anger in his voice. He'd waited too long. "I'm the one in control, not you."

He strokes his thighs, hips, chest, then thrusts forward with a smooth gyration designed to show any onlookers that this is a new move, an example, if they're interested.

He'll have to feed the steel soon.

Another young woman raises her right arm above her head in a graceful arch. Her hand flirts in the disco's sparkles, a butterfly not quite certain where to settle. She dances by herself in this crowded room, eyes scanning for possible partners. He understands her dread of being alone and absorbs it. Every sensuous sway of her slim form tells him she, too, is on the hunt. Her eyes jump from man to man until she meets his. Her mouth opens in a soft inhalation, and she edges away. Satisfaction flows through him. Fear is such a tasty morsel.

Now?

"No, not yet." He strokes his chest. One hand cups his groin as he rises to his toes, and moonwalks until a group of dancers block his movements.

Now!

"Soon. Very, very, soon."

The blade vibrates, demands his attention.

He doesn't like to be rushed. The hunt is his favorite part, and he's been casing this one for a while. A sharp glance along his mark's body admires the way she holds herself. How her eyes continue to focus on those at the tables, the musicians, the dancers.

"I'm tenderizing her."

He twirls through the throng, a whirling dervish. Both hands high in the air, he can't lower them now. He knows she's fascinated with him. That she can't wrench her eyes away. He moves his hips in primal imitation. Invitation. Fierce hunger emanates from the hidden six-inch length of steel. Excitement courses through his veins.

"Be patient," he tells the throbbing shaft.

She dips her head, and instantly, he is there.

"Hello," he says, sets a hand on her shoulder as he leans to speak in her ear. She's surprised he approached her, wonders if he's someone she knows. He smiles, touches her throat oh so lightly. Her pulse quickens under his thumb. His speeds up to match.

A shudder runs through her. She has no idea. The pen she holds rolls off her be-ringed fingers onto the table, stops next to a cardboard coffee container. Red lipstick is thick on the rim. He picks up the cup, touches the spot her lips marked, and sips the now cool brew.

"Yumm," he purrs. Under his thumb, her carotid pushes thick with life against his skin. There is a question in her eyes. Do I know you? Have we met?

He is effervescent, a part of the music, one with the tiny lights thrown off by the silver ball hanging in the center of the club. Wonders if her lipstick is on his mouth, if she sees how alike they are.

He picks up the pen, gold plastic warm from her touch, and sets it on the notebook open to a half-filled page.

"You've been busy tonight." He allows the tip of his tongue to delve into her ear, tastes her.

Delicious!

"Yes," he agrees. "Yes." He settles a hand on her shoulder. She stiffens. But she doesn't fear. They are in public. Gentle as a moth, he trails one hand along her upper arm, grazing the edge of a small breast. He presses his nose near her collarbone and inhales. Ambrosia.

Her fingers quiver. "What—" she begins.

"What do you have here, my sweet?" He glances at the words scribbled on her notebook. The letters she'd used to describe him. "Not bad, dear," he breathes into her ear.

He tilts her head backwards, strokes her hair and searches her wide eyes. Absorbs the horror he sees in their depths. Ah, finally. She knows. Eyes glued to his, she doesn't blink. He shudders.

Yes, yes!

Breath surges hot and heavy in his lungs.

"But this is one story someone else will have to finish." His mouth closes over hers, swallowing her last words as finally, deliciously, and with one exquisite thrust, his blade drinks deep.

Peggy Kassees appears once a month on a local television station, WTXL, The Morning Show, to speak about writing in Tallahassee and the Tallahassee Writers Association. She is a book review contributor to the Southern Literary Review and the Tallahassee Democrat. Kassees recently won first place in the Royal Palm Literary Awards for Dark Fantasy/Horror for her book: *Flocked: Birds of a Feather.*

Kassees is an Imaginist. She likes to take what is, then give it a twist to see what can be. Her favorite question is "What if?" A writer of Paranormal Romance, Urban Fantasy, and Southern Gothic, her stories incorporate elements of myth, mystery, magic, mayhem, and love. Kassees has performed for the public several of her short stories, and has recorded a CD accompanied by Bodega Bob Homme on guitar, "Tales From the Swamp: Swamp Song."

Teen Angel

Judith Turner-Yamamoto

I. Clayton Bishop

The day Donald Ray Spencer was killed he caught four catfish. I found them, right there beside him on the floorboard, wrapped in yesterday's paper. They looked as surprised to be dead as Donald Ray did. He lay there all slumped over the passenger seat, his left eye staring right back at the fish.

I'd come out fishing myself that Friday. A man couldn't work on a spring afternoon like that. Hot, like the first day of summer, the sun made everything green come up looking brighter than you ever remembered. It made you want to sleep the earth was working so hard, and there's no place better to do that than on the end of a fishing pole.

I'd been putting in corn all that morning for my Daddy. Berta Mae says I'm a fool to work for him like I do since I don't get a red cent from what he grows in the fields he still calls his own. And I say look how cheap he rents me the land I do use. Berta Mae never looks at what she has, just at what she thinks she ought to have. That's a big part of what makes her so miserable.

It must have been three o'clock by the time I got my equipment put up and my dinner ate back at the house. When I first came around the bend right before the lake everything looked fine. I saw Buford's car and Donald Ray's parked right in front of it. I remember thinking, 'I'm not the only man that can't think straight in weather like this.' Donald Ray was working third shift, he had his days to kill, and Buford Jones didn't do a thing but lay drunk and he could do that at the lake as well as anywhere else.

Then I saw Buford's car had cut clear through Donald Ray's, right up to the back seat. 'Here's two dead men,' I thought to myself and that crackerjack day took some kind of turn. I got out, not wanting to look, but knowing I had to, being the one to find them and all. Buford's car was empty, and he was nowhere around. Probably down in the woods without a scratch on him, hugging a pint, waiting for the whole thing to clear out.

His radiator was still hissing. Otherwise, there was a complete quiet over things. A fish jumped, hit the lake with a hollow slap. I watched the circles on the water's surface grow and grow until they didn't count as circles anymore.

I opened the passenger door, reached for Donald Ray's wrist where it hung limp over the seat. It's a strange thing to feel warm flesh without life in it. I'd only done it once and that was when my Granddaddy died early one morning before milking. I'd had no idea death was that near on him. But this here was only a boy and it made such an emptiness in me to get nothing back when I touched him.

The clock on Donald Ray's dashboard still worked. I watched the second hand travel from twelve to the fifteen-minute mark, thinking what a mess this was. Then I went on back up the road to Elvin's store to call the Highway Patrol. Drove right past my own house to get there. If Berta Mae was home I'd end up having to tell her the whole thing and I couldn't take her mouth right then, not with what I'd just seen.

The store was dark, cool, empty. Light from the narrow windows behind the counter lit up the dust that trailed in from the road. There was a clean familiar smell about the place, like hay that had been put up to dry.

"Mighty quick trip, Clayton." Elvin padded over to greet me.

It hadn't been a half hour since I was in here buying worms. I might as well of been somebody else, I felt so different. My throat felt rusted shut, that's how hard it was to get the words out. Elvin took the news in stride the way he took everything. He put the phone up on the counter and went on about his business while I got hold of the Patrol.

I had to bend my knees to see to dial the number. Elvin was a midget. His wife, Ethel, was a midget, too. When Elvin retired from his conductor life over at the Tweetsie Railroad Amusement Park, he bought the store and made everything over to fit him. The counters and refrigerator cases were half as tall as the ones at the grocery store in town. Sliding ladders built into the shelves let him put stock away up high. On slow days he did his bookwork at a desk behind the checkout counter that was no bigger than a school child's. He and Ethel lived in the back in tiny rooms full of tiny furniture. She taught the neighbor children music on her miniature piano. In the early evening, Elvin milked his goats, standing below the platform he had built for them. On warm nights, he and Ethel sat side by side on the porch swing he had hung low, their feet just brushing the floor.

Sweat popped out on the bottle Elvin pulled from the drink box. I took the RC he handed me and I went out on the porch, looking for a place to breathe right. I just stood there letting some time pass. I couldn't see waiting down there with Donald Ray. Only thing he was waiting on now was judgment day.

Instead I thought about Elvin. This man who wasn't even big enough to reach the pedals of a car knew all our secrets. He saw the men sitting on his porch in the summer or around his wood burning stove in the winter, every last one of them happier here than at home. He saw the women too, the ones who worked at the mills in town same as the men. They stopped by on their way home to pick up Vienna Sausages or sardines and crackers, something they could open up for supper and not have to think anymore about. And now he saw me, hanging here, putting off a thing that couldn't be put aside.

The Highway Patrol was there measuring skid marks when I got back. It'd take the ambulance a while yet since they'd be in no hurry coming out for a dead man. The officer said Donald Ray probably never knew what hit him. Buford must have been taking that curve pretty fast for those cars to be that far off the road. Close as he could tell without moving Donald Ray it looked like his neck was broke. Anyway, that's what he said he'd tell Darlene, his widow.

They hadn't been married a year. And there she was, not ten miles up the road at her parents' house, thinking she was having catfish for supper. The patrol car would pull up at the house about the time she'd be looking for Donald Ray to be home.

I walked back over to his car. At least he didn't have any disfiguring marks on him. Bad enough to bury a husband at seventeen, but to see him all tore up would be more than a young girl like that could take.

That evening after finishing my supper the best I could I slipped out the side door. Leaving the fluorescent lights and stepping outside was like falling off the end of the earth. The lay of the land and the shaded outlines of the trees led me past the dog lot. The two pointers paced, muzzles snorting ground already worn bare by their worrying. I crossed the cow pasture to where the earth dipped down to meet the little creek running through the far corner of my land.

The creek bed was filled with rocks I'd tossed there years ago clearing the pasture. Water tripped across them making a pretty sound. Listening to the water travel over rocks I'd put in its path always made me feel part of things. Out of the dark, other things came clear, the willow at the bend, its branches draped over the water, new leaves just touching the surface. And further down the bank, the dogwoods, petals like scattered lights in the blackness.

How dark was it where Donald Ray was? The thought made me jump. Coming home, I'd thrown myself into the evening chores with more interest than I'd felt about anything for a long time. At dinner I concentrated on each bite, resisting my usual way of throwing back food like water, indifferent as I am to Berta Mae's cooking. The evening paper took up the rest and Berta Mae going on about this and that. Now here I was, busy tearing up handfuls of grass, hoping to lose Donald Ray again.

Confused, Donald Ray had to be that. Like everybody else all he knew were these rolling hills and fields. One minute he was sitting in his car in that empty moment before you leave one thing and go on to the next. There he was, thinking he'd go home and spread some newspaper out on the front porch, listen to the scales of the fish fly as they pulled away from his knife, dropping on the paper like sleet tapping on a tin roof. He'd watch the sun go low, changing the color of the sky as it went down. And then, he was knocked smack dab into the middle of death, something he'd probably never given a second thought, not at his age.

Berta Mae was another case. She was always threatening to die. That was the thing about her, she was never happy, not anymore. I skipped a stone across the creek and listened to the different tones it made hitting rocks big and small. I couldn't put my finger on exactly when things started going bad.

The world was hard on Berta Mae, and part of me had been drawn to the jumpy unsettled hurt that shown in her dark eyes and the uneasy set of her full mouth. I thought of the calf with the broken ankle Daddy had once left for dead. I had put it in its own stall, away from the careless and deliberate jostling of the herd, giving it time and the care to heal in peace. I'd thought I would be able to do something like that for Berta Mae, but staying ahead of the offenses and slights she saw everywhere had soon exhausted me.

My life had to be half over and here I couldn't speak for the last fifteen years. A panicky feeling came over me. I told myself it was just spending the afternoon with a dead man. But what if the trouble was everything else? I sat back on the coarse grass, the dew seeping through my pants. If I kept going this way, I just might be glad when the burden of living is finally lifted.

I thought of when we first married. I was working third shift like Donald Ray, going to bed in the mornings just as Berta Mae got up. I would roll over, bury my face in her pillow. Still warm and rich with the smell of her dark hair, it lulled me to sleep. Donald Ray had to be lost and sad, cut off from lying down beside his new wife, from feeling the breeze--warm tonight like summer coming—puffing up the curtains, spilling into their room.

II. Darlene Spencer

Darlene sat in the front pew staring hard at Donald Ray through the dim chapel light. She half-closed her eyes trying to make him look the way he did when she'd watched him sleep. Just when she got things fixed her tears carried him off. She ground them away with her fist, and tried looking outside the church at the magnolias instead. A soft rain, like the one falling, that was all they needed to bloom. The blossoms were out when she and Donald Ray married, she'd made sure of that. And here it was not two weeks until their first anniversary. She'd had it in her head that Donald Ray would surprise her with a bouquet of magnolia blossoms he'd sneaked into the churchyard and picked himself. The idea was so set in her mind that she'd smelled their strong perfume for weeks.

She turned back to study Donald Ray. The pallbearers had arranged themselves around the casket. Somehow her mind hadn't let her take the whole thing this far. They were going to shut him up, carry him outside and stick him in the ground. That sick prickly sweat came over her, like she used to feel when she was little and Daddy would lock her in the closet for talking back.

"You can't close him up." Darlene was beside them before she realized she was on her feet. "Ramon, don't you remember how your brother hates being closed up? He can't even ride in the car with the windows rolled up in the wintertime."

Ramon looked anywhere but at her. But he stepped away, motioned for the other pallbearers to do the same. She looked at Donald Ray real good like she hadn't been able to bring herself to do. They had his hair all wrong, parted on the right and swept high up off his face like a blonde Elvis. The make-up on his face and hands was orange. Whatever this was that was left didn't care if it was shut up or not. All smooth and untouched by life, he looked like something out of that wax museum they saw on their way to Myrtle Beach.

"You don't have to touch it," Donald Ray had said, pulling back her hand. But he was wrong. Her fingers ached to know if what her eyes told her was the truth. Clark Gable's face was as cool to the touch as the mulberry candles her mother brought out at Christmas time, the stubble of his beard worked in with a different color of wax. It was so perfect it made Darlene want to dig her nails into the surface to see what lay underneath.

She touched Donald Ray. He felt as solid and cold as a piece of granite. Her fingers snagged on the rough growth of his beard. It'd been two days since they laid him out all smooth and straight in his wedding suit but those little hairs didn't know he was dead anymore than she did. His beard looked like it always did in the late afternoon. She could almost feel it on the nape of her neck: fine-grained sandpaper making the red down stand on end.

She turned around, nodded her thanks to Ramon, and stumbled back to her pew. Her chest tightened and her breath refused to come, as if it was her shut up in that box. The murmurs of the congregation swelled, a giant wave ready to break. Darlene heard people rise, rustling, adjusting, but she didn't have the strength to stand up. Mama and Daddy each took an elbow. She somehow shook herself free and fell in alone behind the pallbearers and their slow shuffle up the aisle under the burden of the casket.

Stares, some curious, some sympathetic burrowed into her. She didn't want them here, none of them. This felt private, not like the wedding. It was one thing for people to see you happier than you've ever been and in the prettiest dress you ever saw, and something else when it was all you could do to put one foot in front of the other without passing out. Darlene hadn't as much as combed her hair in three days and she wouldn't let Mama near her head with a brush either. It was Mama went to town for Darlene's dress, and she hadn't let her pick out her clothes since she was five. The dress Mama came back with was dowdy and hung way down below her knees, not that it mattered what she had on.

She told herself if she just kept her eyes on the open doors and the drizzle falling outside she could make it to the graveyard. The sadness was mostly gone. Looking at Donald Ray had taken all that out of her. She was lonely. Lonely for the Donald Ray left in her head.

Darlene followed the pallbearers right to the grave, ignoring Mama's frantic motioning to her from under the from under the dark green canopy the funeral home had set up a respectable distance from the grave. Out of the corner of her eye she saw her mother hold out her umbrella, her eyes pleading with her daughter to take it, to not embarrass her like this. Last night her mother had lain beside her on top of the covers, watching her toss and turn instead of trying to sleep herself. Her mother's tenderness brought her to tears again. Maybe Mama was just afraid that without her Darlene would get swept so far away from herself she'd never make it back.

Darlene's white high heels sank slowly into the wet clay right along with the lowering of the casket into the vault. It hit bottom, the sound of metal on metal ricocheting off the smooth walls. It was the kind of thing Darlene had hoped she would hear, a sound that held the promise of nothing.

She wiped the mist of rain off her face, batted the frizz it brought out in her coarse red hair. There were beads of water on the lid of Donald Ray's casket; she'd seen them last thing. What would happen to that rain, sealed up tight in the vault? Would it evaporate and fall over and over using the little pocket of air that must be trapped there? Visiting his grave, she knew she would stand by the headstone, breathing softly, listening for the rain.

"Teen Angel, can you hear me? Teen Angel, can you see me?" Darlene leaned over the phonograph on the floor by the bed, moved the arm back to the beginning of the record.

On the way home from the funeral she kept hearing Donald Ray sing the song, holding on to each word like he was trying to hold onto the life he'd already lost. She insisted on driving into Potter to the record store even though Daddy said it was a pure-T disgrace to be seen in such a place with Donald Ray's grave not even filled in yet. She figured if she could play the record she wouldn't hear Donald Ray singing, over and over.

She settled into her throw pillows, willed the tears back in her eyes. Things became softer, their edges melting. She could see Donald Ray, his blonde hair all lit up with heavenly light. He was smiling just the way he always did when he came home after working all night. By the time he got in, her father was in the fields, her mother busy in another part of the house. Her little sister, Chrissie, was out at the main road, waiting for the school bus. Those quiet mornings in the kitchen her parents' house was theirs.

Donald Ray read to her from the morning paper, the sizzle of the eggs and ham she fried rising and falling against the steady flow of his voice. She turned to watch him, his gold head bent over the paper. Sometimes the light from the window would catch his hair and she'd sense the presence of something that reached beyond him yet was a part of him. She decided it was the child they would have, making itself known to those that could see. She kept it for herself, making it a part of her special knowing about how things would work between them.

Fridays her parents drove into Potter first thing. Donald Ray began pulling his clothes off before he was halfway in the side door, letting them fall on the kitchen floor until he stood, finally, naked beside her. There in the low morning light their gasps and sighs echoed through the still house. All the days she could remember began in that room. It was right that she had made him a part of it. The tears flooded Darlene's eyes and she lost him.

"Darlene?" She heard her mother's timid knock, the door open. She closed the door behind her. "You shouldn't be lying there like that, honey. What if somebody opens your door by mistake? And can't you turn that record down a little? You can hear it all the way into the living room."

Mama leaned over and moved the arm off the record. Darlene could tell she wanted to say something about her wearing red at a time like this. The bra and panties were her Valentine's present from Donald Ray. But if Mama didn't understand why she was playing the record, she'd never understand the underwear.

"I brought you something to eat," her mother said. She held the plate out to Darlene. "You've been holed up in here all afternoon and it's past supper time."

Darlene stared at the food. "What is it?"

"Baked ham, candied yams, and Mrs. Freeman's potato salad with pickles."

Mama had used the same coaxing voice to trick her into eating when she was little and went through that stage where she turned her nose up at everything on the table. She looked away, picked at the fringe on a pillow.

"You've got to eat something," her mother tried again. "You can't starve yourself to death." She hesitated, her face turning red, then stumbled on. "You haven't had a thing since that dry biscuit at breakfast."

"Well, I sure don't want to die." Darlene patted the nightstand beside her. "Leave it right here, Mama."

Darlene followed her mother's glance to her mourning dress where it lay discarded at the foot of the bed. In the cedar closet upstairs were all the black dresses Mama had worn to funerals over the years. Sometimes, when Darlene was upstairs alone, she would open the closet and stand there, breathing in the sweet dry smell of cedar, her fingers lightly running over the different materials. Heavy wools for winter deaths, thin cottons for summer ones, all worn once then put away. When her mother undressed tonight she would hang the rayon dress she was wearing in that closet. Here she was about to pick Darlene's dress up and take it right upstairs and put it in that closet. Then she'd be part of it, part of the whole thing of death. Every time she walked past that closet, she'd see her dress in there, all closed up, dark and airless, like Donald Ray in his grave. Her chest froze, just like it did when they closed Donald Ray's coffin. "Don't," she gasped, fighting for air.

"My poor sweet girl, I'm so sorry." Mama reached down to stroke her head.

Darlene dodged her hand. "Don't, just leave it, leave me be."

Mama paused at the door, her hand curled up on her chest like a broken bird. "I'll check on you later."

"Get those people out of here, Mama. They've stayed long enough."

Mama nodded, her chin trembling the way it did when Darlene wore her down. In the visitors' low murmur, Darlene heard her name, then Donald Ray's, followed by hushed whispers. It was as if the two of them were sleeping and no one wanted to disturb them. She stuffed the corner of her pillow in her mouth to stifle her sobs.

Since his death, nothing tore her up more than unexpected kindness. Last night at the funeral home, Mrs. Routh, her fifth grade teacher, had appeared out of nowhere, pulling Darlene into her baby-powdered bulk. The simple familiar smell cut through the heady scent of roses and lilies surrounding Donald Ray to touch off a surge of memories: Mrs. Routh leaning over Darlene's desk to check her long division; sitting with her after school and learning to knit while she waited for the bus; her teacher kneeling at recess to clean a cut on her knee. Longing welled up in her. She wanted to be ten again, to not know about death and loss and change. What was left for her? Losing her parents, her own death? Darlene clung to Mrs. Routh, giving over the full weight of her grief. The funeral director had eased Darlene out of her arms and whisked her away behind a wall of green velvet drapes and into a separate room until she calmed down.

She started the record over, but Donald Ray had disappeared, refusing to sing to her. No matter how many times she told herself he was dead it didn't stick. They were supposed to be together, together forever, he had promised. It was just like they had broken up. She had the record, she had his ring, but they were finished. She lay back, running her hands over her Valentine nylon and lace, uncertain how to begin. Her fingers fell into the familiar pattern of Donald Ray's. They made light swirls around her nipples, moved outward to take in more of her. When the pleasure became unbearable Darlene smiled, thinking to herself, I'm alive yet, I know I am.

III. Clayton Bishop

I never did really know Donald Ray, just by sight is all. Just enough to throw my hand up when I passed him on the road. The best look I ever had at him was the day I found him dead down by the lake.

He was one of Dallas Spencer's boys. I say it like that because Dallas had so many of them. I forget now if it was six or seven. But Donald Ray was the baby and had more looks than the rest of them put together. Everybody said he should have been spoilt being the youngest and looking like he did, but he wasn't. He was smart too, played varsity basketball. Saturday nights when there was a home game we'd all go just to watch that boy run and make baskets. I don't remember ever seeing him miss a one. That can't be right but it does seem like that's how it was. Played good enough that they said he could of had a scholarship to play ball at Carolina.

Then he got married and went to work like everybody else around here. Worked down at the hosiery mill. I never saw him though. They start all the young boys off on third shift and keep them there as long as they can take it.

It was that little redheaded Caveness girl that Donald Ray married. Darlene didn't have that white-faced surprised look you see on most redheads. And she had brown eyes; you don't see that much either. That alone was enough to make her stand out. But there was something else about her. Even when she was real young, back when I'd see her buying soft drinks at Elvin's after the school bus let her off, even then, her eyes were so dark they made you think she'd seen a thing or two.

I guess Donald Ray noticed that, too. She wasn't but sixteen when they got engaged; it was Donald Ray's last year of school. They got married a week after her brother burned up in that car wreck on Troglin Hill. One week folks were sending flowers to the funeral home, the next they were taking wedding gifts to the Caveness's.

Her mother was embarrassed by the whole thing, but that didn't stop her from giving in to Darlene. They went right on, married in the same church where they'd held the services for her brother not seven days before. It had something to do with the magnolia trees in the churchyard. She had her head set on the windows being open during the ceremony and the smell of magnolia blossoms filling the church. Planned the whole thing around the blooming of those trees. Now, almost a year to the day, she was back there again, burying her husband.

Berta Mae says she's spoiled goods now, that nobody will have her except some old widower. Says God is getting even with her for being so self-centered and disrespectful. I don't see it like that though. Donald Ray just picked the wrong day to go fishing, is all.

I saw Darlene down at Elvin's the other day. He ran off somewhere, wide-eyed and uneasy with the coincidence of us. Darlene didn't even notice, all her mind fixed on that hateful little gold cellophane string on her new pack of Lucky Strikes. The minute she looked up, I realized how wrong Berta Mae was. I saw something in her, something that had no business being there. A man might risk a whole lot just to find out what fires up those eyes of hers.

Judith Turner-Yamamoto's awards include residency fellowships from the Virginia Center for the Creative Arts and Fundacíon Valparaiso; Fish International Short Story Prize, Runner-Up; Manchester Fiction Prize, Short List; StoryQuarterly Scholar, Sewanee Writers' Conference; the Thomas Wolfe Fiction Prize, the Virginia Governor's Screenwriting Award, two Individual Artist Fellowships from the Virginia Commission on the Arts, and a Moving Words Poetry Prize from Arlington County, Virginia Arts Council. She has been a finalist for numerous additional awards, including the Sundance Institute Screenwriters Workshop and the 2015 Eludia Award, Sowilo Press.

A novel, IRIS AND TRUDY, is forthcoming from Upper Hand Press. Her stories and poems have appeared in magazines and journals, including *The Mississippi Review, The American Literary Review, Verdad, The Village Rambler, Parting Gifts, Potomac Review, Dash,* and *Snake Nation Review.* Anthologies featuring her work include *Fish Anthology 2016, Gravity Dancers, Double Lives, Farm Wives and Other Iowa Stories,* and *Best New Poets 2005.* She has taught fiction at the Writers' Center at the Chautauqua Institution, the Danville Writer's Conference, and at the Writers' Center in Bethesda, Maryland.

Winnie Nunez on T. Cannon

Jane Arrowsmith Edwards

I just got word T. died. He deserves at least a few words. So first off, I understand if you think he was just another of my husbands, but you better have yourself another think. T. was the one. I was brought up to get married and stay put, like it was all settled, what everybody including me figured. Didn't work out that way, but I can say this and look you in the eye. If T. had been my first, he'd've been my last.

But Woody was first. He was a temperate boy and that's what ruined it. Like when I'd go to him when he was alone down at the sawmill in the woods. I'd drive the sedan he bought me down there and say the way you say it when you mean something else, "Need some help?" and he'd say, "Nope" or "Hold the board steady." T., on the other hand, I'd walk across the junk yard to the garage where he'd be working on a car that was promised six months ago until the owner's calling, his lawyer's calling, and I'd say, "Need some help?" and I'd be arch-backed on a pile of cardboard before I could make a run for it. He made me forget how to run.

Woody and me didn't stay married long, nobody's fault but my temper's. Regular as sin I'd say, "Let's do something different," and he'd say, "No surprises, no disappointments," until one day I said, "Well, screw it, Woody," and surprised him. He was also disappointed. And that was that, his decision, which I admire, stuck to his guns. Right now, you ride 12 miles west up CR 326 and you'll see him and his second and I promise you absolutely last wife working in the yard with their teenagers cheerful to be helping out. A regular Life magazine spread. She heads some church group and always has that cutey-pie I'm-in-charge-of-the-pageant-that-won't-happen-without-me sparkle about her. Now and then, when I can get a ride on a Saturday, I'll drive by there just to have a looksee, and without fail I think Do Jesus, lucky for us both I got a temper. He's friendly enough when I see him. One time he was coming out of the

Little General, his arms full of cleaning supplies, and I was going in and said, "Need some help?" He didn't have a clue. Never did. Just as well.

My mama used to say Woody and me didn't work out because I held my A.A. degree over him, which I did not. She said I ought to take a good look at her, content as a bug running her yard-sale booth at the flea market. "Too much education makes your mind a mess," she used to say, which I'd hear later from T.'s daddy. See, T. didn't give high school a go, junior high having been humiliation enough. My guess is he had dyslexia, a word neither him or his daddy ever heard. He said T. wasn't a book learner and why should he be when he could turn any engine inside out while the kids down the road were learning to pedal their first bikes. Can't argue that.

Along the way I married Someone Else, whose name I am to this day sent a monthly check not to remember but if I told you your eyebrows would jump off your head. Nope, don't guess. I'm not telling and I'm not making it up. That was a long time ago when you best believe I was an eyeful. High heels, tight dress, strapless bra, pearls, eyeliner, all that and more. Now you just see a cripple needs dentures and to cut back on the cigs. Cutting back on the Millers wouldn't hurt either, as I'm first to admit, but that's not happening. Yeah, I figured you'd say you like what you see, but I guarantee you wouldn't in the morning, so do us both a favor and forget about it.

Anyhow, there was no reason in this whole entire g.d. universe for that other husband to pay me a red dime except for him making two mistakes. First, he had his next wife, the honey blonde, to call me and, this is second, ask what it would take to forget I was ever married to the senator-elect. Whoops, not supposed to say that. Well, hell, there's been plenty senator-elects and who cares anyhow. I take his money only because he got too fancy to call me himself. And then to offer money, no manners. Turns out it's her money to boot, so, yes, sir, he's paying overly much for thinking less of me. And Blondie, too.

How I met T. was in a bar. Where else? you say. For your information I do get out somewhere else every day to talk to people, nice people. The girl in the book mobile, the Kenyan guy with the tribal scars in the Little General, the waitress and regulars at the diner, and, that day, the bartenders and regulars at the Pop-Top. The game was ending, the Braves were losing, and I was consoling myself with one last beer and watching the two girls behind the counter. No, not like that. I saw you cut your eyes. If that's what you want, take it next door. Two of them checked in this morning and been at it all day. Hear them through the wall? Oh, yes they are. Well, what else could that sound be, dummy?

The young waitress, I was admiring the straight edge of her thigh jutting out of her teeny jean shorts. She was all in motion, swinging her banner of dyed black hair that advertised her momentary perfection. Well, she sure wasn't thinking momentary, who ever does. But having been there, I was. It fades fast, boy don't you know. And then the older one, you've seen her, still there, wears Wranglers tight to smooth her crumpled thighs, her smile stretched over those big teeth loose in the gums. She's worrying herself new wrinkles about her kids' deadbeat dads and how she's going to pay off her loans for night school that's not leading nowhere. And then, between you and me, there's that snake of a boyfriend she's held out hope for longer than's healthy for anybody.

I was sitting there adding it up, trying to figure out if I'd live — if I wanted to live — to see the young one twenty years forward, see how life grinds her down, see when she stops hot-strutting her young stuff, pretending she's just filling orders, twisting at the waist to slide matches or an ashtray down the bar. Then bending in two, her legs spread straight as a sawhorse when she drops rinsed empties in milk crates under the sink, offering up paradise to wayward husbands and big-tip truckers just enough to make them strain, then her popping up doe-eyed like she didn't know. She's good.

To my right, around the horseshoe bar, a bubba kept smiling into my eye space. No one had done that since before the postal truck mangled my leg, but there he was. I'll be damned, I thought, and began bucking my car coat to head back to the motel where I was receiving mail. I'd go do what I always did, swill mouthwash, ease onto my stale, sunk mattress, prop up my bad leg, and read whatever was next in the line: book, newspaper, catalog, tourist flyer, anything to bore me to sleep. Look, and I'm saying this because you know by now you got no business here. What you see is a woman who gave over twenty years to jumping into wrong arms to avoid setting a goal. My family got just as sick to death of nagging me to go make something of myself as I was of hearing them. A chain on a semi's bumper couldn't have pried me away from any of that, not until sunrise when I'd pull on my dress and whisper goddamn if I'm not a fool I'm a double fool. Once you get past the urge, alone in a bed is a g.d. royal set up.

So here's this elf-faced, barrel-chested cracker grinning and tipping his ball cap just when I would've swore that was all over. I made sure he saw my cane: no surprises, no disappointments. He chirped hi so friendly, him with his pointy lips and johnny-reb whiskers a dime apart. Sixteen days later I moved in with him, T., and six months later he was my number four and my one smart decision. Well, him and my capital gains investments. I got a knack for the second, lucked into the first. Moved out of the motel and into the six Silver Streams he'd welded together to make a house in the back corner of his junkyard, for a grand total of eighty-four months, my lifetime record. Thirty-five years old, the happiest I ever was and ever will be. There's no more detour signs on this road and that's a fact.

With T. I quit smoking, talked more, read less, stopped using my cane, planted azaleas to dress up the cattle gate. I picked up trash, pulled carburetors and radiators, watched the mechanical maw crush cars, and went along when T. hauled them to Deetville to the Scrap Metal Baron, then circled around to Tiny's Repo Auction to buy more. Never go home with an empty bed, T. used to say.

Each car had a story. Loved that. One was a mint-green limo custom made for Lucille Ball, you know her. Found red hair pins deep in the mint leather seats. And then there was that totaled Valiant that two kids got thrown from on their way to church camp. What a sorry sight. Didn't have to know them to shed a tear. When T. cut away the crushed trunk we found two red fiber-fill jackets that we put to good use. Not that we weren't observant of the tragedy of the deceased previous wearers.

Okay, I knew you were going to ask that. I don't know how, I just knew. Yeah, T. was married. Well, so was I, but so what, I hadn't seen that mistake in months. I don't pride myself on busting up T.'s marriage, if you want to call it a marriage. He snuck around some, he was first to admit, and he would've stayed married to the little red-haired roller-skating drunk, what with the five kids. But when they drove the kids over to Daytona for a swim she hopped on the back of someone's motorcycle who she'd met when she went to buy the kids' ice cream cones and just rode off. No ice cream, no mama. Wasn't the first time.

It was after that that T. and I discovered our mutual appetites for each other. Blessed down south already, T., after we married, was run over by a tractor he was pretending to consider buying, just for something to do on a Sunday. It mashed his back in such a way that he was able to maintain interest three, four times a night. I swear the times we had. He could've sued John Deere and won a big piece of pie, but he suspected part of the deal would've been he had to have surgery. He chose the stabbing back pain and brass-ring pecker.

Now don't for a minute think I'm calling the first wife a drunk to butter over busting them up. After Daytona she never showed up except for the big holidays, like people do church. The kids were failing school and she was working as a motel maid for beer money and living with a former preacher who'd done time before he met her at the roller rink. The kids failing might of seemed normal to her, a family tradition binding them like barbwire. Personally and truthfully, I never wanted kids, but T.'s were nearly grown, the youngest already eleven, about to be on their own. And since I had some education I drilled them every summer and sent them to summer enrichment camps. And they brought up their grades.

I tugged them out their bunks every weekday morning for our own little summer school out on the screened porch and picnic table before I headed off to work. On weekends I told them to do their homework while me and T. went to the lake to rehab his back. If the kids wanted to go, they could ride their bikes the six miles, thereby allowing us twenty-five minutes of blue-light-special privacy. T. would fly down the dirt road a hundred miles an hour and I'd pull off our t-shirts and beg faster. We'd dive in and not come up 'til we had to. I liked seeing and touching him underwater, smooth as a fish.

They all graduated high school, not a GED in the bunch and the last one with high honors, thank you very much. I told them they had earned themselves a lot of skills so they had no excuse to get stuck. The youngest one called me mom, believe that? Then they left home, what I was waiting for all along and told them so often they'd say it before I could.

That's when I dipped into my capital and paid off the junkyard so I could quit my job and stay home. At last. And I wouldn't have divorced T. in one million years except when we took to closing the junkyard to go to stock car races or hammer a few nails in the little house we were building on a lot we bought on the lake, his fat daddy took it upon himself to drive down the highway from his junkyard to ask what the hell was going on, why was the g.d. cattle gate chained? I'd sit there thinking it's none of your g.d. concern, while T. nearly fell backwards explaining. Keep in mind, T. was 47 and me not quite 42. The best times were two weeks each spring when his daddy flew to Belize to look for a wife that couldn't drive, could cook, and was willing to give and take what he wanted. Four requirements, English optional. Never found her but did his share of sampling. Two weeks wasn't near long enough for me.

So when the last of the kids moved out and the gate was on occasion chained, not all the time mind you, T.'s daddy drove over to tell us that people with too much education don't appreciate hard work. Apparently he had been ruminating on his little bitch fest because it was nothing if not memorized. He said all those years of us sending the kids to math summer camp and science summer camp and computer summer camp was just my way of getting them out from underfoot. When T. didn't say a word I went ahead and said well, yeah, what did you think?

By the way, this is something I didn't say, but he knew I worked a second job to pay for those camps, he knew me and the kids got along fine. He was steamy about the kids' mama who'd made a career of dropping in and out of detox on his nickel. But that wasn't what he was revved about. It was she'd stopped calling the kids because they stopped calling her and she wasn't that broke up about it because all they'd ever talked about was our car trips and happy us. We went all over the place and had good times, learned stuff, like at Williamsburg and St. Augustine and Moab. Too much education rocks the boat, according to T.'s daddy. He said their mama felt squeezed out because I took over everything. After seven years she was saying this? Then excuse me for not doing a half-assed job. Know what I mean?

For the record, she wasn't drinking over me and T. Truth is that girl drank as far back as when she was pregnant with the twins. Plus, it came out later, she'd had somebody steady on the side long before, even before they got married. I was surprised that T. gave a rat's ass when he found out and that what ate him up most was she wouldn't say who. He said why wouldn't she say? He'd always told her, just to be decent, in case she ran into one of them, so she knew the score. So how bad could it be? He kept guessing, puzzling it out. You can imagine I grew pure weary of that.

Having somebody on the side didn't happen with me and T. Change had been barreling straight at us for a long time simply and only because he would not say boo to his daddy. When it hit I so did not want to see leaving coming.

I walked in the house to pack and thought I'd cry till winter. Before his daddy showed up, it had been just another morning for us out under the bay tree, severing dandelion heads with a putter from the flea market, deciding where to go on a gnat-thick sticky

Saturday. Then here comes fatso rumbling along in his black pick-up with oversize tires to yell why the hell's that g.d. gate chained again.

He rattled on about an education making a body forget what they got, whether it's a good man or five country kids that ought to have stuck close to home or twenty-five acres that makes money just sitting there, and so on and so forth until I thought my arteries would pop. I was boiling but waited for T. to set the old fart straight.

When his daddy finished, spit, and drove off, I once again, except hotter, said that I could not abide that old man misrepresenting our happenstance one more time. It turns out that time was the last. T. looked away and said, I'll never forget this, he said his daddy didn't miss often and if I didn't see it his way now, I would later. Which told me they'd had them a talk. One of them had. Then T. walked down the dirt road and unlocked the gate. I plunked right down on a steaming stack of roof shingles and watched him. Didn't give a royal flip if my shorts got tarred or not. Lord knows I did not want to leave that man, not one bit. I watched him walk back, his hands deep in his jeans pockets, his shoulders up to his ears, how he did when he was tore up, love that man. I said, "T. hon, I wish I didn't have to, but this is it, sugar. I'm going." He dropped his head and put a finger on my hand and said, "I know but don't." He was crying some, but so was I, which wasn't enough to keep me.

After that we talked on the phone at least once a week all these years. He worked steady and kept the gate open and his daddy happy, went along to Belize in the spring. He saw plenty local women, too, even more after word got out about his disability. Friends got divorced and wives stopped by seeking solace with their old buddy T. Some of them were big around as hulahoops and some could wear those swim suits go up to the hipbones. The kind of women that do shopping center aerobics where they know everybody by name and don't sweat. He said, "I always wondered what it'd be like to be with a woman like that." Long distance I said, "Thanks a lot." He said close to the phone, "Take you any day." He got asked a couple times but he never married again. Once I asked why. He said, "You're it, Nunez," which all but killed me. Husky, "You're it, Nunez," like that. I can't do it like him but you get the idea. I wanted those three words branded on me. Although before T. I briefly had other names besides Nunez, T. stuck on that one. I believe he entertained the notion that Mr. Nunez was somebody wild and exciting, like a Mexican bandolero, and I let him think that. Whereas the reality of George Nunez, notary public and weekend auction caller, was he's skinny as a fire poker but less fun. Some of my husbands even I don't get.

Each time, just before I married again, I'd think if T. would leave his daddy we could be it again. It was his daddy's stock car he was driving when he crashed. Brakes. Honestly, it never once occurred to me that that man would never come for me, that he would not someday be standing right there in that door frame where you're leaning right now, no matter how far gone to ruin either of us got, he'd come get me. Someday there he'd be and we'd pick up right where we left off, stop at the store on the way home for pork chops and beer and a bag of nails for working on the lake house, you know, that sort of thing.

The kids called to tell me, each remembering some detail of the crash as they passed the phone around all choked up. I reminded them if one of them goes into public service I got the senator connection, just to give them something positive to think about.

No, uh-uh, I do not do funerals, nobody's. Besides, the kids said their mama's going. Their granddaddy sent for her right off. Plain as day he's had a thing for the little drunk from way back. And that's all I'm gonna say about that. We'll see what the police turn up. If I have to, I will call the senator and make a deal.

Hell, it's late and I'm saying too much. Go on and pull the door hard behind you until the lock clicks. I can turn out the light from here.

Jane Arrowsmith Edwards is a sixth generation Floridian who feels lucky to live in Gainesville. She has also written plays, screenplays, and a couple of shelved novels.